Mother's Kiss

MICHAEL CHAMBERS

DEDICATION

For my own children, who taught me what it means
to be a man.

CONTENTS

ACKNOWLEDGMENTS

The following resources were invaluable in the creation of
this novel:

https://www.learnreligions.com/legend-of-lilith-origins-
2076660

https://en.wikipedia.org/wiki/Sekhmet

The King James Bible

https://www.history.com/topics/folklore/vampire-
history

Any historical or Biblical inaccuracies are mine and mine
alone.

CHAPTER ONE

1.

On a long, lonesome stretch of highway just outside a small town, a lone figure walked calmly down the center line. It was a woman, dressed in a simple white shift dress, her feet bare, and her long dark hair down. If the hot blacktop burned her feet, she gave no sign of it.

Just ahead, a Ford F-150 that was more rust and body filler than paint turned onto the highway and headed her way. The driver, a longtime meth addict named Ruth Ann, never saw the woman in the middle of the road. Still, something made her move the truck over to the right as she went past, the draft from the big truck ruffling the woman's white dress. The woman saw Ruth Ann drive past, and blew her a kiss.

Inside the truck, Ruth Ann, who was on her way to meet with her dealer and maybe work out a little something for some rock, let her foot slide off the accelerator. Rather than go the three miles down the highway and turn off onto the dirt road that led to Garrett's trailer, she sat up straight and pulled the truck to a stop on the side of the road.

She knew Garrett would have something for her, if she had something for him; he'd said as much many times.

She'd resisted so far, but the little bit of cash she'd had was gone, and she was hurting. She had told herself it wouldn't be so bad; a little head, and she'd be right in no time. Garrett wasn't into weird shit; he'd happily smoke her up for a simple blowjob.

But something occurred to her as she sat on the side of the road. She didn't actually need the rock. Come to think of it, she didn't even really want it.

Behind her, the woman turned around and watched the truck, a sweet smile spreading across her pretty face. "Go home, my baby. You don't need that man's poison. All you need is Mother."

Back in the truck, Ruth Ann put the transmission in park, put her head down on the steering wheel, and cried. She cried until it was all out of her, completely unaware that by the time she finished and sat up straight, the last bit of meth still in her system from the rock she'd smoked last night had seeped out of her pores and dissipated into the air, where it was sucked out the truck's open window.

Oh, my God, she thought as she sat back. Caitlyn, she thought. Where was her daughter Caitlyn? The state took her, of course. She remembered now. She remembered all of it, and it brought on another crying jag. She gasped as someone stroked her cheek, and she turned to see a beautiful young woman with long, dark hair and bright green eyes standing by the truck, a sweet, loving smile on her face.

"Come, child," the woman said. It was preposterous; Ruth Ann was every bit of twenty years older than the girl, but the way she'd called her "child" seemed completely natural. "What troubles you?"

"M-my daughter," she said, sobbing quietly. "My baby girl. God, I fucked up so bad."

"Shh," the girl said, stroking Ruth Ann's limp, rather dirty bottle blonde hair. "All is well, my child. We'll make it right, together."

Ruth Ann, by now in a perfect paroxysm of despair and

confusion, didn't think twice when she looked over in the passenger seat and saw the girl had somehow made her way into the truck. "Th-they took her," she said. "Child Protective Services. They took my baby girl. Right to, I guess. I ain't much of a mother."

"You are my child," the girl said, and something about that struck Ruth Ann as ridiculous, but she couldn't argue. Literally could not argue with her; she tried to say it was impossible for her to be this young girl's daughter, but she couldn't. "And my daughters make wonderful mothers. What happened to you is not your fault, my sweet girl. You were corrupted. Corrupted with poisons and lies, by a man no doubt."

Well, the chick had that part right, Ruth Ann said. She hadn't seen Ray Fuller since she was nineteen, but she'd lived with his legacy ever since. Every rock she smoked, every prized possession she sold or stole to get it, all the times she'd degraded herself just for another rock could all be laid right at that handsome bastard's feet. He'd taught her how to smoke, after all.

"I," Ruth Ann said, but the girl stopped her.

"It doesn't matter," she said, with a patient smile that Ruth Ann thought could only belong to a mother. An understanding, loving, kind mother, one who would correct a wayward child as gently as possible. "We're going to make it all right now, my sweet girl. There are lots of my children here, and too many have been corrupted by poison, damaged by men and their base, selfish needs."

"They ain't all bad," Ruth Ann said, thinking of Donnie. Big, sweet, tough, lovably stupid Donnie, who'd stayed by her side longer than she had any right to expect. Of course, she'd managed to drive him off, too.

"No," she said with that same comforting smile. "Of course not. There are good men in the world, too. And they have nothing to fear from me."

"But the others?" Ruth Ann said, the waterworks

finally drying up. "Men like Garrett?" Or Ray, for that matter, she thought but did not add.

The smile never faltered, but her green eyes went from warm and soothing to ice-cold. "A mother protects her children," she said. "That's why I'm here, after all."

2.

Jim Harlow was caught in the whirlwind, again.

It was a familiar feeling, although one he'd thought he was done with once he'd entered the supposedly calmer waters of his forties. His temper had been damn near legendary when he was younger; only a stint in the Army saved him from real trouble. Getting your ass knocked into the dirt by a crusty old drill instructor who could eat six of you for breakfast taught a man more about anger management than a thousand hours of therapy.

He'd worked hard over the years to get a firm grip on that temper, and for the most part had succeeded. Not even the divorce, which had been the stuff of acrimonious legend, had riled him to the point of lost control. Hours of honest introspection had taught him that more often than not, he didn't really lose control of his anger so much as just let it off the leash. Understanding that had let him keep it in check for the last ten years, at least until today.

He stepped out of the station, his face stony and calm as he put his regulation Stetson on and started down the street, in the direction of the town square and the park. A part of him—it was a small part, true, but it was there just the same—told him that he should stop, right now, before he went too far. He hadn't crossed a line yet.

He told that part it was already too late; he was caught in the whirlwind now.

3.

"Oh, my Lord," Brenda Hardy said as she looked out the beauty parlor's big plate glass window. "There goes Big Jim."

"Hmm?" Wanda Burkett said, looking up from the copy of RedBook she was reading. Like most of the older single women in town, the mention of Big Jim Harlow always made Wanda's ears perk up a bit. "Lord, but he sure doesn't look happy."

"No," Brenda said, her lips pursed into a thin line. "He doesn't. He looks mad enough to slap a bear."

"You don't think--" Wanda said, letting the thought trail off. Brenda didn't answer. She was too busy dialing.

"Mark, it's Brenda. You need to get out onto Main Street now. It's Jim Harlow. He's headed to the square, and he looks mad enough to chew up nails and spit out carpet tacks."

"Shit," Mark Gillette said, and the line went dead. She didn't even get the chance to chastise him for his language, although she wouldn't have this time. It seemed to sum things up perfectly.

"Is he finally gonna do it?" Wanda said, an unmistakable gleam in her eye. Brenda felt a brief but powerful surge of dislike for the woman; brief because her sentiment was entirely understandable, and powerful because it mirrored her own.

"He didn't look like he was going to check the parking meters downtown," Brenda said. "Watch the shop for me."

"Oh, to hell with that," Wanda said, putting her Redbook down. "No way I'm missing this."

Brenda almost reminded her who actually signed her paychecks, but let it go. Instead, she grabbed her keys and locked up as they headed out to see what was about to happen.

4.

"I'm sorry," Ruth Ann said as they stepped inside her trailer. "It's a mess. I'm a mess." The girl smiled sweetly as Ruth Ann fumbled around, picking up empty beer bottles and takeout containers. She promptly dropped one of the bottles, and it shattered on the floor. Before she knew it, she'd dropped to her knees, sobbing as a shard of glass cut the knees of her jeans and gave her a superficial cut.

"Oh," the woman said, her voice full of concern and sadness. "There, there. Don't fret, my sweet girl. Come," she said, helping Ruth Ann up to her feet. She led Ruth Ann through her filthy trailer to the bedroom, where she lay down on the bare mattress on the floor.

"I need to clean up," she said, but she was so tired. It felt as if she hadn't slept in days, which she understood was basically the truth; she'd crashed once or twice, but never really slept.

"All will be well, my sweet child," she said. "Right now, you must rest. But first, we should see to that," she added, pointing to the small cut on her knee. She watched as the girl touched the tips of her fingers to her own lips, then placed them over the cut. She felt warmth flooding through her, starting at her knee and suffusing her whole body. When the girl removed her fingertips, the cut was gone. Not healed; there was no small white scar, no mark to indicate there had ever been an injury there at all.

No, she realized; more than that. That was her trick knee, the one she'd blown out on the hurdles her senior year. It always ached these days, but now the ache was gone.

"What did you do?" Ruth Ann asked, her voice clear and firm for the first time in years. Her mouth felt strange, her tongue hitting obstacles they weren't used to. It took her a moment to recognize them as her teeth. Most had rotted out long ago, but now they were whole and strong.

"A mother's kiss heals all wounds," she said, placing a warm, soft hand on her forehead. "Sleep, my child. When you wake, we have much to do."

"Anything," Ruth Ann said, already drowsy. "I'd do anything for you."

She wasn't sure she heard what came next. As Ruth Ann faded into sleep, it sounded like the beautiful young woman who, impossibly as it seemed felt like her mother, had said two words.

"I know."

Ruth Ann slept.

5.

There were times when Mark Gillette wished he'd never moved to this little backwater, and never more than right at that moment as he parked the cruiser two doors down from Brenda's salon and ran after the massive figure up ahead that was his boss and best friend.

"Jim," he said, stepping in front of him and walking backward to keep from being bowled over. "Jim, just stop."

"No time," Jim said. Mark stopped in front of him, barely managing not to cringe. Jim stopped, looking him full in the eye. "You're gonna want to get out of the way, Mark."

"Jim, just stop," Mark said. "Stop and think it through."

"Been enough of that already, don't you think?" Jim said. "We've been through all this shit before. Too many times. And every goddamn time, it's 'Wait, Jim. Be patient, Jim. Go slow, go easy, Jim.' No more." When Mark didn't move, Jim just stepped around him and continued down the street. He was less than two blocks from the square now.

Mark almost reached out to grab him by the arm; if it had been anyone else, he would have done it. Would have, in fact, taken them down and cuffed them until they calmed down. But the simple fact was he had about as much chance of taking down Big Jim Harlow as he had swallowing a live bear.

People were standing in doorways, watching as Jim made his way down the street. Mark saw several nods of

7

what he assumed were approval and appreciation, if not outright awe. He could understand that; this had probably been coming for a long time, and many of them had just been waiting for it. He didn't necessarily disagree that it was almost certainly bound to happen sooner or later, but he didn't have to like it. They had the luxury of not caring what happened after, but he didn't.

"Shit," he said again, because it was all he could think to say. With the sick feeling in his gut that he was about to watch a slow-motion train wreck, he did the only thing he could do.

He went to back up his partner.

6.

The whirlwind was growing stronger as Jim walked; his hands had clenched themselves into fists of their own accord, and he could feel his pulse pounding in his temples as he strode down the sidewalk. He was only peripherally aware that people were gathering behind him, no doubt coming to see the show. They didn't matter. Mark, who he liked and respected, didn't matter. Not even the man approaching him mattered to Jim.

"Jim," Wade Albright said as he stepped forward, hands up. "Jim, stop this. You can't do this."

"Watch me," Jim said, continuing to walk. Mayor Albright followed alongside him, still talking.

"I am ordering you to stand down," Albright said in his best officious tone, which was actually pretty good. Most days it would be enough to at least make Jim pause and listen to what the man had to say. Albright might be a bit of an asshole, but he wasn't a stupid man. He knew the score just as well as everyone else.

"Sorry," Jim said, still walking. Half a block to go; he could see the park up ahead. They'd be there, he was sure of it. They were always there, usually hanging out at the bandstand and drinking. "Can't do that, Mr. Mayor."

"If you won't listen to reason, you give me no choice

but to--"

Jim cut him off by pulling his badge off his shirt and holding it out to him. "You want this? Say the word, Mr. Mayor, and it's yours."

"Well, let's not be hasty," Albright said, crawfishing in the best time-honored tradition of weasel politicians from time immemorial. Jim just put the badge back on and started walking again. "Jim, I'm just saying we need to talk this one through first."

"I'm done talking," Jim said. He left Albright standing on the sidewalk, for once at a loss for words.

Almost there.

This had been coming for a long time, and he for one was damned sick of waiting.

7.

He found them right where he thought they'd be; sitting on the bandstand and laughing as they passed a bottle around. They saw him as he saw them, and he had to give them credit for at least being smart enough to understand that today, things were different. This wasn't going to be another round of the usual bullshit, where he hauled them in until the lawyers could get them right back out. For one, he'd walked here.

He also knew from entirely too much past experience that the look on his face when he was caught in the whirlwind was less than reasonable, and would most definitely not be described as friendly.

Billy Denison was, naturally, in the place of honor at the top of the bandstand steps, his three little fuckhead lackeys sitting at his feet and laughing at something the little asshole had just said. The laughter died as they saw him approaching.

"Denison," Jim said, his voice coming out louder and stronger than he'd expected. It had, in fact, come out almost as a shout. "William Denison."

"Hey," Denison said, his voice cheerful and grating.

"If it isn't Big Jim Harlow. Grab a step, have a drink with us."

"Stand up," Jim said. Denison didn't stand up, but his three pet dipshits did. Jim was vaguely aware he was smiling as he removed his sunglasses and put them in his shirt pocket.

"What's the problem, Officer?" Joe Grady said. He was a tall, sun and surf type with blonde hair and a fairly ridiculous amount of tattoos. Jim scanned him quickly, saw nothing to indicate a weapon of any kind, and promptly dismissed him. He was tall and fairly well muscled, but he was soft; everyone knew that. He was only really tough when he had the advantage.

"Yeah, what's up?" Brad Taylor said, giving Jim the same shit-eating grin the little bastard always seemed to be wearing. "You come to hang out with us?"

"Step aside," Jim said, pointing at Denison. "I want him."

"You got a warrant?" Caleb Hollister asked, stepping forward. He was probably the only really smart one of the bunch, save for Denison himself of course, but he was at heart a coward like the rest of them.

"Get out of my way," Jim said. Even caught up in the whirlwind as he was now, he was still self-aware enough to recognize that what he'd intended to come out as a strong verbal command had instead sounded eager, almost cheerful. Keep it in check, he told himself. You've got to keep it in check. Don't lose control.

"Bill Denison, stand up and put your hands on top of your head," Jim said, struggling to keep what little grip he had on his temper. "The rest of you, get gone."

"We're not breaking any laws," Grady said.

"And unless you've got a warrant, fuck off," Taylor said. Jim had it under control, until he didn't. He was fine, until Taylor poked two fingers into his chest.

Up until that point, he'd at least had marginal control of himself; he'd been aware that some three dozen people were gathered behind him, and no doubt over half of them would have their cell phones out and recording the whole thing. He was aware that Mark was coming up alongside them, and Mayor Albright was with the crowd. He heard someone gasp as Taylor thumped Jim's chest again.

He grabbed Taylor's two fingers in his left hand and twisted them to the left and back, then slammed a fist into the center of the moron's face, his nose crunching. Grady started toward him, fist drawn back and ready to strike, and caught a polished boot squarely in the crotch for his trouble.

He twisted Taylor's hand again, back the other way, and dragged him forward until he hit the ground, and looked up at Hollister.

"Hey, take it easy," Hollister said, hands up and grinning. "No trouble here, right?" Jim saw the sucker punch coming in plenty of time to bat it aside with his right hand, then give the smarmy little dick a hard back-handed shot across the mouth. Blood sprayed onto the concrete sidewalk in front of the bandstand from his split lip.

Taylor was starting to get to his feet, and Jim punched him again, knocking him out cold. He grabbed Hollister by the shirt and shook him twice, then buried a hard right hand into his midsection, folding him in half before tossing him away.

He looked up at Denison, who finally stood up and stepped down off the bandstand. "Guess we've graduated from harassment to police brutality," Denison said, still wearing that same shit-eating grin. "What's the false accusation this week, Harlow?"

"Turn around and put your hands on top of your head," Jim said, some of his self-control returning as he reached for a pair of cuffs.

"Am I under arrest?" Denison said, still making no move to comply. "Am I being detained? On what charge?"

"Jennifer Bennett," Jim said, his voice even and hard. Denison was good, but Jim still saw the barest flicker of real fear on his face before the smart-assed grin returned. Jim smiled. "Yeah, that's right, asshole. She managed to tell us everything. Every detail." He stole a look down at Denison's crotch, and his grinned widened. "Every single tiny, little detail."

Later on, he would blame the whirlwind for what came next. If he hadn't been caught up in it, he would have recognized what Denison was doing in plenty of time to head it off. As it was, when Denison's hand grabbed behind his back, Jim barely had time to register that the shape in his hand was a pistol before he reacted.

CHAPTER TWO

1.

The woman left Ruth Ann to sleep away the last of her pain and poison, and went to see more of her children. At the city limits, she found a small white house with an assortment of broken and battered toys in the front yard, belonging to unfortunately broken and battered children. She felt her children inside, calling out without words or voice for their Mother.

Inside, she found one of her daughters, a high school dropout named Emma, with two of her own children.

"Help you?" Emma said as she answered the door, but the confrontational tone of her voice disappeared as she saw the woman on her front porch.

"My sweet child," the woman said, and Emma burst into tears. Before she knew it had happened, the woman was hugging her in her living room as Emma cried. "You've been hurt so badly, haven't you?"

"He doesn't mean to," Emma said, sniffling. "He just gets so mad sometimes. It's my fault, I know better than to make him mad."

"Shh," the woman said, stroking her cheek. Emma noticed that the woman's hands were small and delicate, the nails perfectly shaped and spotlessly clean. She was entirely clean, come to think of it, which was odd since she was barefoot. Her feet should have been filthy, but they were as immaculate as the rest of her. "Now, I won't mislead you, sweet girl. You've made poor choices. But none of those mean you deserve to be treated so cruelly. And these sweet little children? What could they have possibly done to deserve the same harsh hand you've received?"

Emma sobbed at that, looking at little Aiden's black eye, and her sweet little Carrie's arm, where a large hand-shaped bruise showed under the sleeve of her favorite t-shirt. Five-year-old Aiden had left a stray Lego on the living room floor last night, and seven-year-old Carrie had committed the unpardonable sin of "talking back" to her father. Emma remembered it well enough; Carrie had expressed the opinion that she didn't want to go to bed early.

The steel inside her, which she'd all but forgotten existed, rose up. "Nothing," she said, her voice hard and angry. The woman just smiled and brushed her cheek.

"No tears," the woman said. "No anger. What's done is done, and you cannot change it. But I can help." She pressed her fingers to her lips, and touched Emma's shoulder. It had been sore for days, ever since Brad had shoved her out of the way while she was picking up the living room. She'd tripped over his work boots and crashed into the floor, hearing something let go in that shoulder with a wet pop that had made her sick to her stomach.

She might not have finished high school, but nine years of marriage to Brad Norcroft had taught her a lot. One of the biggest lessons was that you never, ever went to the ER. She'd popped the shoulder back in herself, with help from a video on YouTube.

When the woman touched her shoulder, the pain stopped. It didn't fade away, or dull down; it stopped completely, as if someone had flipped a switch. "My God," Emma said, rotating the arm in a way she hadn't been able to do thirty seconds ago.

"No," the woman said with a slight, sweet laugh. "Just a Mother's love, that's all. And now," she said, turning to the kids. She knelt down on the threadbare carpet, getting down to their level. Carrie came to her first; she was the oldest, and the bravest.

"You poor, sweet thing," the woman said, looking at her arm. "Does that hurt?"

"S'okay," Carrie said with a shrug that made Emma's heart hurt. "I was bad, so Daddy took me up for it."

"Taking up" was what Brad called it. It was a stupidly simplistic euphemism for "beating the shit out of you."

"What could a sweet child like you ever do that could be so bad?" the woman said.

"I talked back," Carrie said, and the woman smiled.

"A woman's voice is all she has sometimes, and some men can't wait to silence it. You speak out loudly, my sweet girl. Be heard." Carrie, who no doubt understood maybe a quarter of what she'd just been told, beamed at the woman nevertheless. The woman touched the bruise on Carrie's arm, and Emma watched in amazement as it disappeared.

She reached over and tousled Aiden's curly hair, then brushed his cheek. When her hand came away, his shiner was gone. "I love you, Momma lady," Aiden said. Not "Mommy," which was what he called Emma. That made her smile.

"And I love you, very much," the woman said. The warmth suffusing Emma's whole being started to fade as she heard a familiar truck pull into the driveway. She looked up at the clock; it was barely eleven.

"Oh, hell," she said, near panic as she turned to the woman. "He's early, and that's bad. It means no work today. He'll be mad."

The woman's warm, loving smile broadened, and she touched Emma's cheek.

"You needn't worry, child," she said. "You have nothing to fear. I'm here now."

When Brad came through the door, his face dark and his brow furrowed in a way that meant nothing but trouble, he stopped for a moment as he looked up and saw Emma standing there with the woman in front of her.

"Children," the woman said, her voice light and friendly as she turned and bent down to speak to them. "I saw some wildflowers in the backyard. Would you like to pick a nice, pretty bunch for the table?"

"Okay," Carrie said, smiling. "Come on, Aide. We gotta get some real pretty flowers."

"Okay," Aiden said, following his sister out the back door. The woman's smile never faded as she watched them leave. It lasted until she turned back to face Brad.

"The fuck is this?" Brad said. "Look at this fucking pigsty. You sitting around gabbing with some random broad instead of cleaning now?"

"Emma keeps a perfectly lovely home," the woman said, looking around. Emma couldn't believe it; the living room was spotless. The toys that had been scattered on the carpet were neatly put away, the coffee table gleaming under the artfully careless spread of magazines that had been an untidy pile moments before.

"Who the fuck are you?" Brad said, stepping forward. He was a big man, solid muscle under a layer of hard-earned beer fat, and Emma wondered why she wasn't flinching. Why she wasn't herself scared shitless, for that matter. Brad was obviously "in a mood," and someone was bound to be "taken up" before the day was half-over.

"If you must have a name, I prefer Lilith," she said. "But who I am is unimportant. What I am, however, is very important."

"Oh yeah?" Brad said, sneering. "Lemme guess. You're one of them dyke social workers, right? Get the fuck outta my house."

"I'm not done with my visit," Lilith said, still smiling. Brad snorted laughter and grabbed her by the wrist, obviously intending to throw her out. No one looked more surprised than Brad when he tried to drag her to the door, and stopped as if he'd just tried to tow his truck by hand.

Lilith looked down at the hand on her wrist, and Emma saw her beautiful green eyes flash cold. "I will not be pawed at by any man, let alone you," she said, and grabbed his hand. She twisted the wrist around, and Brad let out a sharp, surprised gasp as Emma clearly heard bone crack.

Lilith stepped forward, forcing Brad to move back as she continued to twist his now-broken arm. "A man's entire duty is to love and protect his family," she said. "That is how they are made. You have failed in your duty, Brad. I'm very disappointed in you."

What happened next seemed to be both completely unbelievable and utterly inevitable, all at once. Lilith reached up with one small, delicate hand, gripped Brad by the chin, and lifted him off the floor. His boots dangled over the carpet, twitching as Lilith held him aloft, as if he weighed no more than, say, a glass of iced tea.

Brad tried to say something, but Lilith just shook her head. "I don't need to hear your lies," she said. "You hurt my children." She slammed Brad down onto the floor, and he let out a soft grunt as the air was driven from him.

Lilith stepped down on Brad's chest with one dainty, immaculately clean foot. "For too long, you and so many others have treated my children poorly. That ends now. I'm here now, and I will do whatever I must to keep my lovely children safe."

Emma didn't even flinch when Lilith stepped down, crushing Brad's chest. His boots thumped as his legs twitched, then he lay still. "You killed him," she said, and Lilith turned to her.

"I punished him," she said. "A mother always protects her children. I have been away for far too long, and I have neglected my duty to you. To all my children. I'm here to make that right, in any way I must."

She bent down and grabbed a handful of Brad's shirt, lifting him as if he were a small tote bag. Emma watched in equal parts joy and horror as Brad's body disintegrated in front of her eyes. Once he was gone, Lilith dusted her hands, ridding them of a mess that disappeared as soon as it floated into the air.

"There now," she said, smiling. "All better."

"I don't know what to say," Emma said, tearing up again. "I love you."

"And I love you, my child," Lilith said with a pleased smile. "And I may have chores for you later. For now, I think you should see about lunch. Those beautiful babies will need feeding soon."

"Of course," Emma said. "Will you have lunch with us?"

"I wish I could," Lilith said. "But another of my children is suffering badly, and I must go to her."

"How can I help?" Emma said, wishing more than anything she could just curl up at her feet out of sheer relief.

"My sweet girl," she said, kissing her cheek. "I'm the one who's here to help you."

Before Emma could say anything else, Lilith turned and walked out the front door. She let out a wistful sigh, closed the door, and went to start lunch for the kids.

2.

Mark watched the whole thing play out in slow motion. Although it was over in a matter of seconds, it felt like he spent at least a week watching Denison bring the gun out from behind his back and raise it. Big Jim, hardly a green rookie, seemed to see it coming before anyone else. He punched Denison in the nose, blood splattering as he grabbed Denison's wrist and twisted the arm. Denison dropped to his knees as the gun, one of the new Springfield Hellcats, clattered to the cement.

Mark's ass finally received the message his brain was

sending and threw itself into gear. He pulled his sidearm and covered the other three as they started to get up. One of them, Caleb Hollister, looked like he was considering reaching for the gun until Mark kicked it aside.

"Don't even fucking think about it," he said, and Hollister backed off. "You three, over there. Against the bandstand, hands on the railing." They did as he ordered, although Taylor hesitated a bit, obviously thinking over the odds.

"You're not deaf, Taylor. Put your fucking hands on that rail, or give me an excuse to kick your ass."

Taylor eventually complied, and Mark found himself with a decision to make. He could put a stop to things now; Jim had Denison on the ground in an arm lock. He seemed frozen, as if he couldn't decide what to do next, and Mark knew he was wrestling with the world-famous Big Jim Harlow temper.

God knew Mark could understand; Billy Denison was a first-class asshole on his best day. And after they'd seen what had happened to poor little Jenny Bennett, Mark had been sick with rage and the desire to just beat the little motherfucker to death himself. But unlike Jim, he had his anger in check.

Big Jim made his decision; he shoved Denison onto the ground and stood up, taking two big steps back. Mark had a brief moment to think maybe he'd finally won some control, and then the very last thing in the world he'd wanted to see happened.

Big Jim Harlow, his best friend, his boss and partner, the chief of police, unbuckled his duty belt and hung it on the bandstand railing, and Mark knew things had just gone to shit.

"Stand up," Jim said to Denison, who was already getting to his feet.

"Jim?" Mark said, still covering the Three Stooges. "Jimmy, we don't do it this way, man. Come on. Just cuff him."

"Take those three back to the house, Mark," Jim said, never taking his eyes off Denison. "This won't take long."

"Jim, come on," Mark said, aware that he was whining and hating it. God knew Denison deserved one hell of an ass-kicking, it wasn't that. It wasn't the idea of tuning this little bastard up that bothered him; it was that his friend was about to throw away his entire career in the process, maybe the rest of his life.

"Tell me something," Denison said as he stood up straight, and Mark knew from the grin on his face that things were about to go well and truly right to shit.

"You're under arrest," Jim said, and Mark wanted to groan as he saw the same grin spreading across his face. "Eventually."

"Was she walking funny?" Denison said, still smiling. "I mean, because if I had hit that, she'd definitely be walking funny."

Mark saw the look on Denison's face, and on Big Jim's, and made his decision. "Chief Harlow, I believe this suspect is resisting arrest," he said.

"That's bullshit," Hollister said, but he was alone; his two butt buddies were busy studying the paint on the bandstand, and he was quickly shouted down by the small crowd that had gathered in the park. Mark recognized Tim Wilson, the athletic director at the high school who had been beaten by unknown assailants after cutting Taylor from the football team, and dear old Janie Miller, the town librarian who had found her beloved little Corgi Snickers hung from a fence post for some offense or other. There was Gus, who ran the used bookstore on the square and had been hit by Denison in one of his drunken driving accidents, and the young couple who'd just opened a coffee shop in the old computer repair building next door to City Hall. They'd made the mistake of expecting the Great Bill Denison to pay for his coffee, and had found most of the plate glass in their shop broken the next morning. He saw the Renny brothers, who owned the town's laundromat and, if rumors were to be believed, at least half of the adult book emporium three miles out of town, near the highway. Jim thought Denison and his cronies had targeted them simply because they weren't afraid enough. Solid citizens, people he'd known for years. Good people, all of them, and he realized that every single one of them was currently vouching for the fact that Bill Denison was resisting arrest. It made sense; Denison and his band of happy assholes had victimized all of them over the years.

"Take off," Mark said to Hollister, Taylor, and Grady.

"What?" Grady, who would never be a candidate for Mensa, asked.

"Get gone, all of you," Mark said. "Start running and don't stop. Never let me see any of you again, or I'll beat the shit out of you myself."

The others started to go, but Hollister held back. "This isn't over," he said, and Mark nodded.

"Probably not," he said. "But if I see anything but shoe soles and assholes in ten seconds, you're gonna regret it." Hollister grinned, but let his buddies lead him off.

Denison turned from Jim to Mark, still grinning. "You know this is bullshit, Gillette."

"Stop resisting," Mark said in a loud clear voice; with the decision made, there was nothing left to do but commit to it.

He holstered his sidearm and picked up the gun Denison had pulled, and gave Jim the nod. Denison sighed and put his hands up.

"Why not?" he said. "I've always wanted to try you, Harlow. I bet I can take you, old man."

"Just tell me when it hurts," Jim said, still grinning.

Mark, fully aware that both he and Jim would probably end the day in a cell and no longer giving a shit, leaned up against the bandstand to watch as Jim did what he'd wanted to do for over a year now, which was to well and truly beat the ever-loving shit out of a psychotic asshole who desperately needed it.

3.

At her full adult height of four foot ten, five even in heels thank you, and roughly one hundred pounds, Jennifer Bennett had long since come to accept that she was never going to be the sort of leggy bombshell or corn-fed Midwestern beauty most local guys wanted, but she was okay with it. She might not have legs for days, but she knew darned well she had a cute little ass, and overall she'd always seemed okay in her own skin. She might not have believed it if someone had told her, but Sharon had always thought she was just about the prettiest girl in town.

She didn't look quite as pretty now.

Her long black hair, of which Sharon had always been more than a little jealous, was missing in several small patches that had been ripped out; patches of scalp were visible among the bloody tangles of what remained. Her face was a mass of bruises and cuts; whoever had worked her over wore a big ring. She was missing a total of eight teeth; all four upper incisors, three lower incisors, and one lower molar that had been shattered. Her nose had been shattered, as well as her left cheekbone. Her jaw was cracked, and her lips were a shredded mess.

There were ugly strangulation bruises on the poor girl's neck; Sharon had had a hell of a time intubating the poor thing in the ER due to the swelling. But, hard as it seemed to be to believe, the damage got worse.

Eight of her ribs were broken; the clear impressions of shoe tread were visible inside the bruises now that some of the swelling was going down. Her petite torso was a road map of bruises and abrasions, and she could only guess at the internal damage until the scans came back. The left shoulder had been dislocated, and her right hand looked as if someone had ground it under the heel of a work boot. All the bones in that hand were broken. Her pelvic bone was all but powder, and would require extensive reconstructive surgery that probably wouldn't let her walk again anyway. But none of that was what made Dr. Sharon Emmett, late of Boston and newly relocated to the middle of Nowhere, Missouri to be near her parents, want to cry.

She'd suffered extensive anogenital trauma, both external and internal. In layman's terms, the poor thing had been beaten and raped nearly to death. She almost surely would have died of blood loss and shock had she not been found quickly; might still die, as a matter of fact.

Sharon privately thought that might be the best outcome; the poor girl had a lot of suffering and lifelong disfigurement to look forward to if she survived. Sighing, she pushed the thought away and checked the girl's vitals, which in spite of everything were strong. She was tough, always had been.

"God in Heaven," someone said behind her. She turned to see the charge nurse, a tough old campaigner named Marnie, standing in the doorway. Of course, Sharon thought. Shift change. "That's Jenny Bennett. What in God's name happened to you, little girl?"

"Pretty sure God had nothing to do with this one," Sharon said. Like it or not, she still had other patients that needed her attention. "Ortho should be sending someone down to consult sooner or later."

"You mean after they finish playing the back nine," Marnie said with some justifiable contempt, and Sharon nodded. She could even agree with her on that point, most of the time. "Still, I guess there's no point just yet."

Marnie was a twenty-year veteran of the ER, and she probably knew the girl's odds better than Sharon did. What she had just said without saying it was simple; there was no point in consulting on surgery until it was clear the poor thing would survive the night. "Police been in yet?" Marnie asked, and Sharon nodded.

"She was still awake when they brought her in," Sharon said, more than a little surprised to find she was near tears.

"Even somewhat lucid, can you believe it?"

"Jesus," Marnie said, shaking her head. "She give Big Jim a name?"

"She did," Sharon said. "Not that it was a big surprise, you know."

"Of course," Marnie said, shaking her head. "Denison. Someone needs to step on that little fucking cockroach."

"Don't let Squeaky hear you talk like that," she said, and Marnie gave her a sad smile. Dr. Walter "Squeaky" Barnes was the medical director, and a notoriously boring little prude.

"Fuck him, too," she said, and Sharon laughed with her. "You said Big Jim was here?"

"Took her statement himself," Sharon said. She followed Marnie back to the triage desk, grabbing the next folder. Of course, it would be Mikey Simms, she thought.

Mikey Simms was twelve years old, and had the unfortunate combination of a wild daredevil streak combined with utter clumsiness, which made him a frequent flier in the ER. "Return engagement," she said, showing Marnie the folder.

"Lord, what did he do to himself now?" Marnie said, but she was smiling. Despite his frequent adventure-induced injuries, Mikey was just about the sweetest kid you could ever meet. "Shoot himself out of a cannon?"

"Wouldn't surprise me," she said, looking at the chart. The admit slip said he had a laceration of the left forearm. "You know, if it was anyone else, I'd be calling CPS."

"Please," Marnie said, smiling. "Everyone in town knows that boy is just an accident looking for a place to happen." Sharon laughed and took the chart into exam room four, where Mikey was lying on the bed. His mother, looking tired beyond belief, sat holding his hand. Dear God, but I don't envy that woman in the least, she thought. Mary Simms was only thirty-six, but today she looked closer to fifty.

"Hey, Champ," Sharon said, smiling as she came in and

closed the door behind her. Mikey smiled and held up his left arm, which had been fairly expertly wrapped with a clean dish towel and taped neatly in place. Of course, Sharon thought. His mother no doubt had plenty of experience. "So, whatcha do this time?"

"Wrecked my bike," Mikey said, still grinning. "Total wipeout."

"Tell the doctor what you were doing when you wrecked," Mary said sternly, and Mikey gave her a sheepish grin.

"We read about it in history class, and we wanted to try it out," Mikey said, looking properly embarrassed even as his eyes lit up. "And it was awesome."

"Do I wanna know?" Sharon said, chuckling despite herself.

"Jousting," Mary said with a tired sigh. "My idiot son and his friends were jousting with broom handles on their bikes."

"We padded the ends," Mikey said in his own defense, as if that made the whole thing perfectly reasonable. Sharon just shook her head and proceeded to cut the tape holding the makeshift bandage over his arm.

"Well, that one's a blue ribbon winner, Champ," she said, looking at the five inch gash in his arm. "Can you move your fingers?"

Mikey obediently opened and closed his fingers, and flexed his wrist for good measure. "No tendons this time," Mikey said with some pride. He showed her the scar on his right palm for good measure. Sharon had treated him for that one as well, the result of a horrifying attempt at juggling with his mother's kitchen knives. That one had taken surgery to repair three cut tendons.

"Young man, you can stop sounding so proud of yourself," Mary scolded. "You or one of your friends could have been hurt badly."

Sharon resisted the urge to laugh at the boy's enthusiasm, and nodded. "She's not wrong, Mikey. You got lucky this time. Looks like we're just gonna drop some stitches in there, and you're on your way."

She was just finishing up and admonishing Mikey once again to be careful when she heard the alarm tones she'd been waiting for all morning.

"Excuse me, please," she said, stripping off her gloves and dropping them in the red biohazard trash bin. Mary just nodded; they were also ER veterans, and knew well enough that something big would take priority over them.

Forty minutes later, she once again pulled off a pair of bloody gloves and tossed them in the trash, shaking her head. Marnie started turning off the monitors one by one without a word, which brought it home in a way that was somehow more real. "Time of death, one twenty-six PM," she said, looking down at what remained of the prettiest girl in town.

Fifteen minutes later, she made the call to Jim Harlow that sent him into the street after Bill Denison and his posse, with predictable if unforeseen results.

CHAPTER THREE

1.

This was not the first time Lilith had come back to see her children. Far from it; she had visited often, moving from place to place and helping those she could. But never in all her long memory could she recall a time so absolutely fraught with danger for her children, particularly her daughters.

Nor was it the first time she'd revealed herself to her children, although that didn't always work out as well as she hoped. Many who met her and recognized her as Mother thought she disliked or even hated men, which of course couldn't be farther from the truth. She had as many sons as daughters, and loved them all. Even when they misbehaved, sometimes especially when they misbehaved, she loved all her children.

Of course, not everyone walking the Earth was her child. Most were the sons and daughters of the one who came after her. She cared for them, as well, in her own way. She even tried to love them as she loved her own children, but they could be so cruel.

It was that other's children who brought war, and carnage. It was that woman's children who gave the poisons that controlled so many of her children, who used and debased her precious ones so cruelly, often for nothing more than their own amusement.

It was true, her children were not perfect; no being was, after all. She herself had her own failings, although she wasn't entirely convinced that all of them were negatives. She loved her children deeply, would go anywhere or do anything to help them. If that meant that sometimes, just sometimes, she was forced to punish the children of that Other Mother, was that so bad? After all, their own mother had abandoned them all long ago. And children needed a mother's love and guidance, didn't they?

The man in charge of the room where one of her daughters lay dead was not one of her children, but he was not a bad person. He seemed upset at the death of her precious little girl, and when she asked in her sweetest voice if she could see her dear one, he agreed immediately.

"I knew her, you know," he said, following Lilith into the room with the word MORGUE painted in clean, red stenciled paint. "She was just a sweet kid, you know? I don't think she even knew what a sweetheart she was."

"Yes, she was a dear," Lilith agreed. He was not her child, but she could still comfort him. She put a hand on his arm, letting her love flow into him. The pain across his face faded, and she understood. He'd been very fond of her, indeed. "And I want to thank you, Curtis, for taking such good care of her."

Curtis just smiled at her. "You're so beautiful," he said. "I love you, I think. Not like some weird instant sex thing, I think. More like--"

"Like you love your own mother," she suggested, and his smile grew impossibly wider.

"Yeah, that's it," he said.

"And I love you, Curtis. Could I maybe have a moment alone with poor Jennifer?"

"Oh, yeah," he said, remembering. He led her to the drawer, quite unnecessarily. She could feel Jennifer from where she stood. "Uh, I should warn you. We, well I cleaned her up as best I could, but she's still in rough shape. The bastard did a number on her face."

"I am aware," Lilith said, forcing herself to keep her temper in check. If she had a truly detrimental trait, it was her temper. And nothing riled her anger more than someone hurting her children. She pushed it away, and turned back to Curtis with a warm smile. "But you are truly kind to be concerned for me." She brushed his cheek with her fingertips, and he smiled again.

Her smile didn't falter until Curtis opened the drawer, pulled down the sheet over poor Jennifer's face, and left her alone. "Oh, my sweet baby girl," Lilith said, touching her battered face. "What did they do to you?"

Jennifer had been dead for some small time, and it took her a moment to answer. Lilith cried as she listened to the tale of woe her daughter spun from behind the veil, then leaned down and kissed her lips, ever so gently.

"Thank you for telling me," Lilith said. "The men who did this to you will not go unpunished." She saw them through Jennifer's eyes, and knew they were not her children. They were from the Other mother, and they had been very bad, indeed.

It was a very difficult thing to do, but there were certain old magics available to her, things the Other mother would never have learned. It drained her terribly, but in her mind there was no question of whether or not she should do it. Jennifer had been her daughter, and she had been taken before her time.

She could see Jennifer's intended life spin out in front of her; the man she would have met in only a few more weeks, the work she would do, the children she would bear. Her natural death, many decades from now, with all her children, grandchildren, and even great-grandchildren around her.

"It's not fair," Lilith said, the anger creeping into her voice. She controlled it with great effort, because anger was useless for what she intended to do. Love was required for this task; love, and a mother's infinite capacity for sacrifice.

She found what she needed on a nearby table. The scalpel was small but sharp. She drew it across the palm of her left hand, and blood so darkly red it was almost black welled into her cupped hand. She bent down and kissed poor Jennifer's lips again, then opened her mouth and tipped the edge of her cupped palm to them. The blood flowed into her mouth and pooled there until Lilith lifted the poor child's battered head and let gravity carry it into her body.

"Rest now, my sweet one," she said, closing her right hand over her left palm. When she removed it, the cut was gone, the palm as smooth and unlined as it had been before. "When you rise, we will make it right."

She pulled the sheet back over the poor child's face, then closed the drawer and walked out of the morgue. Curtis stood near the door, looking anxious.

"She will come back soon," Lilith said. Curtis looked mildly confused, and she brushed his cheek again with her fingertips. The smile returned, and he nodded. "She will be hungry. You loved her, didn't you?"

"I think maybe I did," he said. "I never really got the chance to find out for sure, though."

"I believe you did," she said, smiling. "And you'll do whatever is necessary to put what happened to her right again, won't you?"

"Anything," he said. "Everyone knows who did it. Say the word, and I'll kill the son of a bitch myself."

"No," she said, with a patient smile. "I would never ask that of you. But there is something you can help with, Curtis. Something wonderful, and it will bring you closer to her than you could ever have imagined."

"Anything," he said, and she knew he meant it. It wasn't just the influence of her touch; he would give anything he could to help her daughter.

She leaned in and kissed his cheek. "Sit with her," she said. "Be with her. When she rises, feed her. She'll know how."

"Sure," he said, without question. She smiled and kissed his cheek. Curtis beamed at her, and went back into the morgue to do as she asked.

It was regrettable that Curtis would have to die to bring her daughter back, but unavoidable. She wished she could bring him back from behind the veil, but sadly that was beyond even her abilities. It required a deep bond, a link only found in blood. But when her special children, as she thought of them, rose, they could only feed on the children of that Other mother.

Jennifer would come to her when she was ready. For now, she had other children who needed her. This small town was full of her children, and so many of them were hurting.

2.

Mark stood outside the bars of cell one, watching as Bill Denison slept in the narrow bunk. He'd fallen asleep within minutes of being deposited there, which to Mark was a pretty solid indication of guilt. Most of them fell asleep as soon as you left them alone, as if they were relieved the whole thing was finally done. He considered letting the asshole sleep, but he had news to deliver.

"Wake up, Denison," he said, tapping the bars with his baton. Denison groaned and rolled over, and Mark managed not to laugh and cheer as he saw just how much progress Jim had made in rearranging the little bastard's face.

"Where's my lawyer?" Denison said, sitting up.

"He'll be here when he gets here," Mark said.

"Then fuck off and leave me alone," Denison said. "Got nothing to say until he gets here."

"Just thought you'd want to know he's really gonna earn Daddy's money this time," Mark said, waiting for it to sink in through Denison's thick skull.

"Yeah, he will," Denison said, looking at him through the one eye that wasn't swollen shut. "Because I'm going to sue the ever-loving shit out of you both, and this little shithole town."

Mark gripped the bars of the cell, mostly to keep himself from reaching for the key, going into the cell, and picking up where Jim left off. "You don't get it, do you?" Mark said. "You honestly have no idea how much shit you're in."

"You're the one in deep shit," Denison said. "You and that fucking asshole Harlow. You let him beat the shit out of me."

Mark nodded. "You think anyone out there saw it that way?" he said quietly. "Because I've already got a dozen witness statements saying you not only pulled a gun, but you fought when we tried to arrest you. But that's not the big issue right now, Denison. The hospital called. She didn't make it." Denison looked at him for a moment, as if he were trying to understand what he'd just said.

"That's right, asshole," Mark said, banging on the bars again mostly because he knew Denison would have one mighty blue fuck of a headache. "You just hit the big time, Billy Boy. DA was just waiting for the call, practically giggled at the thought. You know what the phrase 'special circumstances' means for you?"

"Another few zeros added to the settlement," Denison said. "Do me a favor and get the back deck refinished at that shithole house of yours before you sign it over to me."

"In this case, 'special circumstances' is a modifier to the original homicide charge. They only use it for the really evil shit, like killing a kid. Or raping someone to death. You know why the DA had such a boner when he said it? Because it's one of the qualifiers for the death penalty."

He took three steps away from the cell door before turning his back on Denison, just in case he decided to rush the bars and grab at him. "Happy trails, motherfucker," Mark said, closing the door to the holding cell wing as Denison sat on his bunk, his face turning pale.

3.

Harlan Denison wasn't sure he'd heard that right, and he was confused. It was not a feeling he tolerated. A man like Harlan made himself clear when he spoke, and he expected the same of others. But the three morons in front of him were, saints preserve us, actually being intentionally vague.

"Come again?" he said. "And stop fucking about. Tell me exactly what happened." Grady, Taylor, and Hollister were standing on the rug in front of his desk. Hollister's face was blank, but at least the other two morons had the good sense to look scared.

To Harlan, there was a certain order to things; birds flew, fish swam, and underlings cowered. Hollister didn't look particularly scared, and that bugged him. At least the other two were being quiet; Grady was too fucking stupid to put three words together on a good day, and listening to Taylor's voice made him want to crap himself.

Hollister went through it again, starting with Harlow approaching them in the park and ending with that little faggot Gillette running them off. That in itself was troubling, but he'd deal with it later. Right now, there was something else bugging him.

"And you three little wet farts just let this happen?" he said. Grady was busy studying his shoes like the secret to infinite riches was written on the toe, and Taylor actually cringed.

"There was very little in the way of active decision involved," Hollister said. "We were outmatched and unarmed."

"Of course you were outmatched," Harlan snapped. "Jim Harlow could beat the balls off a brass bull. As for Gillette, he might be a fucking homo but he's at least got balls, unlike you three. That's not what bugs me. You know what bugs me?"

"No, sir," Hollister said, his face blank. God damn if

the little fuck doesn't look bored, Harlan thought.

"What did you walking assholes get into to put my son on Harlow's radar in the first place?" he asked, watching the Hollister asshole's face as he spoke.

"Nothing," Hollister said, and there it was; the tell-tale twitch of the eye, up and to the left. Harlan stood up and brought his not inconsiderable bulk around the desk to stand in front of them. Grady and Taylor once again showed they at least knew how fucked they were, because they stepped back. Hollister stayed put, not even lowering his eyes. Definitely getting on my nerves, Harlan thought.

He punched Hollister in the gut, hard enough to lift him off his feet. He fell to the carpet on his knees, gagging and coughing.

"If you puke on my rug, I swear to God I'll make you eat every last fucking chunk," Harlan said. Hollister managed not to puke as he knelt on the rug, holding his stomach. He looked over at the other two idiots. "Well, help him up," he snapped, and they did.

He paused for a five count so he didn't lose it completely, and took a deep breath. "I'm going to ask one more time," Harlan said carefully. "And you want to believe me when I tell you that if you lie to me again, I'll murder you right here and now. What did you do?"

"It was the Bennett chick," Grady said, still not looking up. "Billy's been working on her for weeks, but she wasn't into him. He tried to hook up with her last night, and she shot him down."

"Understandable," Harlan said. "She actually has standards. That doesn't explain why Harlow went after him."

"It, well, it got a little rough," Taylor said, and oh dear friends and good neighbors, was this little shit smear actually grinning?

"And what does 'a little rough' mean?" Harlan asked. Grady and Taylor both looked at each other, and yes, there it was; they were grinning. Sweet mother of fucking God, these three dicks were actually standing in his office and smirking about what he was pretty sure had happened.

"Jesus give me strength," he said. "Are you three fucking abortions standing here and telling me my son raped that girl?"

"It wasn't rape, not really," Hollister said. "We just kinda--"

Harlan kneed him in the balls. He did it right, grabbing him by the back of the head and drawing him into the shot. He took a good handful of the smarmy fuck's hair in his left hand and punched him in the mouth with his right, knocking him out cold. As Hollister fell, he turned and backhanded Taylor to the floor, then grabbed Grady by his jacket.

"Please, sir," Grady said, whining. "I tried to talk them out of it."

He shoved Grady backward, where he tripped and landed on his ass. He ran a hand through his hair, just beginning to thin out at the top. God knew it was a small wonder he wasn't totally bald by now, given the sort of shit he had to deal with.

"Get these two fucks on their feet, and out of my sight," he said to the cowering Grady. Taylor got up, touched his fingers to his split lip, and then helped Grady pick up the barely conscious Hollister.

"You three idiots go home and stay there," he said. "Keep your fucking heads down while I deal with this, and then you're gone, understand?"

"Yes, sir," Grady said. They left, and he pulled his iPhone out of his jacket and dialed a number from the memory. He explained the situation as well as he understood it to his lawyer, who agreed he'd head down to the DA's office immediately to see Billy and try to figure out how bad it was.

With that taken care of, he poured himself a knock of bourbon from the bottle in his desk, and pulled out his address book, wondering if he still had any markers left he could call in that were remotely big enough to get his idiot son out of this one.

4.

Christ on a pony, Billy thought as he woke up again with his head pounding. His nose felt like it had been stuffed with cotton, and he was reasonably sure someone had run over him with a truck at some point.

A gentle exploratory feel told him that yes, his nose actually had been stuffed with cotton and taped up; apparently Big Jim Harlow had, alongside other injuries like a couple of broken ribs and what felt like one blue mother of a shiner, broken his nose.

Just wait until his Dad got word of this, and sent Gary Rich down here, Billy thought. What little slice of this town they didn't already own would soon be theirs once it was all said and done.

Assuming he wasn't in prison, he corrected himself. The news the faggot Gillette had brought him about Jenny Bennett dying had been like getting his ass kicked all over again. He wasn't really capable of what any rational person would call guilt or remorse, but he felt bad about it. After all, if she'd just played her role and given him what he'd wanted, he wouldn't have had to take it. Maybe if she'd just given it up like a good little cooze, he wouldn't have let the boys have her when he was done. Probably not, anyway.

He sat up on the jail cell bunk slowly, feeling every little ache and pain; that big motherfucker had worked him over like a punching bag, and had anyone stepped in to stop it? Christ no, and don't think for a moment that little mistake wasn't going to come back and bite a whole lot of asses before this was over. He'd recognized quite a few faces in that crowd, faces that belonged to people who owed his father a lot of loyalty. That old faggot who ran the bookstore, for instance; if it hadn't been for his family, that abysmal shithole would have folded years ago.

But all that shit could wait, he decided as he lifted his shirt and saw the spreading bruises. It could wait, because he heard something coming from upstairs that gave him, if not real hope, then at least a fair impression of it. No one had a deep baritone quite like Gary Rich. He heard footsteps on the stairs leading down into the holding cells, and stood up carefully, bracing himself on the wall until the worst of the dizziness passed.

Gary came down with the faggot right behind him, briefcase swinging from one hand. "I assume the recording devices are switched off?" Gary said, looking up at the cameras in the center aisle.

"Yeah," Gillette said. "No cameras, no mics. You've got thirty minutes."

"Thanks," Gary said, and Gillette gave him one more dose of stinkeye before leaving them alone.

"Jesus Christ, Gary," Billy said. "Tell me you're here to get me out. You see what that big fucking monster did to me?"

"I see it," Gary said, and Billy saw something in Gary's face he'd never seen before. The lawyer had been annoyed with him virtually every time they'd met, and had on occasion been outright testy with him, particularly the last time, but he'd never seen the look he now wore before.

Gary Rich was looking at Billy with what could only be described as utter contempt. He looked at Billy, not to put too fine a point on it, like a pile of dogshit someone had just smeared on his living room rug. "So, where are we?" Billy said with the first real glimmer of understanding. "How fast can you get bail set?"

"Are you aware of what you're being charged with, young man?" Gary asked him, still looking at him as if he'd just farted at his grandmother's dinner table.

"Some bogus rape thing," Billy said. "It's pure bullshit, Gary."

"Oh, that's just for starters," Gary said. "You really have no clue just how screwed you are, son. The girl,

Jennifer Bennett? She's dead. You could be arraigned as early as tomorrow morning, probably in front of Judge Sherman. Drew the shit end of the stick there, I'm afraid. She's one hell of a ballbuster. Good luck with that."

"Gary?" Billy said as Gary turned to walk away. "Gary, come on. We gotta talk, man. How are we getting me out of here?"

"There's no 'we,' Bill," Gary said, shaking his head. "I told you the last time was the last time. Apparently, you either didn't believe me, or you're just too stupid to understand what that means."

"You're my fucking lawyer," Billy said, hating how whiny he sounded.

Gary just shook his head. "Not anymore," he said. "Your old man will find you someone; God knows he can afford it."

"You—you can't do this, Gary," Billy said, finally getting angry. "You don't just walk out on me. We own you."

Gary turned back to him, and for just a moment Billy was happy to have the bars between them. For just a bare instant, Billy would have sworn on a stack of Bibles that good old Gary Rich, who had gotten him out of more than one serious scrape with the law, wanted to tune him up a little himself. More than a little, even.

"I told your dad the last time we went through this, he needed to put you on a short leash. Honestly, I think a good old-fashioned trip to the woodshed years ago would have prevented a lot of this."

"You sure didn't mind the money," Billy sneered, and Gary just nodded with a sad smile. "Or did you not cash those checks?"

"You're right," he said. "And everyone's entitled to defense under the law. I'm good at it, and I made a goddamn fortune in the process. I don't deny that. If it makes you feel any better, not all of this is about you. Honestly, you're too much of a fucking numbskull to be worth the trouble. Bottom line is, I'm out. I'm on my way to tell your old man the same thing, so I'll give you the same advice I'm about to give him."

He stepped closer to the bars, until their faces were only inches apart. "Don't you ever fucking threaten me again, you little bastard, or when you finally do hit prison, I'll personally see to it that you spend the rest of your life getting your tender ass reamed by every bull queer on the block. Nod your head if you're understanding me, Billy, because I don't repeat myself."

Billy just nodded. "I don't know if you've got anything resembling a conscience, son," Gary said, "but if you do, I hope you'll at least try to do the right thing here."

"I didn't--" he started, but Gary didn't let him finish.

"I saw the photos upstairs," Gary said, his voice barely above a whisper. "I saw what you and those others did to that poor girl, Billy. God knows I'm at least partly to blame, mostly because I liked your dad's money too much to do the right thing and let them put your sorry ass away before you could go that far. But the things you did to her? I don't know how anyone can live with themselves after that."

Billy was left, for what might have been the first time in his life, utterly speechless as Gary turned and walked back up the stairs, leaving him alone in the holding cells.

CHAPTER FOUR

1.

Oh, fuck me, Brad thought as the stupid bitch started crying. She actually started fucking crying, as if this were one of her stupid tween romances or some shit. Well, he supposed he couldn't really expect anything else; it was what he got for screwing around with freshmen chicks, after all.

Over the girl's shoulder, he saw Gabe and the others watching. Most were doing a pretty shitty job of trying to hide their laughter as Gabe gave him a big smile and a thumbs-up. Behind Gabe, Wes grabbed two fistfuls of air and pulled back as he thrust his hips forward, making a humping motion in the air.

He let her ramble on for a bit longer, then cut it short by saying he had to get to class. She stared at him for a moment longer, and the look of sheer horror on her face was almost enough to make him feel bad before she thankfully scampered off.

Gabe and the others broke out into raucous laughter as he approached. "Okay," Gabe said, still chuckling. "What's the score?"

"Five point deduction because she's a freshman," Wes said, and Brad rolled his eyes. "But, you get a bonus for dumping her in public, so it balances out. Call it fifteen."

"Fifteen?" Brad said. "That's all? Fucking fifteen

points? I fucking nutted all over her face, man. Where's my facial bonus?"

"That's with the facial, man," Wes said. "She was only ten points to start with. I mean, it was just a blowjob, dude. Not like you hit that."

"Man's got a point," Gabe said. "Hey, don't look so down, man. You're still ahead in totals."

"Fucking-A, I am," Brad said, grinning.

They were all still laughing when the front door opened wide. Both doors, actually; they swung open like the old batwing doors in a Western saloon as a chick walked into the main hallway.

Not just a chick, Brad realized. A woman, and a stone-cold fucking hottie at that. Long, dark hair, full hips and long legs, and an absolutely marvelous set of titties. They were, in fact, exactly the sort of perfectly sized and firm titties that he always pictured when one of these A-cup bitches was slobbering on his dick. It never failed to push him over the top.

"Holy shit," Brad said. "Guys. Hey, guys. You seeing this?"

It was an entirely unnecessary question; all of them were staring at the woman as the doors closed behind her. Come to think of it, they weren't the only ones; the entire hallway, which was normally a zoo just before lunch period ended, had gone quiet enough to hear the air whooshing through the vents at the top of the walls. Every guy in the hall was staring at her, and quite a few of the chicks, too.

"Jesus," Gabe said as the girl turned, looking in every direction. "That has to be the ass of the fucking century. Jesus, you could sharpen a machete on that."

A locker door closed; a sound that would have normally been lost in the racket sounding as loud as a bomb in the suddenly quiet hallway. The stupid frosh chick was slinging a backpack over her shoulder, and of course she was still fucking crying. Christ, did they all have to do that shit? It was fucking nerve-wracking.

The woman turned to her, and Brad saw she was barefoot as she stepped toward her. She reached out and put her hands on the frosh chick's shoulders, then touched her cheek. Holy shit, he thought. Is she about to kiss her?

"No fucking way," Gabe said as the woman leaned in and kissed the girl on the cheek. "Dude, I call it."

"Yeah, bullshit," Wes said. "First come, first served."

"Oh, she's gonna come," Gabe said, slugging Wes in the shoulder. "You'll hear her screaming."

Brad stood in something like shock, just watching as she spoke quietly to the freshman chick. Kris, he remembered finally. Her name was Kris. It suddenly seemed important that he remember her name.

The woman touched Kris's cheek one more time, then turned to look directly at them from down the hall. It felt as if she were staring directly at Brad, at least to him. The others would all swear later she'd been staring holes in them. Brad was vaguely aware of two conflicting, almost warring emotions at once. He was simultaneously scared shitless, and horny enough to fuck an angry bear as she started walking toward them.

No, he thought. She's not walking. She's strutting. Every set of eyes is on her, and she fucking well knows it. He himself was unable to look away, even as Vice Principal Grove, the bald old fuck, stepped out of the office and tried to intercept her.

"Uh, can I help you, Miss?" he said, trying to block her way. Brad could just see her face around the bald little bastard, and the smile she gave him was probably the sweetest thing he'd ever seen.

"No," she said, her voice light and cheerful. "But it's very kind of you to ask." She stroked Grove's cheek, and he stepped aside. When he turned to watch her progress, Brad saw that he was wearing the same dopey grin on his face that he saw on others.

Even Gabe, who could be counted on to be an absolute pig in front of anyone, was quiet. "You boys," she said with a sigh, shaking her head. Brad was suddenly reminded of his mother, particularly the way she would shake her head in exasperation when they fucked up, which was often. "What to do with you boys?"

Gabe apparently found his dick again. "Well, I've got a couple of ideas," he said, but it lacked his usual confidence. What he'd probably meant to come out as charmingly dirty just sounded weak, like a kid trying to pick up a real woman and failing miserably.

She smiled. "Oh, I bet you do," she said, and looked away, dismissing him. Brad was expecting Gabe to say something then; he was a senior, an All-State linebacker, and in his world, no one dismissed him.

But Gabe didn't say anything at all as her gaze moved from him to each of them, in turn. "You," she said to Wes. "Last week, you convinced one of my sweet girls to do something utterly unspeakable, then took pictures. I understand that little prank earned you almost forty points."

Wes said nothing, and Brad saw he was staring at his shoes. Her gaze slid over to Mike, who looked decidedly nervous. "You've fallen quite low in the rankings, young man," she said, almost chiding him. "What's the matter? Couldn't find anything to top Wesley's stunt? Well, I suppose convincing a girl to put a cucumber in her rectum while you take pictures is a pretty big coup." Mike said nothing, and Brad was suddenly terrified as she turned her gaze on him.

"I'll get to you in a minute, Bradley," she said. "I'm particularly disappointed in you, young man, because you're not like these others. You're actually one of my children, which makes me sad."

Brad had a fleeting thought

I'm not your kid, lady

but it flew away as fast as it came. She stared at him for a moment longer, then shook her head. Her smile faded briefly, which for some reason made Brad feel worse than anything he'd ever done before.

"Gabriel," she said, turning to him. He was the only one who managed to meet her gaze, even giving her what he thought of as a charming smile. "Hard to believe, but I've actually lost count of how many of my sweet girls you've hurt. And not just emotionally, either. I understand Jeannette was in some pain for days after you finished with her."

"What can I say?" he said with a shrug. "I'm gifted."

"If that's what you wish to call it," she said, looking down at his crotch with a sarcastic grin. It was the first time Brad had ever seen anyone actually dismiss Gabe's cock, the size of which was damn near legendary. "Personally, I doubt you could do much to satisfy someone who isn't intimidated by you."

Brad felt an insane urge to laugh at that, but the look of anger on Gabe's face chased it away. He started to say something, but she actually reached out and put a finger on his lips, shushing him.

"You boys," she said again, with another shake of her head. "I wonder if you can even begin to comprehend the damage you've done. Maybe I should show you."

She reached out and grabbed Wes by his letter jacket, actually picking him up off his feet. She did it effortlessly, as if he weighed nothing. She smiled again, and set him back down on his feet, quite gently. "No," she said, shaking her head. "I doubt that would do much good. No, I think something special is in order for this, don't you?"

She turned her focus on Brad. "And you, young man," she said. "I understand you're very far ahead in points. How many of my sweet daughters have you debased and ruined for this little game?"

"I don't know," he said quietly. The lie felt wrong on his tongue. She clucked and shook her head at him, and he told the truth. "Twenty-nine," he said, and she sighed.

"Twenty-nine," she repeated, and now she was

genuinely angry. "Well, I guess the question is, what do I do with you?"

"I'm sorry," Brad said, his voice barely above a whisper. It was the truth, too; with her looking at him like that, he could feel every single shitty thing he'd done over the last three and a half years.

"I know," she said, and her smile returned. She had a playful gleam in her eye as she touched one slender finger to her chin. "I think we should give the others a chance to catch up on points, don't you? How about it, children?"

Several of the other students in the hall expressed their agreement, with varying tones of anger and hostility. One girl, a junior he'd scored twenty-five points off last semester when he talked her into a threesome with her step-sister, was staring at him with absolute murder in her eyes.

"Ladies, if you'll come with me," the woman said, and all the girls in the hall stepped behind her, leaving Brad and the others surrounded by guys. Many of them looked as angry as the junior chick, or worse. "I think we'll leave the boys to their game. Boys enjoy their foolish games, you know. It's not a bad thing, most of the time."

She turned to walk away, with the girls trailing behind her. "Game on, boys. Let's see. Wes and Mike are worth a good two hundred points each. Gabe is a solid five hundred. And Brad? Why, he's the grand prize. First one to get Brad earns himself two thousand points."

Brad had time to wonder what the fuck she was talking about as the girls all left, and then the guys surrounded them. Someone grabbed Wes and threw him against a locker as Mike was forced down to his knees.

Gabe put his hands up, ready to fight, but he was quickly swarmed. Brad watched as a group of juniors, most of them on the chess team, dragged him kicking and screaming into the nearest classroom. He was vaguely aware that at least one of them was already ripping at Gabe's warmup pants as the door closed.

Someone tackled him from behind, and his head slammed into the floor. Two thousand points, he thought, and closed his eyes as he waited for it to be over.

2.

Such a shame, Lilith thought as she connected with the girls in front of her. More than thirty of them altogether, and only a handful were her daughters. She touched each of these gently, caressing her cheek, and they stood aside from the others.

"I thank you all for your love," she said to the rest. "I only wish I could be your Mother, because I love each and every one of you."

"We love you," a pretty girl with blonde hair so light it was almost white said. She had a lovely face, and Lilith could see that even though she was a child of that Other, she had a good heart.

"You should all go home now," Lilith told them. "Rest, and wait. I will come to all of you in time, and you will have an important part to play, if you wish."

"Anything for you," a sweet but rather homely girl said. She couldn't change her into one of her special children, but that didn't mean she couldn't help the poor thing.

She hugged the girl, and kissed her cheek. She stood back and watched as her skin cleared, the cheekbones refined, the too-thin lips plumped into a soft and kissable mouth. Her somewhat shapeless body refined itself into something curvy and toned, and Lilith smiled.

"What--" the girl said, looking at herself. "What did you do to me?"

"I simply let others see you the way I do," Lilith said. "You are strong, and beautiful, Kelly. Never let anyone tell you differently."

She kissed Kelly's cheek, and blew kisses to them all. They all beamed at her, and then did as she asked, wandering away toward their homes. Only the five who were her daughters remained, and she turned to them now.

"Come, my beautiful ones," she said. "I have a special place for you, where you can become all you were meant to be."

"I can't wait," Kris said, and Lilith smiled.

"Then we should go," Lilith said, holding the girl's hand. "We have much to do."

She was just walking back toward Ruth Ann's trailer when she felt something rip through her, forcing out a scream of anguish and terror as she felt several of her children die at once.

3.

Harlan Denison hadn't set out to become a criminal when he got out of the Army. He'd taken the small inheritance he'd received from his otherwise worthless father, combined it with what he'd managed to scrimp together while he was in the service, and gotten down to business.

He'd started by getting a job working the bagging line at Surima Mills, making a smidge more than minimum wage because he was willing to work the night shift. He'd also picked up a nice side gig at the local flea market, selling furniture he'd scrounge from the dump and carefully repair and refinish himself. He wasn't entirely adverse to a little creative marketing, however, and more than one "authentic Amish-made" kitchen table, headboard, or crib had been sold out of his stall after the "Made in China" or "Handcrafted in the Philippines" logo had been carefully sanded away and covered with stain.

Still, he had been no stranger to hard work, and the Army made a man somewhat allergic to tardiness. He'd quickly been promoted to supervisor of Bagging Line B on the overnight shift, and then moved to days six months later when the day shift Line B supervisor took an early retirement when he threw his back out.

Between the pay bump and his side business, which had grown to include other resale items of sometimes questionable history, mostly cheap jewelry and such acquired at auction, he had been well on his way to modest comfort when a golden opportunity had fallen practically into his lap.

Surima Pet Foods was a family business, and it had been in moderate trouble when he hired on. Three years later, shortly after he'd been promoted once again to the foreman spot over all three bagging lines, the general manager had called him into his office with harsh news.

When he was told he needed to find six positions to cut, meaning he needed to decide which six guys over both shifts to fire, an epiphany had struck him. He hadn't said anything to Pete Guilder, the GM, because Pete was a short timer waiting for his first chance to call it quits and head off to Florida.

What he'd done instead had been to go home after telling Pete he'd think on it, and made sure his best suit was clean before jumping in the shower. Cleaned up, freshly shaved and his hair neatly combed, Harlan had put on his suit and hat, and driven out to the house on top of Pettymore Hill—the very house he now lived in, as a matter of fact—and introduced himself to one Gladys Rollins, the matriarch of the Rollins family and the owner of Surima Pet Foods. After some polite conversation in which he was gently but thoroughly grilled by the sharpest old woman he'd ever met, Harlan had made his proposal.

It was a logical enough idea; Surima was in financial dire straits, and Harlan Denison was a man looking for an investment. After some lovely Earl Grey and some tough negotiations, Harlan walked out of the Rollins family home with a handshake deal, which the lawyers would put together for him to sign three days later, making him forty percent owner in the business. Instead of finding six sad sacks to can to save a little on labor costs, he'd replaced the fairly inept plant manager and brought in someone who could actually make the whole operation efficient again.

And from there, the ball had started rolling, and it so far hadn't stopped.

When Gladys Rollins died of congestive heart failure, leaving the three Rollins kids without a lick of financial sense between them and more actual responsibility than anyone could rightfully expect three such utter morons to shoulder, Harlan had stepped in. All three of them would have sincerely sworn that Harlan Denison hung the moon when he agreed to take a small percentage of the business in lieu of monthly dividends, thus saving them from a minor outlay of cash and slowly bleeding away their only real source of income. Within five years, Harlan owned the vast majority of the company, and between their own inept business sense and their mounting debts, it wasn't long before he'd pushed them out completely. A year after he'd taken the business, he'd bought out their home at fire sale prices, once again using his own predatory nature and their total inability to function in the real world against them.

By the time Billy Denison left college and came back home to work for his old man, the last surviving Rollins kid was living with his grandchildren in some shithole in New Mexico and collecting Social Security.

That alone had made Harlan a very wealthy man, but like any overachiever, he'd never really stopped hustling. With his financial base secure—the business hadn't really been under financial strain so much as suffering from terminal neglect, a situation he'd remedied quickly—he'd gone to work with a vengeance, expanding his ever-growing empire.

He'd moved into real estate, which had done well until the market shit the bed in the early 2000s. He'd bought substantial interests in a trucking company, in the local waste disposal company, and numerous other independent ventures that were only too happy for a quick shot of cash. By 2009, Harlan was worth somewhere between thirty and forty million dollars altogether, and quite happy with it.

Then he'd met a young man who'd reminded him entirely too much of himself, and everything changed.

Jerry Hartman had rented a small warehouse from him in October of 2009, and by September of the following year had made quite a tidy bundle himself, although hardly through the same channels Harlan had. What Jerry did mostly was store things; someone brought him something to hold onto, and for a hefty fee he kept it safe until they came for it.

Most of these things were completely legitimate; wholesale merchandise bought from failing companies and held until shipment to different outlets could be arranged, or short-term storage for industrial equipment. But, like Harlan, Jerry was always looking for a side gig. What he found was, of course, a gold mine.

It had started with the usual; first pot, then meth, coke, and the occasional hijacked truckload of high-end electronics or cigarettes. Harlan, having learned first-hand from the Rollins family what happened to someone who did not keep his hand in his own business matters, quickly found out about Jerry's side gig, and by March of 2011 they were partners. Harlan took a cut off the top, hidden as warehouse rent, and Jerry found himself under the protective umbrella of the richest man in town. And then, as these things so often did, everything had changed and gotten way out of hand, until he found himself in the unenviable position he'd been in when he called Jerry to tell him to shut it all down and erase the evidence.

It was only at times like these, when Harlan was waiting to hear from his lawyer before going to the police station and jail to see just what sort of absurd fuckery his only son had gotten himself into this time, that he regretted ever getting into bed with Jerry.

4.

Three hours later, and even Harlan's masterly control over his temper was being sorely tried. "What?" he said as

Gary Rich, the lawyer he'd had on retainer for the last twenty years, shook his head.

"I can't do this anymore, Harlan," he said. "I'm out."

"What the fuck are you talking about?" he said. Gary just shook his head and pulled something from his breast pocket, then unfolded it and put it on Harlan's desk. It was a check for twenty-five thousand dollars, the exact amount of his retainer.

"I told you last year you needed to get that boy under control," he said, sounding genuinely pissed off. "I told you I'd gotten him off for the last time, and I meant it. This one isn't going away, Harlan, and you need to wrap your head around that fact now. Billy's in a hell of a jam, and I don't think Perry Mason could get him out of it. At any rate, I also work for the girl's father, so it's a conflict of interest."

"Then why aren't you giving him his retainer back?" Harlan snapped. He clenched his fists and counted to five, but that trick had stopped working two hours ago.

"Because his daughter didn't rape someone to death," Gary snapped right back. This was exactly the opposite of how these sorts of interactions were supposed to go; there was a noticeable lack of cowering on Gary's part, although he'd never really expected it from him. "Yeah, that's right. The girl, Jennifer Bennett. She died six hours ago, Harlan, as a direct result of the injuries she received when your son and his asshole friends gang-raped her and beat her senseless. They said it's a fucking miracle she lasted as long as she did."

"You're finished," Harlan said. "You're done in this town, Gary."

"That's not even remotely up to you," Gary said, staring him down. "You don't scare me, Harlan. You forget I know everything you've covered up over the last twenty years? Not just the stupid shit your delinquent son has done, either. I know your whole business, inside and out. Even Surima," he added, making Harlan's heart skip a beat. He turned and started for the door.

"Don't ever threaten me again, Harlan," Gary said, turning back toward him. "You might be the big man locally, but you don't want to try that shit with me." He left on this last note, and Harlan found himself in a perfect paroxysm of frustrated rage.

"God fucking damn it," he said, picking up the stress ball from his desk and squeezing it viciously. That last bit about Surima had hit home, and hard. If Gary knew half of what he was up to out there, then there was nothing he could do to move against him. In short, Gary had him over a barrel, and unless he was a very good boy, Harlan could end up getting cornholed.

He called a number he never dared to store anywhere but in his own brain, and someone answered right away. Thank God for small favors, it was at least the right someone. Jerry Hartman was his right-hand man out there, and probably the only man he could completely trust right now, simply because if it all went tits up on them, Jerry would probably end up in the cell next to his.

"It's me," Harlan said, careful not to use names. He was reasonably sure no one knew enough to bother tapping any of the phones, or whatever they did now, but he was a cautious man by nature. "Shut it down."

"Sir?" Jerry said. Not questioning him, but simply making sure he understood what he'd just heard.

"Shut it down," he said again. "Shut the whole thing down. I might be under a lot of attention right now."

"Understood," Jerry said. "And the product on hand?"

Harlan took a moment to consider what he was about to say, and went ahead. "Get rid of it. All of it. No trace," he said, and he heard Jerry gulp.

"I--"

"I understand, son," he said. "And I get what you're thinking, but you're my guy. I know you can do it."

After a moment that made Harlan more nervous than he'd ever admit, he heard Jerry sigh. "I understand. I'll take care of it personally."

"Atta boy," Harlan said. "Make it clean, no traces."

"Harlan, this attention," he said. "Is it coming from where I think it is?"

"As always," Harlan said, suddenly exhausted. He was a patient man, God knew. He'd put up with Billy's stupidity for years. And, as much as he loved his son, if Billy had been in front of him at that moment, he'd have cheerfully shot him dead.

He knew what was coming next, and if it had come from anyone but Jerry, they'd be dead very soon. But Jerry was his right-hand man for a reason. "Harlan," he said carefully. "Should I take care of that?" Even though he knew it was coming, it was still something of a shock to understand that Jerry had just asked if he should kill Billy.

"No, just shut everything down and clean it up." After a moment, he had what he thought was a stroke of real genius. "I'm sending three guys to you to help out. No loose ends, understand?"

"Understood," Jerry said again, and ended the call.

"God forgive me," Harlan said, and went to see his son. But first, he called Hollister, Grady, and Taylor, and told them that if they wanted to see the sun rise with their asses intact, they'd be out at Surima in thirty minutes.

CHAPTER FIVE

1.

Jerry watched as the three morons Harlan had sent him, whom he'd immediately dubbed Larry, Moe, and Curly, finished loading the last of the defunct merchandise into the back of a panel truck. "That's all?" he asked. Taylor, the big one, looked like he was about to whoops his cookies and soil his pants all at the same time as they all three nodded.

"Jesus fucking Christ," Grady said. He had indeed whoopsed his cookies several times, but to his credit he'd kept working the entire time. "We didn't know it would be this kinda shit, man."

Jerry looked at him for a moment, and the boy squirmed. "Would it have mattered if you did?" he said finally, and the kid blanched again. "You're not being paid to think, son. Just bend your back and shut your mouth."

"Got it," he said, and went back to work. He and Taylor each grabbed hoses from the hooks on the wall and attached them to the spigots, then began hosing down the inside of the storage room.

"Hey, pay attention," Jerry said. "The whole room means the whole goddamn room. Start at the ceiling and work your way down. Rinse everything, then scrub it all down. There's buckets and cleaner in the closet there."

He didn't like these two, but they were at least

tolerable; the third one he found he actively hated, almost on sight. He was a smarmy dick, entirely too sure that his own particular shit did not stink at all. Jerry turned to him as he pulled the door down and locked it. "The fuck you looking at?" Jerry said as the asshole just stood there. "Get in there and help, Princess."

The kid gave him a smart-assed salute that made Jerry want to beat the balls off him, and went in to start filling the scrub buckets. Ordinarily he didn't like what came next, but these three assholes just bugged him. Besides, after the morning's work, this would be like nothing at all.

Once they'd rinsed down the ceiling, the walls, and the floors, he watched as they each grabbed scrub brushes and started scrubbing down the entire holding room. The water running down the central drain in the floor turned from pink to foamy white as they rinsed everything down.

"You," he said, pointing to Grady. "Take all that shit out back. There's a burn pile there. Throw it all in and get it burning."

"It's plastic," Grady said, and Jerry resisted the urge to stab him in the eye.

"It'll melt," Jerry said. "And eventually it'll burn. It'll also destroy anything that might be evidence."

The moron shrugged and did as he was told, carrying all three buckets and all the brushes around to the back. "You," he said to Taylor. "In the back of the closet. Two cases of bleach. Pour every bit of it down that drain."

"Sure," Taylor said, and actually hustled his way over to the supply closet. Once they were done, he motioned to the truck.

"Throw the empty bottles in the back," he said.

"I just locked it," Hollister said.

"And did I tell you to lock it, fucknuts?" Jerry said. "No. So how about you stop trying to think and just do what you're told?"

Jerry managed to ignore the way the asshole rolled his eyes as he unlocked the truck and they tossed in the twelve empty bleach jugs. Grady came back at a half-assed jog as they finished up. He looked into the storage room, double-checking their work. It wasn't perfect, there was really no such animal, but it would be good enough, especially if no one had any reason to look for what had been there in the first place.

"What now?" Grady asked.

"Yeah," Hollister said. "And how much longer is this gonna take? I have something to do later."

That was it, Jerry decided. The very last straw. He grabbed Hollister by the ear and pulled, hard. "You don't have shit to do, asshole. Don't you get it? Mr. Denison owns your sorry asses. Now, for whatever reason, maybe just my own shitty karma, he's given you to me. That means I own you, understand?" When no one answered, he twisted the ear harder. He could feel blood seeping through his fingers. "I can't hear you, bitch. You understand me?"

"Jesus, yes," Hollister whined. "I hear you."

Jerry let go of his ear and wiped his hand on the asshole's shirt. "Good." He closed the back door of the panel truck. "Now, you three assholes get in this fucking thing and follow me."

"Where we going?" Grady asked, and he was sure he could actually feel the other two cringing. That was good; he liked it when assholes like this were afraid of him.

"There's a service road on the other side of the plant," he said. "You're going to stay right behind me. You understand? Right fucking behind me. If I look in my rearview and I don't see the grill of this fucking truck, I will personally feed you each other's nuts."

"Got it," Taylor said quickly, shoving the other two toward the cab of the truck. "Right behind you, no problem."

Satisfied he'd made his point, he got in behind the wheel of his pickup and drove out slowly, giving the Three Stooges time to figure out how to start the truck and follow him.

The access road led to a small gravel pit that had played out into clay years ago. Denison had bought the property mostly because it was adjacent to the plant, and he'd been planning expansions once upon a time. That idea had fallen by the wayside, but the pit would make a handy place for Jerry to dispose of broken or defective merchandise. He parked off to one side and got out.

"Back it up here, to the edge," he said, and Taylor gave him a nod before turning the panel truck around and backing up slowly. He thumped on the side, and the truck stopped. All three of them climbed out, and judging by the looks on their faces, they knew exactly what came next.

"Okay, no time to waste. Get it unloaded," he said. They moved slowly, and he clapped his hands together twice. "Come on, hustle up. Ain't got all day, boys."

They groaned and started unloading the truck, tossing each piece of broken merchandise into the pit, where it rolled down the sloped sides to the bottom. It went faster this time, because gravity was on their side.

"All done," Taylor said as they climbed out of the back of the truck. "What next?"

"You guys understand what it is you just dumped here, right?" Jerry said, catching them off guard. "I mean, I know they were wrapped up and all, but--"

"Yeah," Hollister said. "Kinda hard not to, you know?"

"Good," he said. "Then you understand that from the second you touched the first one, you all became accomplices after the fact. Just as guilty as if you'd done it yourselves. That means if I go down, you all go down. Are we clear?"

"Crystal clear," Hollister said. "Your business, which means it's none of ours."

"Good boy," Jerry said, smiling as he patted Hollister on the cheek. The smile helped them relax. That was good; relaxed was always a good way to be.

He was still smiling as he pulled the gun from his waistband and shot each one of them in the forehead. One shot each, quick and clean, before any of them had time to react. "Well, shit," he said as he saw that none of them actually fell down the embankment. Oh well, can't have it easy all the time, he thought to himself as he put the gun away and rolled each of them over the side, one by one. He had time; the little .22 didn't have much of a report in the first place, and out here no one would so much as raise an eyebrow at the sound of gunshots anyway. Plus, the segmented lead rounds fragmented inside the skull, meaning no exit wound or mess to clean up. Just one shot to the brain, quick and clean.

Whistling to himself, he grabbed a pick and shovel from the back of his truck and made his way carefully down the shallow end of the pit wall to the center. His watch said it was only four in the afternoon, which meant he had plenty of daylight left. It broke his heart a little to lose all that prime merchandise, but he supposed Denison knew what he was doing. It'd be so much easier if he'd just let him get rid of the boy too, but he supposed that was asking a little too much. Still, it was just such a damned waste.

"Well, at least you assholes will have company," he said, poking Grady's shoe with the tip of the spade. He looked around once more, then stripped off his shirt and got to work scooping and shoveling loose gravel over the bodies of the Three Stooges and the thirteen girls, most of them smuggled in illegally from South America, that he'd shot earlier in the day on Denison's orders.

"Such a waste," he said, shaking his head, and went back to work.

I could use a burger, he thought as he worked, dumping a shovel full of gravel over a hand. A very small hand, but he didn't let himself think about that. Just merchandise, he told himself. Nothing but merchandise. If he finished up here in time, he'd grab a shower and head into town for a big, greasy cheeseburger and some fries. No, not fries.

Onion rings. Definitely onion rings.

2.

"Mother?" one of the girls said as Lilith fell to her knees, sobbing as she felt the pain of her children dying. Thirteen, she thought, and sobbed. Thirteen, all at once. What could cause such a terrible loss?

But of course, there was only one real answer. She had well over a billion children, all over the world. They were constantly being born and dying, all part of the natural course of life. She could notice their passing if she focused, but mostly she chose not to; it was too sad. But these thirteen, these beautiful daughters of hers, had not died as part of the natural course of life and death. They had been murdered. By a man, she understood as the first of their collective memories came to her. A tall man, handsome and intelligent. Not one of her children, of course; her children had the capacity to be cruel, as did all human souls, but rarely were they responsible for such a massive loss of life, at least not like this.

Her children were strong, often much stronger than those of the Other mother. Her sons, in particular, were well suited to war, and made excellent soldiers. She felt a distinct pride in this; her children had been at the front of virtually every conquering army in history. And while such men rarely hesitated when it came time to kill the enemy, she could only remember a small handful of times, no more than two or three in all of history, when her own children had been responsible for such a senseless mass killing.

Senseless murder was the trademark of the Other mother's children, not hers.

She let Kris help her to her feet, smiling so the girl wouldn't be afraid. "Mother, what happened?" Kris asked.

"Nothing for you to be concerned about, my beautiful

child," she said, holding her hand. "Come, let's get you children home."

"Mother," one of them said. It was a small, heart-breakingly beautiful Korean girl, with gorgeous brown eyes and a shy, sweet smile. "The cops, they'll be looking for us. We're truant."

"Ah," Lilith said, and patted the girl's small, smooth cheek. "Of course. We have somewhere we need to go, and while it isn't far, I'm not quite familiar with this town."

She told them where they needed to go, and Kris shared a smile with two other girls. Teresa was a vision of soft seduction; plump and inviting. Melanie was her almost exact opposite; tall instead of short, with a smooth, muscular body and a compact but quite lovely bustline.

"We know how we can get there," Kris said. Melanie held up a set of keys.

"I used to complain about having to drive my Mom's old minivan," Melanie said. "But now, I love it."

"Your mother," Lilith said, feeling the girl's presence in her mind. Her lineage stretched back through time, and Lilith smiled. "Deborah. How is she? Is that horrible disease under control now?"

"What, the cancer?" Melanie said, completely unsurprised that Lilith would know such a thing. "Oh, yeah. Total remission, going on three years now."

"Wonderful," Lilith said, smiling and clapping her hands. She looked closely at the girl, and a twitch struck her left eye. "But hold on. I see—yes, there it is. Well, I simply can't allow that."

Before anyone knew what she was even talking about, Lilith had kissed her fingertips and touched them to Melanie's pelvis, just above her untried sex, and destroyed the seeds of the cervical cancer that had been slumbering there, waiting for the biological signal to awaken and take one of her special children.

Melanie gasped and placed a hand over her flat stomach, giggling. "You cured it," she said. "I didn't even know it was there, but now I can feel it dying inside me."

"My beautiful children," she said, looking at all of them. "I would do anything, for any of you. That's what a Mother does. Now, will you do something for me?"

"Anything," Melanie said, her eyes shining with tears. "Anything for you." The others all murmured their agreement.

"Then listen closely, my loves," Lilith said. "Once we get to where we need to go, I have something very special for all of you. A gift, one you'll treasure forever. And I think," she said, pausing as she felt out with that primeval sense, the one that let her feel all of her children, wherever they were. It took a second for it to focus, but she found the one she needed, and smiled. "Yes. And there will be someone special there, waiting for us. A sister, in more ways than I can explain."

"A sister," Kris said, tears now sliding down her smooth cheek. "I always wanted a sister."

"Now you have many sisters," Lilith said, gesturing to the girls with her. "And together, you will all help me set right what has been made wrong."

She watched as they all stared at her in awe, their eyes glimmering. "I love you all," she said, and let Melanie lead them to her vehicle.

3.

Curtis Standhope was not a particularly imaginative young man. He preferred reality TV and documentaries to sitcoms, dramas, or fantasy; he brought the same lunch to work every day. He was methodical, bordering on plodding, but that was what made him so good at his job. He did things by the book, every time.

So he was aware, at least on some level, that letting a random woman off the street into the morgue was definitely not in the book. Neither was just sitting on a rolling chair parked next to the cooler where a homicide victim lay and waiting patiently instead of starting the postmortem exam, but that's exactly what he was doing, and it felt right.

Of course it felt right; that was what she wanted, after all. And he loved her, he knew that much. She felt like home to him, maybe like a favorite aunt who had always doted on him. He wanted to please her, to make her turn that beautiful smile on him. He was not a particularly sexual man; he had a few girls he saw now and then, but it never really went anywhere, and he didn't mind. It wasn't that he was devoid of sexual desire, far from it. He'd felt intense attraction for any number of women, and from time to time acted on them, usually at least marginally successfully.

But that woman, she intrigued him. It wasn't just that she was beautiful, although she was easily the most beautiful woman he'd ever seen. It was that she seemed so kind, so utterly wholesome, that surely anyone who saw her must fall in love with her.

Still, it was Jennifer who his mind kept coming back to; sweet, lovable little Jenny Bennett, who'd worked at the liquor store and could brighten even a truly horrible day with just a smile and a "hey, hon." He'd been working up the nerve to ask her out for days now, at least until he found out that Billy Denison, the miserable son of a bitch, had a thing for her.

He wasn't a coward, but he was far from a tough guy. And when a violent bastard like Denison laid claim to something, even if it wasn't his to claim, it was just smart to steer clear. But then he'd gotten notice that he was expecting a body, and had seen the name on the form. No fucking way, he thought, but of course it had been her.

It had taken him all of three minutes to learn that Big Jim Harlow had not only arrested Denison for the murder, but had beaten the holy Jesus-jumping shit out of him in the process. That had helped, a little, but not enough to take away the sting he felt whenever he'd remembered who was currently waiting for him to autopsy.

But now, he didn't know what to expect. The woman, Lilith, had said to wait, so he'd wait. She'd said Jenny would be hungry when she woke up, and something about that felt extremely wrong, but he waited just the same. He didn't play on his phone, didn't work on his never-ending backlog of paperwork, or even clean the exam suite in preparation for the autopsy. He sat on his rolling stool patiently and waited. And when the cooler drawer with Bennett, J written on the white card in its pocket began to slide open, he just turned and smiled.

"Curtis," Jennifer said, and sat up. She swung her short but very shapely legs over the side, hopping down to the floor. Something pinged deep in his subconscious, something telling him to quit gawking, get up, and run the fuck away as fast as he could. He actually managed to stand up before Jenny came to him, gently but firmly pushing him back down onto the stool. She was naked, of course, but there was something wrong.

"Your face," he said, actually touching it in a way he'd never dared before. "It's better now."

"Didn't know there was anything wrong with it before," she said, smiling as she sat down in his lap. "You never seemed to mind it."

"No," he said, intensely aware of the very naked, very robust woman in his lap. Very aware, he realized, and wondered how he could shift it around without tipping her off.

"Oh, don't mind that," she said, smiling, and actually ground against it as she leaned in to whisper. "I don't. I don't mind it at all."

He felt something tickle the side of his throat, and he gasped as her lips left his skin. "I know you used to look at me all the time, Curt," she whispered in his ear. "I always knew. I saw how you watched me. And you know what? I liked it." She nibbled his earlobe, and his eyes rolled back in his head.

She slid around and straddled his lap, backing the

rolling stool up against the coolers, and put his hands on her waist. Her small, firm breasts pushed against him as she continued to grind, moaning softly in his ear. "You have something I need, Curt," she said, her voice breathy and soft. "I know, because Mother told me. Can I have it?"

"Anything," Curtis said. And when he felt small, sharp teeth slide effortlessly into his throat, he didn't even make a sound.

4.

"Shut up," Harlan said as soon as Billy opened his mouth. "Not one word, boy. They're probably recording this right now."

"Isn't that illegal?" Billy asked, and Harlan shook his head.

"I've got a lawyer coming down from Kansas City. He'll be here in time for your arraignment. In the meantime, have you said anything, to any of them? Harlow, Gillette, anyone?"

"Just that I want my lawyer," he said, and Harlan nodded. He looked the boy over for a bit.

"I have to guess who worked you over like that?" he asked, and Billy shook his head.

"Kept saying I was 'resisting arrest' or some shit," Billy said.

Harlan nodded again. "You pull a gun on him?" he asked. He could see Billy mulling it over, wondering how much he already knew. "You lie to me boy, and I'll leave you here to rot."

He didn't say anything, just nodded. "Stupid," Harlan said, shaking his head. "Means you can pretty much kiss any sort of lawsuit goodbye."

"But he--," Billy started, but stopped when he saw the look on his father's face. "Yes, sir. I figure it's a wash."

"Smart," Harlan said, nodding. "Might be the first smart thing you've ever said, son."

"How soon can I get out?" he asked, and Harlan shook his head.

"You still don't get it, do you?" he said, shaking his head. "You're being charged with murder, boy. Murder in the course of a sexual assault, no less. Felony murder, Bill. That's a capital crime. It'll be a goddamn miracle if I can keep you off death row. You really think Judge Sherman's gonna grant you bail on that?"

"She's played ball with us before," he said, his voice low. Harlan shook his head, simply aghast at his own son's stupidity.

"This is a hell of a lot bigger than another DUI or a bar fight, son," he said. "That burning feeling you've got right now? That's the puddle of boiling shit you've gotten yourself into this time, boy. Time to start taking this seriously. The lawyer will be here for the arraignment. You're to shut your hole and do exactly as he says, am I clear?"

"Yes sir," Billy said. "What about the guys? What happens to my friends?"

Right about now they're probably rotting in a hole somewhere, he thought but didn't say. "They're gonna go on a nice, extended vacation," he said. "And, on the off chance we somehow keep your stupid ass out of prison, you'll never have anything to do with any of them, ever again. I won't go so far as to say they're bad influences, because we both know they're too stupid for that. But it's obvious you've had just a little too much free time on your hands. If you're granted bail, and I highly doubt that, you're going to spend every waking minute of it working your ass off out at the plant."

"You mean with Jerry?" he said, almost hopefully. Harlan just shook his head.

"Of course not," he said. He wanted to curse at the mention of Jerry's name in association with anything, but he let it go. That Jerry worked at the plant was no secret. "You'll be working the loading docks. Twelve hour shifts, six days a week. I figure that way, you'll be too dog-ass tired to do anything stupid."

"Dad, come on," Billy said, and Harlan held up a finger to shut him up, just as he had his whole life.

"That's how it's gonna be, son," he said. "But honestly, I doubt even Judge Sherman will give you bail."

"If she does," Billy said, swallowing hard. "If she does, are you going to put it up?"

Harlan considered this briefly. There were a number of reasons he shouldn't do it, but one overriding reason he was going to just the same. "I'll do it, because that's what your mama would have wanted me to do," he said. "The same reason I'm going to do everything I can to get you out from under this. But you need to understand the situation, son. There's a good chance you're going to prison over this, and all the money and favors in the world may not be enough to stop it."

"Daddy, I--"

"If it's within my power, I'll do it," he said. "But you're a grown man, son, and you need to understand the reality of the situation."

He didn't want to say this next part. God knew he didn't want to, but it had to be done. He loved the boy, always would, but there had to be a line. "I need you to listen to me, Bill," he said. "I only got the heart to say it just the one time, so listen up good. You listening?"

"Yes, sir," Billy said, and Harlan saw he knew what was coming. "I'm listening."

Here goes, Harlan thought, and pressed on. "This is the last time, son," he said. "I have protected you, I have covered for you. I've made problems go away, when maybe I shouldn't have. I've done all that because you're my son, and I love you. It's what your mama, God rest her soul, would have wanted me to do. But like I said, you're a grown man now, and it's time you stood on your own."

"Can I ask you something, sir?" he said, taking a deep breath. Harlan nodded.

"Of course," he said.

"Do you think I did this?" he asked. Harlan looked the boy in the eye for a moment, then reached through the bars and cupped the back of his head, leaning in as close as he could.

"Son, do you honestly think it would make a difference to me either way?" he said. "I love you, boy. Stay strong, and we'll get through this."

"Yes, sir," he said, close to tears.

CHAPTER SIX

1.

Ruth Ann's trailer was vastly improved when they arrived. Emma greeted her at the door with a smile and a warm hug. "I'm so glad you're here," Emma said as the kids played in the backyard.

"And I can't tell you how happy I am to see you, Emma," Lilith said, kissing her cheek. "And how sweet was it of you to help Ruth Ann while she sleeps?"

"She's my sister," was all Emma said. It was all the explanation needed. She saw the group of girls climbing out of the van behind Lilith. "Oh, more sisters?"

"Yes," Lilith said, smiling.

"I did what you asked," Emma said. "There's plenty of room for them to sleep."

"Thank you," Lilith said, and kissed her cheek. Emma beamed at her again, and began crying. "Oh, what's this?" she said.

"I'm just so happy," Emma said, and Lilith smiled. Kris and the others came forward, stopping at the porch steps.

"Emma," Lilith said. "This is Kris."

"Welcome," Emma said, hugging the girl as warmly as if they were long lost friends, reunited after years. Kris stepped into the trailer, and each of the girls came forward one at a time as Lilith introduced them.

"Oh, my," Emma said as she hugged Teresa. "You know, you look almost exactly like Betty Page. Absolutely gorgeous." Teresa blushed and kissed her cheek, and went inside. Emma had similar praise for each of the girls. She marveled at Melanie's toned muscle, and told a shy Black girl named Melissa that hiding a beautiful face like hers must be a crime somewhere. The girl instantly stood up straight, brushing her long braids out of her face to smile. Lilith nodded her approval.

Last to come to Emma was a tall brunette named Amber. Amber's pain ran deep, more than most. The things those boys at the school had done to her were nothing compared to what her own father had been doing since she was nine years old. She had been wandering the halls of that school, broken and lost, for years, and no one had even noticed. It made Lilith incredibly sad, and was there a touch of anger behind the sadness? Yes, there was. That someone could break something so beautiful was, to her, unforgivable.

But in the van, something had begun to change inside Amber. It started small, smiling as she crammed in with the others instead of shrinking away. She'd laughed at something silly Kris had said when they passed a group of men in a work truck who had been ogling them. She'd even held Melissa's hand at one point as the girls began to bond.

Lilith put an arm around Amber's waist as she came forward. What might have been invisible to others was plain to see for Emma, who was still riding high on influence of Lilith's power. "Oh," Emma said, holding out her arms. "Come here, sweetheart."

"I don't need your pity," Amber said, finally showing a little of that core of strength her children had. It made both Lilith and Emma smile.

"No pity, sweetheart," Emma said. "Just love. We're sisters, you know. We all love you, Amber. And we'll all protect you. No one will hurt you, ever again."

"That's right," Lilith said, hugging the poor child. "Never again. You're strong, Amber. Stronger than you know, and once you've become what you were truly meant to be, you'll be even stronger. You all will."

"I love you," Amber said to Lilith, and kissed her cheek. "And you," she added, hugging Emma.

"I love you so much," Emma said, squeezing her tightly. "Go inside with the others. There's food, and soda."

"Thank you," Amber said, and joined her sisters. Lilith came to Emma then, and kissed her cheek.

"Thank you for all you've done," she said, brushing Emma's hair with her fingertips.

"Anything for you, Mother," Emma said. It made Lilith's heart swell. "Will I be joining my sisters?"

"Oh, no," Lilith said. "I have something very important for you to do, my sweet girl. Something particularly suited to a big sister."

"The father," she said. She was still in tune with Lilith's thoughts and feelings, and she knew exactly what Lilith needed. Lilith nodded.

"They'll be hungry when they wake," she said, looking into the open trailer, where the girls were sitting in a circle on the floor, sharing sandwiches and Cokes and laughing happily. "And we'll provide them with all they need. But I think young Amber deserves a special first meal, don't you?"

"He's not worthy of that honor," Emma said, her face twitching. "He's a monster. Please, Mother. Can I kill him?"

"Do as I say, Emma," Lilith said, her voice still pleasant, but firm. Emma looked crestfallen, but nodded. Lilith took her hands, and kissed them. "I understand how you feel. I know about your father, as well. How could I not? But Amber needs this, more than we do. Don't you think so?"

"Yes," Emma said, nodding. Her smile returned. "She

should get what I never could. I'll make it happen."

"Thank you, love," Lilith said. "Once they're asleep, you'll go to him. Bring him to her, and she'll finally be able to take back all he stole from her."

"Will you stay with us?" she said. Lilith touched her cheek with a sad smile.

"I'm always with you, Emma," she said. "And we'll all be together soon. But I have to see about my other children."

"I felt something," Emma said. "I don't know what it was, but it was horrible." Lilith didn't have the heart to tell her that she'd felt thirteen of her beautiful sisters die; it would break her precious heart, and there had been enough heartbreak in Emma's life.

"I know, and I'm sorry," Lilith said. "It hurts me to know you felt that pain, my sweet one. But I'll make it right, I promise you. Now, come inside, and let's tend to your sisters."

They were just about to go inside when a car pulled up, parking next to Melanie's van. Lilith smiled as she felt who was driving. Emma turned and stared, not in horror but wonder as a petite girl, completely nude with blood still trickling from the corner of her pretty mouth, got out of the car.

"Jennifer," Lilith said, and embraced the woman as she came forward.

"Mother," Jennifer Bennett said.

They went into the trailer together, and no one was the least bit surprised to see the naked woman with them. They all stood, and everyone exchanged hugs. Somehow, she knew all their names, and they knew hers. It didn't seem the least bit strange to anyone inside the trailer that this was so.

They were sisters, after all.

2.

"Jim?" Mark said, knocking at his door. "Just got back

71

from one hell of a weird call out to the high school."

"Oh, Lord," Jim said. "What is it?"

"Not exactly sure," Mark said. "Best I can tell, half a dozen girls just walked out."

"Not exactly the crime of the century," Jim said, and Mark laughed.

"No, but it gets weirder," Mark said. "I swung by and took the statement, and while I'm there, one of the students pulls me aside. Does the whole 'you didn't hear this from me' bit, and tells me at least four male students were gang-raped at about the same time."

"What?" Jim said, almost spitting coffee all over his desk. Mark just nodded, as if to acknowledge just how crazy it was. "You talk to them?"

"I tried," Mark said. "Couple of them had some bumps and bruises, but they said it was from a rough football practice. None of them would admit anything."

"Christ," Jim said. "You follow up with anyone?"

"No idea where to even start," Mark said. "None of the alleged victims will even acknowledge they were attacked, and I don't have any names to follow up on."

"Shit," Jim said. "You talk to the guidance counselor?"

"Just got done with her," he said. "She said she'd start trying to reach out to them."

"Doesn't the school have surveillance cameras?"

"Not in the classrooms," he said. "And the cameras in the main hallway didn't catch anything. You know, I hate to even say it, but--"

"Nothing else we can do," Jim admitted. "Write it up so we have documentation, but that's all we can do."

"Just about to get started," Mark said as the door to the cells opened. "Uh oh."

"Stay close," Jim said. He wasn't remotely scared of Harlan Denison; he just wanted someone nearby to be able to swear he didn't beat the balls off him.

3.

Harlan knocked on Chief Harlow's office door once before walking in without waiting for a response. "Mr. Denison," Harlow said, standing up. "Have a seat."

"Save the small talk," Harlan said, waving a hand in the air. "We've got a lot to talk about."

"Sir, if this is about your son, you should know I can't comment on--"

"Save it," he said again. "I love my son, but he's had that ass-kicking coming for quite some time now. Honestly, I wish I'd done it myself years ago. Might have saved everyone a lot of trouble. That's not why I'm here."

"Then why are you here, Mr. Denison?" Harlow said, sitting back down. Harlan saw his knuckles were scraped up, and restrained the urge to attack the man.

"Like I said, what Billy got he's had coming, and for a long time," Harlan said. "That's all water under the bridge. My way of saying there'll be no stink raised about it. But what concerns me is what happens to him from here on out."

"He'll most likely be arraigned in the morning," Harlow said. "In the unlikely event Judge Sherman grants bail, he'll be released with severe conditions. House arrest, ankle monitor, the works if I have anything to say about it."

"That's fine," he said with another dismissal wave of his hand. "But I want your word, Chief. No one else lays a hand on him while he's in custody."

"You have it," Harlow said, nodding. He felt Harlow studying him, and knew something else was coming. "You know he did it, don't you?" he said. "He and his asshole buddies raped that poor girl, repeatedly. They beat her and broke her, and tore her insides up."

"If that were true, and if these young men were involved, why aren't they sitting in the cells next to him?" he said. "Because you couldn't get much of a statement from her, is my guess. Maybe she whispered a name, maybe not even that. Am I right?"

"I can't comment on an open investigation," Harlow said, which was all the confirmation Harlan needed. "But we're collecting and sorting evidence from multiple avenues of investigation."

"Two hundred," Harlan said, ready to play his hole card.

"Excuse me?" Harlow said. "I don't follow you."

"Two hundred men," he said. "Two hundred men over three shifts, that's what my plant employs. It also pays a large portion of the tax base for this county. Be a shame if all those jobs and all those taxes just dried up and blew away."

Harlow nodded. "Let me see if I understand you, Mr. Denison," he said, and Harlan knew he had to be careful; if he needed any proof of the big man's temper, all he needed to do was go back downstairs and take a good look at his son. "You're telling me that if I push this, you'll close down your plant in retaliation."

"I said nothing like that," he said, smiling. "Just pointing out certain facts. After all, I like it here. Grew up just down the road, came back here after the Army. It's a nice little town, but if my son is gonna be the first place you look for a scapegoat for every crime, maybe this isn't such a nice town anymore."

"Cut the shit," Harlow said. With some people, the profanity might have shocked him into losing his poker face, but Harlan Denison wasn't easily shocked. "We both know your son and his friends killed Jenny Bennett."

"I don't have a bit of problem believing those three little shits could do something like that," he said. "Bad news, is what they are. But my son couldn't do that, not even with them behind him. You might wanna look them up, find out where they were when this happened. Assuming they didn't take the chance and head for the hills when you were busy beating up my son and arresting him for something they did."

Harlow returned his hard gaze, and he wasn't a bit

surprised. It would take a pure damned fool to mistake Jim Harlow for a soft man. "Oh, I'll find them," he said. "And when I do, you can believe I'll get the truth out of them. All of it."

Harlan nodded. "You do that, Chief," he said, and walked out.

4.

Jim watched as Harlan Denison left the station, wondering exactly how and when this whole thing would blow up in his face. Now that the whirlwind had passed, he could think rationally again, and he knew he'd just bought himself a whole lot of trouble.

And not just him; if he wasn't very careful, this could be trouble for a lot of other people, including the two hundred or so employees of the plant, not to mention all the smaller satellite businesses that catered to those employees. And it hadn't been an idle threat on Harlan's part; Jim knew perfectly well the man was capable of anything. He doubted Harlan would hesitate for a second to close down the plant and put all those people out of work just to punish him for arresting Bill.

He was mulling over this happy thought when someone knocked on his door. "Hey, you got a minute?" Mark said, and Jim nodded.

"Come on in," he said. After a pause, he added. "Close the door if it's gonna be the talk I think we're gonna have." Mark closed the door, and Jim cursed silently.

"Bad news first, I guess," Mark said, and held something out.

"You're kidding me," Jim said as Mark handed him a message slip from Dispatch. "Tell me this is some sort of sick joke, Mark. You're just screwing with me, to teach me a lesson, right?"

"Afraid not," Mark said. "The Bennett girl's body is gone, Jim. No word from Curt Standhope, either."

75

"Shit," Jim said. He was reaching for his hat when Mark shook his head.

"It's County's call, Chief," he said. "They're already on scene. I know the guy who caught it, and he'll call if anything pops."

"Christ, what a mess," Jim said, and Mark nodded. He sat down and cleared his throat, obviously working up to something.

"You, uh, feeling okay now?" he said.

Jim smiled. It wasn't a warm smile. "You mean am I still seeing red?" he asked, and Mark smiled back. "No, I'm good. I'm sorry, Mark. I put you in a hell of a spot out there."

"You didn't put me anywhere," Mark said, shaking his head. "I made the call, backed your play. It'll shake out how it shakes out. I'm good."

Jim looked out the window, where Harlan had stopped on the sidewalk to have a little chat with the one person he'd been dreading seeing since he'd calmed down. Mayor Albright was nodding sympathetically and listening as Harlan talked. "I sure as hell hope so," he said. Mark followed his gaze, where Harlan and the mayor shook hands before Albright started up the steps. "If it comes down to it, I'll try and get them to leave you out of it."

"Bullshit," Mark said, shaking his head. "I meant what I said. I made my own decision out there. That little bastard has needed every square inch of his ass kicked for years now. You know Gus still can't stand up for more than a half hour at a time these days?"

Jim nodded. Last year, Bill Denison had gotten liquored up and driven his brand new pickup onto the sidewalk, managing to avoid killing anyone only by the grace of God. He'd clipped Gus a good one, though, and at sixty-five even a little tap was no joke. Gus had spent three months in the hospital, undergoing a full hip replacement and physical therapy.

"And that's just one of a dozen stories everyone

knows," Mark continued. "Like I said, he's had it coming."

"His father said the same thing," Jim said, making Mark's eyebrows go up. Jim nodded. "Says there won't be a stink about it, although I'll believe that when I see it."

Mark just grunted, and Jim didn't have to ask what that had meant. He knew as well as Jim did that there was something off about Harlan. He had nothing concrete, not even a solid suspicion, but Harlan Denison was a wrong guy, plain and simple. And there was that creepy bastard who worked for him, Hartman. That guy alone was enough trouble for three or four men.

"Uh oh, incoming," Mark said as Mayor Albright hit the front door of the station. He blew past the receptionist and headed straight for Jim's office with a full head of steam, and opened the door.

"It's customary to knock on a closed door before entering," Jim said as Mark stood up. "I'm just in a conference with my officer, Mr. Mayor, but I'll be with you in a moment."

"Cut the shit, Harlow," he snapped, a rare breach of his ever-present decorum. He turned to Mark. "We're gonna need the room."

Mark, bless his cheerfully gay little heart, ignored Albright and looked at Jim for instructions. "Mark, you mind calling your buddy at County for me? Let them know I'd like to see whatever they have on the Bennett girl ASAP."

"Will do," Mark said. He turned to Albright and gave him the barest of nods before leaving. Albright closed the door and paced in the small swatch of floor in front of Jim's desk. He just sat back and closed his hands over his midsection, waiting him out.

"I've got half a mind to ask for your resignation," he said finally, stopping his pacing and leaning with his hands on Jim's desk.

"All you gotta do is ask," Jim said, his voice neutral. "I

was out of line. It shouldn't have happened."

"Bullshit," Albright said, shaking his head and resuming pacing. "I don't give two shits about Bill Denison. What bothers me is that you did it in front of half the damned town."

"I affected an arrest," Jim said. "Not by the book, I'll admit that. I let my emotions get the better of me."

"I'd call that an understatement," Albright said, chuckling.

"Has anyone called your office to complain?" Jim asked, and again Albright shook his head.

"Not a single soul," he said, sitting down. "Privately, I've talked to just about everyone who was there when you had your little prize fight, and all of them say pretty much the same thing. The Denison boy pulled a gun on you, and you took him down. That's not our problem right now."

"Then what is our problem?" Jim asked, although he was already painfully aware of it.

"You know goddamned good and well what the problem is," Albright said. "Shitty arrest, no actual witnesses, and with the body gone before anyone could do an autopsy, shit for physical evidence. Do you have any actual evidence linking young master Denison downstairs to the Bennett case?" he asked. Jim supposed he could pull the "we don't comment on open investigations" card, but thought better of it.

"I've got her statement," he said. "Talked to her when she came into the hospital."

"And she told you he did it?" Albright said. Of course, the smarmy bastard zeroed right in on the weakest point of the whole thing. "She named Denison as her attacker?"

Jim resisted the urge to squirm. "She said 'Billy.' Said it several times, as a matter of fact."

"That's it?" he said, and now Jim was squirming. "That's all she said? She didn't give you a full name, even?"

"He's been after her for months," Jim said. "She even came to me about it, a few weeks ago. Said he was getting a little too aggressive."

"And of course, you wrote up a report, right?" Albright asked, and again Jim couldn't help but squirm.

"I told her I'd have a talk with him," he said. "And I did. He said he'd cool it."

"Right," Albright said, letting out a deep and heavy sigh that could only mean trouble. He stood up and started for the door. "Jim, do I need to even say it here? I know you told them he'd be arraigned in the morning, but come on. You can't tell me anyone actually signed off on that, even before the whole shit show at the morgue. Or do I need to call Wes Nelson down at the DA's office and get his opinion on it first?" He knew better; Albright was still technically a lawyer, although he hadn't been in actual practice for some time.

"They did a rape kit at the ER," Jim said. "Those reports will nail him. I'm just holding him until they come in."

"And that would be perfectly reasonable, if you hadn't beaten the ever-loving shit out of him first," Albright said. "His father's saying everything's copacetic right now, but I don't trust it. You know what he told me on the way in here?"

"We need better coffee?" he said.

"He said he was running late for a meeting," he said. "With a realtor. Said he was 'exploring his options.' I don't have to tell you what happens to this town if he decides to move, do I?"

"No, he made that pretty clear himself," Jim said, sighing. Christ, he hated this part of the job. The back-and-forth, the politics. Then again, if he hadn't let himself get caught up in the whirlwind—and he'd let it happen, no point in kidding himself about that—none of this would be happening. "Aw, for Christ's sweet sake. I have to kick him loose, don't I?"

"Technically, you could hold him for seventy-two hours without charging him," Albright said. "Maybe your forensics come in fast, who knows?"

Jim just shook his head, feeling the first twitches of the old anger stirring. This time, he pushed them down. No more of that shit, he told himself. That's how you ended up here in the first goddamn place.

The girl had managed to croak out the name "Billy" two or three times before she'd lapsed into unconsciousness. He'd already had Billy Denison on his mind when he'd gone out to the hospital to take the report. And it was generally accepted that when you were talking about trouble in this particular small town, there was only one Billy, but that could hardly be called evidence. And when Dr. Emmett had called to inform him that the girl had passed away, he'd seen red.

Twenty-four years old, he'd thought.

Raped and beaten to death, he'd thought.

Bill Denison, he'd thought. Billy fucking Denison.

And then the whirlwind had him, and there was no more thinking.

"No way in hell forensics gets back that fast," he said, shaking his head. "It'll be three days before the HiPo lab even gets those samples, let alone runs them."

"You want some free advice?" Albright said. "Worth every penny you're paying for it."

"Hit me," Jim said. "No, really. Pick up something heavy and clobber me with it, because that'll be better than my day so far."

Albright smiled. "Officially, you were just there to interview Denison," he said. "Like you said, he has a history with the girl, and she said the name 'Billy' before she passed out. But he pulled a gun on you, and you had to defend yourself. That's why he's sitting in a cell right now."

"And, after everyone's had a chance to cool down, I've decided not to press the issue," Jim said, and Albright nodded. "What about the gun?"

"He doesn't have a record, thanks to Daddy," Albright said with a shrug. "And there's no permit required to carry any more. I could get any charge you'd care to bring tossed without leaving my office. He was just turning it over to you while you talked, and you over-reacted. That's how I'd play it."

Jim nodded; it sucked a big fat one, but it all fit. "Fine, I'll kick him. But when those tests come back, I'm coming at him again, and hard."

"Just don't hit him anymore," Albright said. "Because I think you're right. I think he and his little pack of idiots killed that girl, and I'd hate to see the whole thing get tossed because you lost your temper again."

Albright saw himself out as Jim nodded. Okay, he thought. We'll play the long game.

Sighing, he made himself stand up and walk out into the main station. Mark flagged him down, and he headed over to his desk. "Just got off the phone with HiPo," he said. "They have the rape kit, and they swear they'll get to it ASAP."

"Meaning Monday," Jim said, shaking his head. Mark just nodded.

"I made it very clear we need those test results," Mark said. He looked at the door to the station house, where the mayor had just left. "Do I need to ask what that was about?" he said, and Jim shook his head.

"Three guesses, and the first two don't count," Jim said.

"Crap," Mark said. "And we're okay with this?"

"I'm about a million miles from okay with it," Jim said. "But it's how it is."

Mark sighed and pulled the keys to the holding cells from his desk drawer. "This sucks," he said, and Jim nodded. "Maybe, uh, you should sit this one out."

"No," he said, shaking his head. "But you can come along and make sure he can't say I tuned him up again."

CHAPTER SEVEN

1.

"Sleep now, my sweet," Lilith said, kissing Kris's forehead as she tucked the blanket in around her. "And when you wake, all your sisters will be here with you."

"Will it hurt?" Kris asked, and Lilith smiled sweetly at her.

"I would never cause you pain," she said.

"It doesn't hurt, sister," Jennifer said. "It feels wonderful." Kris smiled, and closed her eyes. Lilith kissed her forehead again, and left her to sleep with the others.

Lilith stepped out of the small bedroom and into the living room, where Emma was just finished tidying up after their impromptu picnic. "Please, sister," Jennifer said. "Let me help."

The two of them had the trailer in tip-top shape in moments. Jennifer now wore some of Ruth Ann's clothes, which were only a bit too large. "My beautiful girls," Lilith said, watching as they worked together. "You've both been through so much, I'm ashamed to ask more of you."

"I'd do anything for you," Jennifer said. "You know that, Mother. All you have to do is tell me what you need, and I'll make it happen." Lilith smiled and touched her cheek.

"I don't have to tell either of you that there are evil people in this world. Evil men, certainly. Some of them may come looking for your sisters. When they wake, they'll be almost untouchable, but while they sleep, they are vulnerable."

"I'll protect them," Jennifer said. "You've made me so strong, Mother. Let me use it. I'll keep them safe."

"I know you will," Lilith said, smiling. "They'll be as safe with you as they would be in my arms, I have no doubt of that." This made Jennifer smile, revealing the small points of her elongated canines.

"How can I help, Mother?" Emma asked. "I'm not as strong as my sister, but--"

"My sweet girl," Lilith said, shushing her. "You are stronger than you can possibly know. I can't tell you how proud I am of you. Of all of you. And I have a special job for you, the one we spoke of earlier. Will you do that for me?"

"Of course, Mother," Emma said. "I know where to find him. I don't know how I know, but I do."

"You know because your sister knows," Lilith said. "You are all connected, now and forever. What one knows, all will know. You'll all feel each other's joy, and pain. Let it bond you all together, and nothing will ever touch any of you, ever again."

She kissed each of her daughters with tender care, and left them to do as she'd asked. She had something to do herself, and she could put it off no longer.

2.

Billy was trying to find a comfortable way to sit on the shitty cot in his cell when the door at the top of the stairs opened. He gave up and stood at the cell door as Big Jim and the faggot came down the stairs. Gillette had the keys to the cells in his hand.

"Hey, come on," Billy said as he backed away from the cell door. "You guys can't just come down here and beat on me whenever you feel like it. I got rights."

"Mr. Denison, you're free to go," the faggot said, and

83

Billy could see it on his face; calling him Mr. Denison had left the strong taste of shit in his mouth. "On behalf of the city, we'd like to apologize for today's regrettable misunderstanding."

"Misunderstanding?" Billy said, watching as Gillette unlocked the cell door and swung it open.

"Yes, the misunderstanding," Harlow said. "I came down to ask you a couple of questions about Jennifer Bennett today, and things got out of hand. In the future, Mr. Denison, I'd suggest that before you remove your personal weapon to hand it over during questioning, you inform the officer of what you're doing first."

Billy, who might not have been the smartest man around but certainly wasn't the dumbest, caught on. "Right," he said. "My mistake. Totally should have told you about the gun first."

In a rare stroke of genius, he kept going. "And I'm sorry about the way the boys got in your face. They're morons, but they're good people. I'll make sure they know not to interfere with the cops when they're working again."

Gillette and Harlow looked at each other, and nodded. "There won't be any charges from this today," Harlow said. "But I do still have some questions for you, son. You mind stepping upstairs into my office?"

"Um, no offense or nothing, but I think I'd rather wait until I talk to my lawyer," he said.

"Fair enough," Harlow said, nodding. "I'll expect you and him in my office first thing in the morning. That work for you?"

"Shouldn't be a problem," he said. He started to follow Gillette out of the holding cells when Harlow stopped him with a hand on his elbow.

"Don't kid yourself, Billy," he said, low and quiet. "I know you did it, and I'm going to be up your ass to the shoulders until I can prove it."

Billy looked down at the hand on his arm, and resisted the urge to knock it away, mostly because he had no interest in getting bitch-slapped again. "I'm free to go, right? That's what you just said."

"For now," Harlow said. "And just so we understand each other? The next time you pull a gun on me, I'll kill you."

"Are you threatening me?" Billy asked, because it was all he could think to say. It sounded better than shitting his pants, at any rate.

"You're goddamn right," Harlow said.

"Mr. Denison, if you'll come with me, we'll return your personal property and get you on your way," Gillette said, and Billy smiled.

"Mr. Denison," he said. "I like that."

He was at the foot of the stairs when Harlow spoke again. "Watch your ass, Billy Boy," he said, pointing at him. "Because I'm coming for you."

Billy just gave him his best grin and walked out before Harlow could see how badly his hands were shaking.

3.

Lilith stood at the edge of a large gravel pit, tears streaming down her cheeks as she felt the bodies of her children crying out for her from under the rock. She climbed down, the sharp rocks creating small, bloodless cuts in her feet and hands that healed immediately.

Crying, she knelt in the gravel and dug until she found the first body. It was a young man, not one of her children. She touched his face and saw what he had to tell her. "You were fortunate, young man," she said, and tossed the large young man aside as if he were an empty paper cup. She dug deeper until she came to the body of a petite young woman, barely more than a girl.

"My beautiful girl," she said, brushing away the tears on her cheeks with one hand covered in dust. She cradled the poor darling in her arms, rocking back and forth as she let her grief and anger rage through her. She'd just turned nineteen only a few days ago, although by that time she'd had no idea what the day was, and her birthday had meant nothing to her but another day in chains, waiting for more torture. More pain, more humiliation. More degradation at the hands of men, who thought that money bought them the right to do with her as they pleased.

She bent down and kissed the poor thing's lips. It was too late to help her, as she had Jennifer; the damage to her brain from a man's bullet, along with the damage to her spirit from countless others, was too much. Her soul was still close, though, and she could at least listen to her.

"Tell me, my sweet," she said through her tears. "Tell me what happened to you."

She listened carefully, her own heart breaking over and over again as the girl's spirit poured out its litany of agonies. From the man who'd taken her money to get her into the United States, then promptly sold her to another man, then to the virtually non-stop chain of indignities and abuse as she was sold from one man to another, and to another, until she ended up here.

The other men were not here, not in reach of her anger, but one was. The man who'd stolen her life had to be near, and she wanted to know his face. She listened patiently, caressing the girl's scraped and dirty cheek, as she poured out her woes. A man might push her to tell her who the man she wanted was; would want her to get to the point, he might say. But a mother knew that sometimes, the only thing to do was to listen, and to love.

She continued to rock the poor thing as her soul spoke to her, and eventually she had the man's face in her mind. She didn't know his name, but she knew his face now, and she'd find him. He was not one of her children, which she considered a small blessing. It would compound her torment and grief to know her own son had done this.

She gently laid the poor girl aside, kissed her cheek, and proceeded to look for the rest. She found each one, and repeated the process, letting their souls vent until they found peace. That was all she could do for them now, but it would have to be enough. Once she had all her beautiful, lost babies free from the earth where they'd been dumped like so much garbage, she carried each one into the nearby woods, letting them rest.

The men who'd hurt Jennifer stayed where they lay; it was all they deserved. Not far from the pit was a factory of some sort, and she could feel some of her sons there. They would help her with what she needed to do.

She knew something of the behavior of men, of course, and was not offended or surprised when some of them made lewd noises as she approached the loading dock. She ignored most of them; they were sons of the Other, and at that moment she had no time for them. They could sometimes be persuaded to do as she wished, but only if she could focus her love and energy toward them. At this moment, all she felt was anger and sadness, and neither would help her with them.

Three men, hers, stood up and removed their hats as she approached. "My beautiful, strong boys," she said to them, smiling. "Something terrible has happened, and I need your help."

"I got something that'll help you, sweetheart," another man said. One of her sons turned to him, his fists balled.

"Shut your mouth, buddy," he said. The two of them stood in front of each other, and as if called, more of her sons came out of the nearby door.

"He isn't important," she said to her sons, and they turned back to her. "Will you help me?"

"Of course," one said. "Anything you need, ma'am."

She watched as they fetched shovels and tools from pickup trucks, and followed her into the woods over the shouts of someone she assumed was their supervisor. But he was hers, as well, and a smile from her made it all right again.

The dozen or so men made short work of digging the grave, and soon her beautiful girls rested together. They'd been strangers at one point, but had become true sisters in death, and she would not separate them for anything. "Thank you," she said to them as they stood in front of her. They were dirty and sweat-stained, and they all looked indescribably sad as they waited for her to speak to them. "You've given your sisters a beautiful gift today, and they are all eternally grateful to each of you, as am I. I love all of you, my sons."

"We love you, Mother," one of them said. His name was Roger. He was an older man, the oldest of them at forty-nine, but still strong and virile. He'd bent his back and worked right alongside men half his age, never slowing or faltering.

She came to him, touching his cheek. "There is a man," she said. "A man who is not my child, who has done this to your sisters. He's done unspeakable things to my children, and he must answer for them."

"Who?" one of the younger men, a nineteen-year-old boy named Quentin, asked, his voice trembling. "Who did this? I'll fucking kill him."

"I know you would, my sweet boy," she said, touching his cheek. "But I would no sooner wish that on you than I would this for them."

"Wouldn't be the first man I killed," Roger said. "I'll do it, just so the boy doesn't have to."

"That is not a burden I would put on any of my children," she said. "But you may be able to help me. I know this man's face. Your sisters were able to show me." She took Roger's face in her hands and let him look deeply into her eyes. The connection formed, and she had access to all his memories.

She cried as she saw a young Roger, standing tall in his soldier's uniform, receiving a commendation for valor. She saw the birth of his daughter Caitlyn, who had died of a heart defect at seven. She saw his whole life in an instant, and her heart swelled with sadness at his losses and pride in his strength. She searched through his more recent memories, until she found a name for the face burned into her mind by her children's pain.

"Jerry Hartman," she whispered. The others gasped, and she felt their rage and pain as if they were hers.

"That creepy bastard," Quentin said. "He--"

"Is my concern now, my boy," she said. "I will deal with him, and with anyone who helped him. For now, I need you all to go back to your work and trust me to do as I must. Can you do that for me?"

"Of course, Mother," Roger said. "But all you have to do is say the word, and we'll do whatever you need."

"I don't doubt that at all," Lilith said, caressing his cheek. It was lined with his age and worries, but it was a strong face. He was still a handsome man. "When your employer asks, you will tell him you helped a lady with her vehicle. Will that be enough for him?"

"It'll do fine," Roger said. "Plenty of folks get stuck on these back roads."

"That's good," she said. "For now, return to your work, and say nothing of this." She pointed to the grave where her lost lovelies lay, and repressed the urge to cry again. She would cry for them later, after her own work was done. "And be ready. I may have need for all of you again, and soon."

"We'll be ready," Roger said. "Mother, are you in danger?"

"No," she said, smiling at the thought. "No child of the Other can hurt me, my boy. But you have brothers and sisters who may need your strength and protection. Will you give it if needed?"

"Anything you need," Quentin said, and the others agreed. She kissed each of them on the cheek and left her invisible mark on each. They would feel her call and come to her. She watched as they left, and turned back to the grave.

"I am so sorry I couldn't protect you," she said. "But I can make things right for you, my sweet ones, and I promise you I will."

In the distance, she felt the tug at her center as the first of her newest special children began to wake, and she knew it was time to go to them. The sun was just beginning to set as she began to walk, following not the roads so much as that tug at her center as she went to her special children.

Along the way, she reached out with her special mother's gifts, and left her mark on several of her children. When the time came to cleanse this place, she wanted as many of her children at her side as she could find.

4.

Sam Harrison was drunk.

This wasn't an unusual state for good old Sammy; he spent most of his time in a pleasant state of oblivion. Nothing fancy for Sam; good old Natural Lite did him just fine. But all was not well in Sam's world just then, and it irked him.

For one, the house was a goddamned pig sty. There were empty beer cans everywhere, the ashtray next to his recliner was overflowing, and worst of all, last night's dinner dishes were still in the goddamned sink. And that, good friends and neighbors, was not at all acceptable. Amber was supposed to have taken care of those before bedtime last night, or at least before she left for school. The rest of the housework should have been done when she got home, long before he stumbled in after a long day.

And was any of it done? No sir, and thanks for asking. Not a goddamn thing had been done, as far as he could tell. Shit, there wasn't even anything in the oven waiting for him, and she knew goddamned well she should have dinner at least working by the time he got home. He wasn't an unreasonable man; it wasn't like he expected a hot dinner waiting on the table when he breezed through the door. The kid had school, and there was a lot of work to do around the house, but Jesus please us, was it too much to ask to at least have something planned?

He certainly didn't think so; after all, he worked all day, paid all the bills, and kept a roof over her ungrateful head. And what did he ask in return? Not much, as he saw it. A little dinner, some housework. That was all, most days. On occasion, he wanted a little comfort, but why not? Her useless, good-for-nothing mother had taken off years ago, leaving them both in the lurch. And what woman worth banging wanted to become an instant mother to a teenage girl? None, that's who, and so if he needed a little comfort now and then, who was she to argue?

And come to think of it, where the fuck was Amber? School had been out for hours now, and she knew she was supposed to come straight home from school. No sports or after-school activities for his girl; she had responsibilities at home, after all. But was she here, taking care of those responsibilities? No sir, and you had best believe that shit was not acceptable.

"Fuck her, then," he said finally, crushing the empty Natty in his hand and letting loose a damned healthy belch before hauling himself out of the chair. If she couldn't do her damned job, then he'd do it for her, and she could return the goddamned favor later.

It had been a long day, and he needed a little comfort. But for now, he might as well get to work.

He made a half-assed pass through the living room, collecting empties and crushing them in his meaty fist before dropping them into an empty shopping bag. Once that was done, he carried the overflowing ashtray to the kitchen and dumped it in the trash can, which was, of course, full as full could be.

"Christ," he said, shaking his head and carrying the garbage bag to the can outside. The neighbor's ugly fucking orange cat yowled at him as it scrammed off his porch, aided by a fairly slow kick aimed at its backside. His dusty work boot missed the cat's ass by a fair country mile, but it did the job just the same.

He went back inside after using most of his

impressively large vocabulary of curses at the cat, grabbed another Natty from the fridge, and popped the tab before tackling the sink full of dirty dishes. "Ain't no fucking job for a working man," he mused, but he emptied the sink and filled it with hot, soapy water. At least she'd fucking scraped the goddamned things first, he thought.

Of course she had, because he remembered watching her do it. He had to watch her do certain things, because otherwise she'd half-ass her way through it. Although, half of that particular ass was still mighty fine, he thought, but chased it away. It wasn't about sex, he told himself, although Amber had grown into a fine-looking young thing, even hotter than her mother. It was just comfort, something to let him relax after a hard day at work.

Still, as he washed the dishes, he couldn't help but think of the way Amber did it, often slopping the front of her shirt as she scrubbed and rinsed until she could star in a wet t-shirt contest. The image came to him, unbidden but not necessarily unwelcome, of those fine, perky tits poking out of a wet shirt, the nipples hard and erect, and he had to reach down and adjust his works to a more comfortable position. This did nothing for the situation, though, and it wasn't long before he stood there at the sink, scrubbing dishes with a blue-steeler that could cut glass. Yes sir, he thought. Could definitely use a little comfort right now.

By the time he finished the dishes and had rummaged around in the freezer until he found one of the disgusting little Banquet TV dinners, his erection was throbbing like an infected tooth, and was little Miss Amber anywhere in sight to help him? Of course not, and don't think he wasn't planning on taking her to task for that when she finally showed up.

"Jesus," he said as he sat down in his chair, took one bite of the Salisbury steak, and set the whole mess aside. "That's just fucking nasty."

Still doing his best to ignore his pulsing hard-on, he picked up the remote and started flipping through channels until he found something worth watching.

Well, not actually worth watching, but definitely worth spanking the monkey to, he thought as he stopped on the Disney channel, where they were playing a rerun of that Hannah Montana show. God damn, now that was a fine little ass. He didn't bother with pretense, simply unzipped his fly and grabbed his rod.

He was fairly well into things when the doorbell rang. "God fucking damn it," he said, almost dropping his beer in his surprise.

Ordinarily, the sudden shock of an interruption was enough to kill even the most monstrous boner, but apparently little Sammy had different ideas. Little Sammy didn't give fuck-all for interruptions; he had business to get on with, and to hell with everything else.

Grumbling, he tucked his cock, now sore and swollen, into his pants and went to answer the door. "Better be fucking good," he said as he opened the door. What stood there on the front porch was definitely good.

"Hey there," the woman said, her eyes drifting down to the tent he was currently pitching, and then back up to his face. "That for me?"

"Might be," he said, smiling. "You, uh, wanna come in and talk about it?"

"I think we have a lot to talk about, Sam," she said, stepping inside. She closed the door and leaned up against it, and Sam saw that while she was a little older than what he usually liked, she had one hell of a nice rack. Big, round mommy tits jutted from the open top of her button-up shirt, and he could see the lacy edge of a black bra. She undid two more buttons and pulled the shirt open to give him a view of some world-class cleavage.

"You like what you see, Sam?" she said. He couldn't speak; his tongue felt thick and heavy in his mouth, but he nodded. The woman stepped forward and slipped her hand through his open fly, pulling him free. His cock, which by now was practically screaming for fresh meat, jumped in her hand, and it made her giggle.

"Oh, my," she said. "Someone's very excited." She squeezed him, hard enough to almost hurt, and then started stroking him slowly as she turned him around. He let her push him against the door as she worked on him.

"What--" he started to say, but she shushed him.

"No talking," she said. "You're not one of those wussy men who wants to talk about everything first, are you?"

He responded by groping those amazing tits through her shirt, making her gasp and moan. She led him to the couch and pushed him down, her hand never stopping its torturously slow ministrations. He felt like he'd been on the edge for hours now, and he wondered briefly if it was possible to die from an orgasm.

The woman straddled him, her hand leaving his throbbing dick just long enough to slip out of her shirt and bra. He was right; a pair of amazing tits now hung in his face. Not quite as high or firm as a younger woman's, but full and heavy, the nipples a dark coffee color. He cupped them as her hand went back to him, and she leaned into him.

"Tell me something, Sam," she said as she stroked his cock. He wasn't entirely sure he'd actually be able to speak, but as long as she kept that up, he'd tell her anything she wanted to know. His bank account information, where the deed to the house was, anything. Hell, he'd make shit up if it kept her stroking his cock like that. He'd never been jerked off so expertly in his life, and he was suddenly quite sure than when he did finally blow his load, it might actually physically knock her off his lap.

She slid off him and knelt on the floor in front of him. He waited in equal parts anticipation and abject terror as she leaned down slowly, her lips pausing just above the tip of his dick. "Do you like fucking your daughter with this cock?"

That got through to him. He looked startled as she produced something small and black from her pocket and shoved it into his stomach. A press of the button, and the stun gun made his entire body jerk and spasm.

The shock drove him over the edge, and the last thought he had before he passed out was that she was going to have a hell of a time cleaning that mess off her face.

By the time he woke up, Emma had not only cleaned herself up, but she'd hog-tied him quite efficiently. Sam lay on the threadbare carpet of his living room, hands tied behind his back and ankles bound. A strip of duct tape was wound multiple times around his mouth and head.

"Congratulations, Sam," Emma said, and gave him a sharp kick in the ribs. "Finally got your rocks off with an adult, for once. Don't worry, you'll see Amber again soon enough. But this time, she's not the one who's going to end up getting fucked over."

She kicked him again, this time in the temple, and the world went away as he was knocked out.

5.

Jerry was growing annoyed at a phenomenal pace, which was not a good sign. Well, not good for someone else, anyway. Usually when Jerry grew annoyed, someone paid the price for it. Sometimes it was the person causing the annoyance, and sometimes it was just the next person to fuck with him. But today, he knew exactly who was causing it, and he desperately wanted to take it out on the little fuck. As much as he'd like to pimp-slap Billy Denison up one side of the street and down the other, he held his temper in check. The little shit was Harlan's kid and, like it or not, that bought him a little grace. But only a little.

He stood in the corner of Harlan's office as the man himself sat behind what looked like an acre of desktop, his hands folded neatly in front of him. They were awaiting the arrival of the prodigal son, who would no doubt be somewhat annoyed himself. Harlan had done something

Jerry hadn't honestly thought he would, and refused to send someone to pick him up. Jerry would have gone to meet him, but he'd have made the little shit jog the three miles back to the house, probably with the right front tire of Jerry's truck nipping at his heels the whole time.

"You know," Jerry started, but Harlan held up a hand.

"I do," he said, cutting him off. "And trust me, he's not going to be a problem anymore." Jerry had his doubts on that score, but he held his tongue. He thought Bill Denison was going to be a major pain in the balls so long as he continued to draw breath, but that wasn't the sort of thing you said casually to a man about his son.

"Maybe it's time I kept an eye on him," Jerry said. "Keep him busy, and maybe out of trouble."

Harlan looked up at that. "What, exactly, did you have in mind?"

"I know you're thinking you'll put him on at the factory," he said. "And maybe that's not such a bad idea. But come on, Harlan. There isn't anyone in the county who doesn't know he's your kid, and nobody out there's gonna really bust his chops. You know that."

"But I bet you're not the least bit afraid to bust his chops," Harlan said, and Jerry shrugged.

"We both know what's bad for you is bad for me, and that goes both ways," he said. "And right now, that boy is drawing a lot of attention neither of us can afford."

"We're clean," Harlan said. "Unless you missed something out there."

"There's always the possibility," he admitted. "No cleanup is perfect, and you know it. Come on, Harlan. You're smarter than this. You know damned good and well—"

"Stop fucking telling me what I know," Harlan barked, but Jerry ignored him. It was his best defense.

"--that Jim Harlow is not a stupid man," he continued. "If he even thinks there's something to find, he'll find it sooner or later. And with Junior showing his ass every five minutes, it's only a matter of time until Harlow decides that maybe he needs to take a closer look at Daddy. And, by extension, me."

"You got something on the side you're worried about?" he asked, and Jerry smiled.

"Of course I do," he said. "Just like you've got deals in place I'm not involved with. But there is one we're both hip deep in, and that's what concerns me, Harlan. Now, you can sit here and try to side-track the issue, or we can deal with it head on."

Harlan sighed. "What are you thinking?" he said finally.

"I can put him to use," he said. "We saw today how dicey it is to house merchandise at the plant. Frankly, I was against it from the beginning."

"So you said," Harlan said, nodding. "You have something better in mind?"

"As a matter of fact, I do," he said. "I'm building a warehouse. Well, a number of shell companies are, at any rate. It'll be done next week."

"I didn't know that," Harlan said. "Sounds like the kind of thing I should know, Jerry."

"It was supposed to be for something else," he said. "But it'll work for what we need. It's remote, it's clean, and it can't be traced back to either of us. I can have new merchandise in a few days, and we're back in business."

"I see," Harlan said. "And how much is this gonna cost me?"

Jerry smiled. "I'll front the warehouse. And half the cost of the merchandise, as usual. We'll do the split sixty-forty, instead of down the middle. Sound fair to you?"

"And what, exactly, will you have my son doing?" he asked. Jerry laughed.

"Every single shit job I can find," he said. "Anything that needs doing, so long as he can't fuck it up. Honestly, can you sit there and tell me a little time doing some honest work wouldn't do him some good?"

"I think a hard day's work and a cold beer would probably kill him," Harlan said, and they both chuckled. The door to Harlan's office swung open, and Bill strolled in, looking hot and tired. Christ's sweet sake, Jerry thought. A three-mile walk, and he's almost dead.

"Sit down," Harlan said, pointing to the chair in front of his desk.

"I'm gonna grab a shower first," Bill said. "And thanks for the ride, by the way."

"Sit the fuck down," Harlan said, his voice hard and cold. Bill sat down almost immediately. "I'm going to ask you two questions, son. And believe me when I tell you that if you lie to me, I'll make what Harlow did look like a kiss on the temple from a little old lady. Are you listening?"

"I am," Bill said, trying to find a comfortable way to sit in the hard chair with his inured ribs. Jerry enjoyed watching the little shit squirm, but he didn't have a lot of patience for the big talk that always made it happen.

To Jerry, if you were gonna beat the shit out of someone, telling them was pointless. Either they knew they had a beating coming, or they were too stupid to bother warning.

"Did you and those three assholes intend to kill that girl, or were you just too fucking stupid to know what you were doing?" Harlan said.

Jerry was surprised to see the moron actually thinking it over. "I don't think we meant to kill her," he said. "But she--"

"Go ahead," Harlan said. "Make some bullshit excuse about why it was really her fault. Tell me you four jackoffs were mortally afraid of a hundred pound girl." Jerry was pleased to at least hear a little outrage in the old man's voice as Bill shut up.

"That's the first question," Harlan said. "And the second one is bigger. Did you have anything to do with the Bennett girl's body disappearing from the morgue?"

"Kinda hard to do in a cell," Bill said. Before the idiot understood what was happening, Harlan nodded. Jerry stepped forward and slapped him upside the head, hard.

"The fuck?" Bill said, starting to stand up. Jerry stared him down.

"You feeling froggy now, kid?" Jerry said. "Better be careful. I'm not a tiny chick."

"You don't put your fucking hands on me," Bill said. "Don't you ever put your fucking hands on me, asshole."

Jerry slapped him across the face, knocking him back. "Do something about it," Jerry said. "Go ahead. Take a swing at me, kid. Be a fucking man for once. Or do you need all your girlfriends here to help hold me down first?"

He honestly didn't think the kid had it in him, but he managed to block the half-assed swing Bill threw. He twisted the arm around behind his back and drove him down to the floor, putting a knee in his back.

Leaning in close so that only the kid could really hear, he said "If you ever even open your eyes at me again, I'll snatch the life right out of you, boy. I hope you believe me, because I don't repeat myself." He gave the arm an extra tweak for good measure, then stood up.

"Get off the floor, son," Harlan said. "You're embarrassing me."

"You really gonna let him do that to me?" Bill said, sounding more like a whiny brat than a grown man.

"He did it because I told him to do it," Harlan said. "You still don't understand, and that's a goddamned crying shame, because Lord knows I've explained it to you time and again. You are starting to become more trouble than you're worth, son."

"You know what I noticed?" Bill said, sitting down gingerly. "You asked if I had anything to do with that chick's body going missing. Not if any of the guys did it. You know what I think?"

"I'd be very surprised to find thinking entered into the equation at all," Jerry said. Bill ignored him, looking straight at his father.

"I think you know they didn't," he said. "And I think you know that, because you had this prick kill them. I'm right, aren't I?"

Harlan and Jerry exchanged a look, and Harlan shrugged.

"They were a liability," Jerry said. "Kinda like you."

"You gonna kill me next?" he asked Harlan.

"I'm trying very hard to avoid that, son," Harlan said. "But you don't make it easy. You're drawing attention I can't afford. Still, I'm trying. That's why you're going to work with Jerry for now."

Bill looked over at Jerry, and shook his head. "No fucking way," Bill said. "I'm not doing shit with this psycho."

Harlan sighed. Jerry recognized that sigh; it was the sound of a man at the very end of his patience. He watched as Harlan clenched his hands and then opened them, laying them palms down on the desk. "I apologize," Harlan said. "I see now that maybe I wasn't being clear, although I certainly thought I was. Jerry, was I in any way unclear about what I said?"

"No," Jerry said. "Seemed crystal clear to me."

"Billy, did you somehow get the impression I was asking you to work with Jerry?" he said. When Bill said nothing, Harlan continued. "Still, I suppose I can't force you to do anything, can I?"

"If that's what you need me to do, I guess I can--"

"Best get to packing," Harlan said.

"What?"

"Pack your bags, and get out of my house," Harlan said. "You don't want to do what needs to be done, you want to put my entire business at risk? You don't live under my roof anymore."

"Dad, I--"

"Get out of my office," Harlan said. When Bill didn't move, Jerry stepped forward. That got him out of the chair and headed for the door.

"You sure you wanna do this? Dad?" he said.

"It's done," Harlan said. Bill just shook his head and walked out. Jerry waited until he was gone, and turned to Harlan.

"How do we handle this?" Jerry said.

"It's been handled," Harlan said.

"So you say," Jerry said. "He could make a lot of trouble we don't need."

"He doesn't know shit, and even if he does, he can't prove shit," Harlan said. "Leave him alone."

Jerry knew a lost cause when he saw one; he just shrugged and walked out without another word. He didn't believe in repeating himself, and he'd already warned Harlan every way he knew how that he wasn't going down because he couldn't keep his kid under control.

It was probably long past time to cut his losses.

CHAPTER EIGHT

1.

When Sam woke up, he was aware of two things.

One, he hurt all over, like he'd gotten the absolute shit kicked out of him. It seemed as if every muscle was sore, and he had one blue mother of a headache.

And two, he was absolutely surrounded by grade A prime pussy. All of it young, all of it gorgeous. He almost didn't recognize Amber at first; she'd cleaned herself up. Washed and fixed her hair, and changed into actual girl's clothes for once. Christ Almighty, and she wasn't even the hottest thing there. There were nine of them, including the MILF that had apparently bushwhacked him. As he watched, a woman with flawless olive skin and long, dark hair moved among the girls, touching and being touched. One of them touched her hair, and she kissed the girl's cheek.

It might have started out rough, but the night was definitely picking up. He tried to sit up, but found that he was still bound tightly at the wrists and ankles. Still, he managed to get himself into a sitting position, and looked around.

He seemed to be in a trailer, small and rundown, but spotlessly clean. Hell, he wished Amber could keep the nice house he worked so hard to pay for half this clean. "What's going on here?" he asked, not liking the gravelly sound of his own voice. God, his head hurt; bitch had damn near caved in his skull with that last shot.

"Tell me something, Sam," the olive-skinned woman said. She looked at the group of chicks behind her. One of them stood apart from the others, and it took him a moment to recognize her. It was that really hot little bite-sized from the liquor store. Janey, or some shit like that. But holy fucking shit, she'd somehow gotten even hotter. Something was wrong, though, and it took a moment to click in his mildly concussed brain.

"I know you," he said to her. "Wait, aren't you dead?"

"That's up for debate," Janey or whatever said. "But whatever it is, it seems to agree with me, don't you think?"

"You like young women, don't you, Sam?" the woman who was clearly in charge said. "Very young women."

"Little girls," the MILF said. "You like fucking little girls, right?"

"No need to deny it," the woman said. "I know everything, Sam." She knelt down next to him, shaking her long hair out of her face. He saw that she wasn't just pretty, but absolutely beautiful, the kind of woman he'd always thought only existed in Hollywood. Unbelievably, his cock actually stirred in his pants as the woman and the others all gathered around him.

He wasn't a stupid man; he knew he was in a world of trouble here. If nothing else, they knew about what he'd done with Amber. Her presence here confirmed that much, at least. What was infinitely worse was that he had no idea where he was, but it was obviously in the boonies.

And still, his dick was stiffening just at the sight of them all so close together. Un-fucking-believable.

"Do you love your daughter, Sam?" the woman asked. She motioned over her shoulder, and Amber came forward, kneeling in front of him. Holy shit, he thought as he got a good look down her shirt. Had her tits actually gotten bigger, or was it just that she wasn't trying to hide them anymore?

"Yes," he said. "You know I love you, sweetie."

"And you'd do anything for her, right?"

"Y-yeah," he said. "Of course. Haven't I always taken care of you, baby?" He knew it was a mistake, but he couldn't help looking up at all the others, standing together in a tight little knot. They were all touching each other; a hand on a hip here, an arm around another one's waist there.

The woman giggled. "You like what you see, don't you?" she said. "You don't have to answer. I can see that you do." She looked down at his crotch. "My babies are very beautiful, aren't they?"

"Y-yes," he said, caught somewhere between terrified and insanely horny.

"Then I think we're about to make you very happy, Sam," the woman said. "Tell me, would you like a kiss, Sam? From Amber, from all of my girls?"

"Hell, yes," he said, with no hesitation.

The woman stood up and turned to the girls, smiling. She put a hand out, and Amber slid into her arms. "Amber gets the first kiss," she said. "I think after seven years of what he's done to her, she's earned that. Don't you?"

"Absolutely," a beautifully plump short chick said. God, the things he could do to that one alone. He wasn't even entirely sure he'd fit inside that tight little frame, but he desperately wanted to find out.

"Go ahead, love," she said to Amber. "We're all here, and he can't hurt you now. Not ever again."

Sam watched as Amber strolled over to him and straddled his lap, her hands on the back of his neck. "Do I look pretty now, Daddy?" she said.

"Yes," he said. "And Daddy could use some comfort, honey. It's been a day."

Amber smiled, and there was something wrong with that smile. It was too adult, too knowing. "Oh, it's about to get so much worse," Amber said, and hissed at him.

Actually hissed, like a fucking cat. He saw long, sharply pointed teeth, and by the time she yanked his head back by the hair and sank them into his throat, his hard-on was out of control.

"Don't forget to share, children," the woman said, and Sam passed out as the others fell on him.

2.

Lilith stepped out into the clean, crisp night air as her children fed. It wasn't that it bothered her; they were exactly as she'd made them, after all. It was just that they deserved their moment, and she wanted them to have it. Jennifer and Emma joined her. Emma looked mildly ill, and Lilith hugged her as soon as she saw her face.

"I imagine that must be a terrible thing to see for the first time," she said, and Emma nodded. She stood up tall, though, and put her shoulders back.

"He deserved it," she said. "The things he did to her. The things he would have done to the others, if he could."

Lilith touched her cheek and gave her a warm smile. "Sweet girl," she said. "You don't have to justify your feelings, Emma. That's a man's trick. It's okay if it bothers you. It's okay if it doesn't bother you."

"He deserves it," Emma said again. "And Amber needs it, to finally be free. But it's still hard to watch."

"I know," Lilith said. "And you never have to see it again, if you don't want. I only needed you here for this one so you'd know who your sisters are. What they are."

"Are--" Emma said. "Are they vampires?"

Lilith laughed. It was a musical, beautiful sound that put Emma at ease. "No," she said, still laughing. "Vampires are soulless, dead things. They don't feel, they don't love. They don't do anything but feed. They're my children, that's all. As are you, and Jennifer, and so many others. Some are different, but you're all my children."

"Do I have to--" Emma started, and Lilith shook her head.

"No," she said. "You have your own children to think of, after all. I trust they're asleep inside?"

"Yes," Emma said. "Sleeping soundly, probably for the first time in years. They don't have to be afraid anymore. Because you saved us, Mother."

"A mother keeps her children safe," Lilith said. "And the best way for you to do that is just be the wonderful woman you are, Emma. You're already strong. They needed to be stronger than they were, and now they are."

"They'll feed, and they'll feel better," Jennifer said. "I don't think it's the same as it is with me, but I know they'll feel better."

"I was too late to protect you," Lilith said to Jennifer. "For that, I'll always be sorry. But I did what I could for you."

"You brought me back, Mother," Jennifer said. "You did more for me than anyone else ever has."

"Because I love you," Lilith said, hugging the tiny woman. The door to the trailer opened, and Amber came out, blood on her chin. Her whole face lit up in a smile as she hugged first Jennifer, then Emma, and finally Lilith.

"Thank you, Mother," she said. "Thank you for making me strong."

"I didn't make you strong, my sweet girl," Lilith said with a warm smile. "I only let you become what you were meant to be. You were always strong."

The others came outside, and they stood there in the front yard, embraced in a group hug. Lilith felt their power flowing, and she drank it all in. Her eyes lit up with an amber glow that none of them noticed.

She loved her children, and fed as they loved her back.

"I have something we need to do," Lilith said once the moment was over. "There are men we need to find. Evil men."

"Like my Dad?" Amber said, and Lilith nodded.

"Yes," she said. "These men, they've hurt my children. Your sisters. They must be punished."

"Billy Denison," Jennifer said, and Lilith gave her a loving smile.

"Of course," she said. "He's the first. And when we find him, he belongs to Jennifer, is that understood?"

"Yes, Mother," they all said in unison. She knew they would comply; they were all well fed, and Emma hadn't been changed.

"Then it's time to hunt, my beautiful children," she said. "Go. Search the town, and find this Billy Denison. When you find him, we'll come to you, and Jennifer can have her justice."

"Not revenge?" Jennifer said. Lilith smiled.

"You are a sweet, dear girl," she said. "What you will do is justice. Vengeance is mine."

"Yes, Mother," Jennifer said, and there were tears of gratitude in her beautiful eyes.

Lilith stood on the front porch of Ruth Ann's trailer, and watched as her children disappeared into the night. Emma stood next to her side, looking anxious.

"Will they be safe, Mother?" she asked.

"I would never let them go if I didn't know they'd be safe, my love," Lilith said. "I would never risk any of you."

"I'm sorry," Emma said, and Lilith took her hand.

"You never have to apologize for worrying about your sisters, Emma," she said. "That's what sisters do for each other." Emma swiped at a random tear, and Lilith hugged her.

"I should go clean up," Emma said. "There'll be—there will be leftovers."

"You've done so much," Lilith said, shaking her head. "You need to rest. I need you strong, Emma. Your children need you, too. Go to them, and sleep. I will take care of what needs to be done."

Emma bent down and kissed her cheek, and went inside. Lilith felt her love as she kissed each of her beautiful children in their sleep and lay down next to them.

She was out almost immediately, feeling warm and safe and loved for the first time in too long. It filled her heart to know she finally felt those things, and hurt her that she had ever known anything different.

She dragged what was left of Sam out into the backyard. She knelt down and felt for his soul. He would turn, and perhaps hurt others. That was not acceptable. And besides, he didn't deserve to live another night, even as a vampire. She channeled her energy into her palm, and soon his body burst into flames. It burned quickly, leaving nothing but a scorched patch of grass.

Out in the night, she could feel each of her special children moving through the dark; could see through their eyes, feel what they felt. They had split up to cover more ground, but at the same time they were all together, and she heard their laughter as they hunted.

They were enjoying themselves, and she loved it. "Find him, my babies," she said to the night. "Find him, and we'll show him what happens to those who hurt my children."

Satisfied her daughters would find and punish Bill Denison, she turned her focus on one Jerry Hartman. She could feel him out there somewhere close by. Once Emma was well asleep, she went around the trailer to the front yard. She found a comfortable patch of grass and sat down, her shapely legs crossed under her. She closed her eyes and rested her hands on her knees, and let her consciousness drift up and outward.

Her special children were on a hunt, mostly so they could bond and work together as true sisters, but she had other children, and she'd placed her mark on many of them throughout the day.

She left her earthly body and soared out into the night, reaching out for her children. She found Roger, sitting at his kitchen table and cleaning several guns. She could feel his urgency, his need to protect her and his sisters. She chose not to tap him for her needs, because she didn't want him to add to the load of guilt he already carried.

And of course, young Quentin was similarly unsuitable for her needs; if she sent him to find this Jerry Hartman, his young heart and fiery passion might lead him to kill Hartman instead of bringing him to her.

She let herself soar, and touched each of her children in turn. One of them, a woman in her forties named Margaret who ran the local diner, was working the counter and keeping an eye on the floor when she saw a familiar face come through the door and waved to him.

Lilith smiled as she watched Jerry Hartman take a seat at the counter and order a bacon cheeseburger and onion rings. "Coming right up, Sugar," Lilith said through Margaret's lips, and smiled. She pulled away and let Margaret do her work, and found another of her children on the street. He was young, and she saw no urgent commitments in his memory, so she had him wait and watch for Hartman to leave.

She left young Peter Barnes to watch Hartman, and gave him a gentle suggestion to come to the trailer to tell her when he found where Hartman lived.

She felt a thrill of excitement, and turned her attention to her special children. She sank back into her body, and clapped as she saw that shy young Melissa had not only found Billy Denison, but was keeping him delightfully distracted as her sisters rushed to her.

"That's my girl," she said, laughing. She fell over onto the grass, hands clasped in front of her and a wide, beaming smile on her face as she laughed in pure delight.

3.

Billy drove aimlessly, wandering down back roads and drinking. That alone was a major accomplishment; he'd ended up buying a twelve-pack from the convenience store, paying entirely too much for beer barely below room temperature. He'd made what turned out to be a colossal fuck-up by stopping at the liquor store, purely out of habit.

He always bought his beer there, because they had the best prices and the coldest beer in town.

"You," the old man who owned the place said as soon as he stepped through the door. Billy, not one of the world's great thinkers, actually looked around to see who the old fart was so pissed at.

"What's up?" Billy said. "Just grabbing a--"

But even as monumentally dense as he could sometimes be, Billy understood what happened next. If he had any doubts as to the old man's feelings on the matter, all he had to do was take a good look at the Winchester rifle in the old dude's hands. His very steady, determined hands that racked the Winchester's lever action in one smooth, practiced motion. For that one moment, Billy understood that his life in town might not be destined to last much longer.

"You best get your sorry ass out of my store," the old man said, the rifle coming up to his shoulder. "I ever see you again, and I'll blow your murdering head clean the fuck off. Try me and see, you sumbitch."

Billy had backed out of the store and ran for his car, and astonishingly, had almost dialed 911 before realizing what he was doing. God in heaven, was he actually going to call the police for help? Jim Harlow had practically sworn a blood oath that he was going to nail Billy to the wall by his dick; he doubted the man would be very sympathetic.

"Fuck it," he said, chucking his empty out the window and grabbing another from the cardboard case on the seat next to him. "Bastards ain't running me out of town."

He turned the truck around and headed back into town, where he figured if nothing else, he could grab a motel room for the night and figure out his next move.

The clerk at the only motel in town gave him a sidelong glance, but took his credit card and gave him a room on the third floor. He took the two card keys in their paper envelope and went upstairs, thinking maybe he'd just crash out for the night and think things through in the morning. At least his father hadn't cut off the credit cards yet.

But Billy was a flexible kind of guy, and when a golden opportunity presented itself, he was just the man to jump on it. That golden opportunity tonight came in the form of an insanely gorgeous chick waiting outside the door to room 315, which just happened to be the one he'd just checked into. "Hey," she said, smiling. Good God, he thought as she lifted one leg and planted a heel on the door. Not just any leg, but a tight, firmly muscled leg that disappeared into a skirt that showed them off to their best effect. Even leaning against the door, he could tell she had a killer ass, too. She was Black, but that barely registered. Billy was a modern, open-minded sort of guy, and besides, it was all pink in the middle, right?

"Hey, yourself," he said, smiling as he stopped in front of the door. She didn't move, just stood there, staring up at him. She shook her long, tight braids out of her face to get a better look at him, and probably to give him a better look at her. On the whole, it was a move he strongly agreed with; she was even better-looking up close. Firm titties, not too big but not too small, and gorgeous chocolate skin. "You, uh, lost?"

"I sure hope not," she said, biting her lower lip. "I've been looking for you all night, Billy."

"So you know who I am," Billy said, leaning against the wall. She turned to face him, and smiled.

"I've wanted to meet you for some time," she said. "I've heard all about you."

"Oh, you have?" he said, thinking that the night had definitely taken a turn for the better. "Well, it just happens you're standing right in front of my room."

"Oh, really?" she said, laughing. "Right." She rolled those pretty brown eyes, but she never lost the flirty smile.

"I can prove it," he said.

"Oh, this should be good," she said, crossing her arms under those fabulous titties. He pulled the key card out and slid it into the lock. The light turned green, and the door popped open.

"Well, isn't that a coincidence?" she said, and stepped inside without being asked. He followed her into the room, where she immediately sat down on the bed. She leaned back, and he caught another glimpse of some world-class legs.

He was just thinking he could use a little action, and here was the best piece he'd seen in some time. She was even hotter than Jenny; what was even better, she seemed to really want it.

"So," he said as he sat down next to her. He touched the bare skin of her arm, trailing one finger down it lightly. "What did you have in mind?"

"Well," she said, looking sideways at him. "That depends on you, stud. You the adventurous type?"

"I like to think so," he said, barely containing a shout of joy at the possibilities. She sat forward, shoved him back onto the bed, and straddled him.

"That's good," she said, pinning his arms down. Pinning them down hard, as a matter of fact.

"Wow," he said. "You're pretty strong, aren't you?"

"I like to think so," she said, tossing his line back at him. "And I have a friend who wants to meet you as bad as I do."

"I like the sound of that," he said. "Is she as hot as you?"

"Oh, definitely," the girl said, smiling. She leaned down, her braids brushing his chest as she nibbled at his ear. "And she's got a deadly body, too. You're gonna love it. I know I do."

Halle-fucking-lujah, he thought as she ground against him. "Better give her a call, then," he said, and she giggled.

"I already did," she whispered in his ear. "She'll be here any minute now."

Sure enough, there was a quiet, almost polite knock at

the door. She sat up, trailing her hands down his chest as she ground against him. "Don't go anywhere," she said, smiling as she slid down his body. Instead of standing up immediately, like most people would, she knelt in front of him for a moment, her face tantalizingly close to his junk.

"I can't wait to see this," she said, the statement so full of possibilities that he didn't even know where to start.

She rose up in one fluid motion and turned to the door, thus confirming what he'd suspected; she had an absolutely perfect ass; tight and round, filling out the back of her skirt in a way that made his eyes almost pop.

She strutted to the door and opened it, blocking his view of her friend. "He's here," she said, her voice low and sexy. "And he's everything you said he'd be."

She turned off the room light as her friend stepped inside. Silhouetted against the hallway lights, he saw a familiar tight frame and long hair, but he couldn't quite place it. Her friend, who certainly knew how to make an entrance, stepped inside and immediately began unbuttoning her blouse as she crossed the room and laid down next to him. Soon the other girl joined them, lying down on his other side.

"Do I know you?" he asked the new girl as she ran a hand over his chest.

"Better than you might think," she said. "Cut on the lights, Mel. I want to see the look on his face."

The Black girl, whose name was apparently Mel, rolled over and flipped on the bedside table lamp. Billy looked at the new girl, and his face dropped as fast as his rapidly rising boner.

"You," he said as he saw Jenny lying next to him, looking incredibly hot for a dead chick. "You can't be here. You're dead."

"Honey, you don't know the half of it," she said, laughing as she climbed on top of him and pinned him to the bed. She was, if anything, even stronger than her friend, who got off the bed and turned on the room light.

"What's the matter, Billy?" Jenny said as she ground her ass against his now-limp dick. "Don't I do it for you anymore?"

"Maybe he just needs a little encouragement," Mel said, stretching out beside him. She reached up and pulled down one of Jenny's bra straps, exposing the top of her left breast. Mel moved to the other side of the bed and held Billy's arms down. He tried to pull free, but it was pointless; both of them were stronger than a freaking linebacker, and he had no leverage.

Jenny slipped out of her bra, and cupped her bare breasts in her small hands, tweaking the nipples playfully. "Don't you like what you see?" she said. "You did the last time you saw it."

"What's the matter, Billy?" Mel said in his ear. "Can't get it up unless they fight a little, is that it?"

"Maybe he needs an audience," Jenny said. "He really seemed to enjoy himself when his friends were watching. How about it, Bill?" she said, still groping herself as she moved against him.

I don't believe it, he thought. I'm being dry-humped by a dead chick, and it's actually fucking working. He could feel his dick stirring again, and Jenny smiled.

"You know, I think you're right," Mel said. "We need more people watching."

Both of them closed their eyes, and for a moment he had a brief glimmer of hope that they'd spaced out, and maybe he could get out from under them. At least get his hands free; after that, he could slug one or both of them and take off. But even zoned out like they were, Mel's grip was iron.

The door opened, and Billy actually thought he might be dreaming as more girls came into the room, each one hotter than the next.

"He likes it when someone watches," Jenny said, and the others smiled.

"I like to watch," a tiny blonde said.

"You know, I think what little Billy really needs is to get good and royally fucked," a tall brunette said.

"How about it, Billy?" Jenny said. "Wanna get fucked, good and hard? And not just by me; we'll all take turns. Right, sisters?"

"Sisters?" he said, confused and suddenly horny enough to fuck a brick wall. Fuck it, he thought. Why not? It's probably just a dream anyway. "Sure," he said, laughing. "I could use a good fuck."

"Well, you're in luck," Jenny said, running one hand up his chest, then to his face before grasping a handful of his hair. She yanked his head to one side, hard enough he heard something pop. She bent down and licked a long, slow line up his throat to his jaw, making him shiver.

"You're definitely fucked now," someone said, and he had just a moment to wonder what the hell was happening and hear feminine laughter as Jenny hissed at him, exposing long, needle-like fangs. He started to scream, but an impossibly strong, small hand clamped over his mouth as Jenny lunged forward, sinking her new fangs into his throat.

Jenny sat up, his blood on her chin, and smiled with a crazed gleam in her eye. "Don't be shy, sisters," she said. "I've always wanted to try a group thing."

The full reality of his situation now finally settling in on him, Billy had just enough time to think he should have just left her alone before they all fell on him.

4.

Lilith sat calmly on the front porch rocker as her daughters came home, arms around each other and laughing. She rose and came to them as they stopped at the front steps. She hugged Jennifer, feeling the intense strength in her body as it flowed to her. "I hope it was everything you needed it to be, sweetheart," she said, and Jenny smiled.

"It was better," she said, and looked at the others. "It

was even better, because I did it with my sisters."

She smiled at that, and let her love flow freely to them all. Each of them closed their eyes and basked in it, holding each other and swaying slightly. "I love all of you so much," she said. "And I can feel how you love each other. It's so beautiful. You're all so beautiful."

"We are what you made us, Mother," Melissa said. She hugged the girl tightly.

"I'm so proud of you, Melissa," she said. "Is this the same shy girl who hid behind her hair?"

"Not anymore," Melissa said, her head up and her eyes full of life and fire.

"No, I can see that," Lilith said, smiling. "You're so much more now. All of you. You're not just girls anymore. You're not prey now, but predators. I couldn't be more proud."

She led them all inside the trailer. "You've all done amazing things today," she said. "It makes me so happy to see you become what you were always meant to be. And now, I need to rest."

"Mother?" Kris said, looking concerned. "Are you okay?"

"Yes, sweetie," she said, smiling. "But even I have limits, and I've done much today myself. Besides, we'll all need our rest for what comes next."

"Mother," Jennifer said. "Earlier, you said there were men we needed to find. More than one."

"Yes," she said. "And I know where the next one is. But I will need rest before I deal with him, and you will, as well. He isn't a fool like Bill Denison, or a coward like Amber's father. He is a very dangerous man, and he's killed many of my children. Your brothers and sisters. We must take him seriously."

"Aren't we, like, invincible now, or something?" Melanie asked. "I mean, we could probably pick up Ruth Ann's trailer and move it for her. Maybe over there, in the shade." A few of the girls chuckled, and Lilith smiled. It was a warm, patient smile. A man would have snapped at her for joking, told her to be "serious." Lilith enjoyed their levity, and their new-found confidence was a source of constant joy for her.

"You are all so incredibly strong, and beautiful," she said. "But nothing is invincible, children. Not even me. You will not age, and you won't fall to sickness. But your bodies are still vulnerable to injury, as is mine."

"We're not afraid, Mother," Jennifer said. "How can we help?"

"Soon," Lilith said. "We'll have our revenge soon. For now, rest, and love each other."

They all nodded, and each stopped to give her a kiss on the cheek as they went to bed. She held onto Jennifer's hand for a moment, and the girl stayed behind as the others left.

"Were you the first to taste him?" she asked, and Jennifer nodded, smiling.

"My sisters were very generous," she said. Lilith smiled.

"That's good," Lilith said, hugging the poor thing. "I just wanted you to know that he will never hurt anyone, ever again. He did something terrible to you, Jennifer, but he paid for it. You don't have to carry the hate anymore."

"But I do hate him," Jennifer said, weeping suddenly. "I hate him for what he did to me. For what he did to so many other people. I saw it all when I fed, everything he did. You didn't know him, Mother."

"He was a cruel, drunken bully," Lilith said. "I see through your eyes, through your heart and mind, remember? I see everything you've been through, everything you've watched others go through, and I felt your heart break for each of them. I know your heart, my sweet girl, and it is every bit as beautiful as your face. There's no room for hate in a heart so beautiful, Jennifer. Let me take it away."

"But--" Jennifer started, and Lilith touched her lips with one finger.

"I can handle it," she said, smiling. "I have experienced the darkest impulses of all my children, since the beginning of time. Let me take away that hate from your heart, before it poisons you."

Jennifer, now crying freely, nodded. Lilith cupped her face in both hands, thumbing away tears, and kissed her. A light touch of the lips, nothing more. A mother's kiss. That brief contact drew from the girl not just her hatred of the worthless bastard she'd just killed, but his memories that had been transferred to her with his blood.

She saw everything that Billy Denison had done to her beautiful girl, and to so many of her children in his short time. She saw the things no one had ever known about; sadly, Jennifer had not been the first of her daughters he'd killed. There was a girl he'd stalked, the real reason he'd been forced to leave school. He'd strangled her in her bedroom after she'd rejected him.

His punishment had been far too light, but there was nothing to be done for it now. When Jennifer opened her pretty eyes, she could see the light returning to them.

"There," she said, a tear running down her own face. "A mother's kiss makes it all better."

"I love you, Mother," Jennifer said as a single, blood-tinged tear leaked down her face. Lilith wiped it away before it could stain.

"And I love you, my child," she said. "Go now. Be with your sisters. Rest, and tomorrow we'll find the man we seek."

Jennifer did as she asked, and Lilith waited until she was out of the room before stepping back outside, into the comfort of the night air. She'd seen everything Bill Denison had known, including more about Jerry Hartman than anyone had suspected.

It wasn't just Hartman she needed to punish, but his partner, as well. Maybe others; Billy hadn't known that much. But she knew who his partner was, and between the two of them, they would tell her what she needed to know.

Closing her eyes, she let her consciousness drift out into the night, finding each of her sleeping children and mining their dreams and nightmares for any information about Harlan Denison. She smiled as she saw their dreams, comforted them as best she could through their nightmares, and pried into their darkest secrets in search of what she needed. She was almost done when the impossible happened.

She touched a mind that was not her child, but did not taste of the Other's line, either. "No," she said, snapping back to herself instantly. Her eyes flew open, and a feeling she hadn't experienced in millennia attacked her, causing her slight shoulders to shudder.

There was a child of neither line in this town, and he was strong. Oh, God, he was so strong. It took her a moment to understand what she was feeling, but once she did understand it, she took a firm grip on her fear and pushed it down.

CHAPTER NINE

1.

Jim woke up with a start, sitting straight up in his empty bed as the nightmare broke. He only recalled fragments of it, something about a dark entity chasing him through the empty town. He looked down at his hand, and found he'd actually picked up the gun he kept on the nightstand out of reflex.

Hands shaking, he swung his legs over the side of the bed, put the gun back on the nightstand, and rubbed a hand over the back of his neck, rubbing away the tension before plodding his way to the bathroom down the hall.

The last remaining scraps of the dream faded away as he urinated but the feeling of deep dread they'd inspired remained, and he knew there was no point in trying to go back to sleep. Instead, he went back to the bedroom, pulled on some workout clothes, and prepared to go for a little late-night run.

But before he left the house, he went to the gun closet, wrapped the Velcro belly band holster around his midsection, and tucked his off-duty gun, a Smith and Wesson J-frame .38 Special, into it, along with a flashlight and his favorite Benchmade knife. He rarely ran while armed, but tonight he couldn't bring himself to leave the weapon behind.

2.

One of the things he liked about this place was that it wasn't a large town. He ran for time, not distance, and his two-hour run took him through most of the town. He didn't have a set route, but just sort of followed his intuition as he ran. His house was at the end of a dead-end street that led to the Square, and he almost always took at least one lap around before striking off in whatever direction took his fancy.

Tonight he did two laps around the square, the weight of the revolver strapped to his stomach a comfort rather than a hindrance. Eventually he went south, into the mostly residential section of town. He ran past the park, which was deserted at this time of night save for a couple of old-timers he knew well enough to not bother rousting. They were insomniacs looking to fill their empty nights, not screwing kids or looking to score dope, and tonight he could empathize. His own night felt decidedly empty, as well.

He turned down the main path into the park, waving to the old guys sitting at one of the picnic tables and shooting the shit around a battery-powered lantern. They waved back, looking mildly surprised to see him out so late. He didn't stop to chat, but just ran on, through the park and out onto the street at the other side. He turned left, by now settled into his rhythm and enjoying the warmth spreading through his legs as he worked his body.

The more he worked his body, the better his mind worked. As he ran, he let it go where it wanted to go, without trying to steer it, and it eventually came around to the nightmare that had broken his sleep so violently.

He remembered a woman. Medium height, dark brown hair, classically beautiful features. Trim waist, good hips and legs, and high, firm breasts. She wore some sort of white shift dress, no shoes, and she seemed angry at him.

He remembered the way she'd recoiled when she saw

him on the street, and the insane urge to turn and run, something he'd never done once in real life. Jim Harlow was not the man who ran away from danger, but went right at it. But dreams had their own logic, and he'd turned on his heels, running down the street and across the Square.

He remembered passing Denison and his band of happy assholes on the bandstand, but they were dead. Denison himself looked horrible, pale, shriveled, and sunken-eyed as he raised a bottle wrapped in a brown paper bag.

"Pull up a seat, Jim," Denison croaked, his voice rough and harsh. "Pull up a seat and have a drink with us. Might as well, you know. She's gonna get you too, sooner or later."

He ran past them as they laughed, feeling that dark woman coming after him. She wasn't running, just moving along at a steady pace like some 80's slasher movie villain, but she was somehow gaining on him all the same.

His feet pounded the pavement, and he saw that his route had wandered back to the Square. He stopped at the bandstand, stretching out his hamstrings as he looked at the piece of ground where he'd beaten Denison so badly. It had been stupid, he knew that now. Pointless, and probably detrimental to any sort of real justice, but damned if it hadn't felt good at the time.

Standing at the foot of the stairs leading up to the bandstand, breathing heavily and coated in a light sheen of sweat as he stretched, he saw everything for what it was. He could see everything that had led up to that moment, all the times he'd been caught up in the whirlwind of his own deep-seated anger.

He started to dismiss the train of thought, to distract himself with his memories of the nightmare or just random thoughts about the long day he had coming, but he didn't. If the middle of the night wasn't a good time for a little self-examination, then when was?

His early life hadn't been what anyone would call stable; absent father, distant mother. At least until she died at fifty-two from the three packs a day she'd smoked, and then he'd been shipped off to relatives in Oklahoma. Uncle Oren wasn't the most expressive man in the world, at least unless he was drunk. He expressed himself quite well then, usually with a hard right hand.

His aunt Carolyn had been okay, though. She'd loved him, in her own way, and when he had felt homesick, first in the Army and then in college, it had been Aunt Carolyn he'd thought of. Aunt Carolyn and her cinnamon rolls. The only time Jim couldn't remember feeling that anger rolling just under the surface was when he'd spent time with Carolyn.

But she was gone now, too; she'd outlived Uncle Oren by fifteen years. He'd died not long after Jim had come to live with them, and to Jim the cause of death should have been as predictable as the sun rising in the east; he'd picked the exact wrong drunken moment to work on his aging pickup, and had accidentally kicked the jack holding it up off the garage floor. Oren, he of the hard right hand, had died slowly, crushed under the weight of his '62 Chevy pickup. Jim imagined him lying there, two tons on his chest and slowly squeezing the life from him as crankcase oil slowly dripped on his forehead. It was a horrible death, surely, but Jim still found it hard to empathize with the man. At the funeral, he still hadn't been able to see out of his swollen left eye, a last parting gift from good old Uncle Oren just hours before the accident.

He had been amazed that Aunt Carolyn had found it in herself to actually cry for the man.

But the anger had deeper roots than one old drunk and a few black eyes; he knew that much. A shrink would tell him it came from his early home life, and he supposed there was some truth to that. He'd asked his mother for a bicycle when he was nine; all the other kids had one, and it didn't have to be anything special. Her response still rang in his ears, some forty years later.

"Bikes and such are luxuries," she said. "You eat three times a day, your ass is covered, and you've got a place to sleep. Everything else is for boys whose Daddies stick around to pay the goddamned bills." She'd tossed this little nugget of poison at him on her way out the door to her second job, waitressing at a truck stop on the highway.

He hadn't gotten the bike. Had never owned a bicycle, come to think of it. Maybe he should be operating in classic man-child fashion, and buying himself the things he'd never had as a kid. He grinned at the thought, and started running again before he could stiffen up.

A man could only unpack so much baggage at one time, unless he wanted to spend two or three afternoons a week lying on a couch and telling some doctor about when he'd learned to use the toilet. And as a rule, men who spent that much time in a shrink's office were not often given the Chief of Police's chair.

He ran instead, and wondered what, if anything, the dream about the beautiful, terrifying woman might mean. He supposed the obvious wasn't out of the question; he hadn't had anyone steady in his life since his divorce some eight years ago, and while he wasn't exactly a misanthrope, he liked being by himself well enough to feel no pressing need to change that. He wasn't afraid of women, but he was leery of the sort of entanglements and complications they always seem to bring into his life. If nothing else, the divorce had taught him that.

Eventually he ended up back where he'd started, and let himself into the house. He stopped at the closet to put the gun away, but found he couldn't quite bring himself to do it just yet. Instead, he left it on the bathroom counter as he showered, and carried it with him into the bedroom as he dressed. The clock on the nightstand said it was just now coming up on four in the morning; it was going to be a very long day, he thought as he went to start the coffee pot.

Later, he would think he hadn't had any idea what a long day really was before that one.

3.

Jerry checked his phone again, seeing that the tracker he'd put on Billy's phone hadn't moved. He'd spent a few hours rip-assing around on backroads, probably drunk and working himself up to doing something stupid. When the little blip on the map had changed direction, headed back into town, Jerry had thought he might finally get his chance to deal with the little bastard, once and for all. Billy wasn't the sharpest knife in the drawer, so he'd figured if this was going to happen, it was up to him to be easy to find. But Billy had gone right to the motel, and hadn't left.

Maybe he'd been a little too easy to find, he thought as he walked, checking out the reflection in a dark window and spotting the kid right away. He'd known he had someone following him almost the second the kid picked him up outside the diner. It would have been simplicity itself to shake the tail, but he was curious. It was a kid, he saw, barely old enough to buy the cigarette he was currently smoking. Cops didn't use kids for surveillance, and even the local yokels were better at it than this kid.

He led the kid on a merry little walking tour of the town, occasionally pausing to look at his phone, tie his shoes, or anything else he could think of to keep from accidentally losing his follower. Still, the game had been going on for too long, and he was getting bored.

Not the kid, though; he had dedication in spades. Jerry was a little surprised to find himself grudgingly admiring the kid; anyone else would have given up hours ago. But this was a small town, and there was only so much walking a man could do before it became obvious he wasn't going anywhere.

He stopped in at the convenience store, bought a cup of bad coffee, and stood outside drinking it and pretending to be absorbed in his phone as he watched the kid watching him. He wasn't on a phone, wasn't taking notes or pictures. He was just watching Jerry, hidden poorly in the shadows of the funeral home across the street. His phone told him it was almost three in the morning. "Christ," he said under his breath. "I'm not that fucking interesting, kid. Make your damned move."

The kid didn't make his move. He didn't move at all; just stood there in his shitty, amateur hiding spot and watched Jerry do nothing at all. Drinking a cup of bad coffee was about as exciting as it had gotten since the kid had started tailing him, but the kid was as devoted as a horny teenager looking through a woman's window.

"Enough is enough," he said. He tossed the half-empty coffee into the trash and started walking in a diagonal, toward the bank on the corner. Once he was out of sight of the funeral home, he ducked into a blind spot, pulled the knife in his waistband from its sheath, and waited.

Predictably, the kid came bopping along right on schedule, completely oblivious. He let the kid get a step ahead of him, and pounced.

He grabbed the kid by the jacket and tossed him backward, into the shadows. He shoved him up against the wall, one arm across his chest to pin him, and put the point of the knife under his chin. The kid didn't react. No protests or questions, just looked at him. "Come on. Do I really gotta ask, kid?"

The kid continued his long spiel of nothing at all, and it was starting to piss Jerry off. "Why are you following me, son?" he said. He nicked the skin under his chin. Nothing messy, just a little scratch. Just enough to get his attention. "If I have to ask you twice, it's not gonna matter what the answer is, you dig?"

"Mother is very upset with you, Mr. Hartman," the kid said, grinning. "Very upset."

"The fuck does your mom have to do with anything?" he said. "I bang her or something?"

"Mother is coming for you, Jerry," the kid said. "She's very angry at you, for what you did to my sisters."

Fuck it, Jerry thought. The kid's off his nut. "I should just bleed you out right now," he said. "But that's a complication I don't need. So instead, I'm going to do you a favor. You're going to turn around and walk your narrow ass home, and forget all about me. If you try following me again, I'll know. That will be bad for you, son, because if I see you again, I'll kill you. You understand?"

The kid looked at him, his smile growing. "You've been very bad, Mr. Hartman." And before Jerry could even register the crazy shit the kid was saying, a knee drove upward into his balls at the same time a thumb was driven into his throat. He staggered backward, trying to slash at the kid. His wrist was caught and twisted, and the knife fell from his hand just before an elbow smashed into his temple, knocking him down.

Christ, he thought randomly. Where in the holy hell did that come from? He didn't have time to think much about it, because the kid was already in the wind. He staggered to his feet, picking up the knife as he looked all around for the kid, but when he saw no sign of him, he put the knife away and started walking back to where he'd left his truck.

Shit was definitely going sideways, and the last thing he needed was more complications. It was time to cut his losses, no doubt about that. And the first order of business was making sure a certain swinging dick moron couldn't take what little he might or might not know to the cops. "Sorry, Harlan," he said as he got behind the wheel and pulled away. "But it's gotta be done."

He drove to the hotel and parked in the visitor's lot, and started planning his next move. Eventually he decided that simplicity was beautiful, and walked into the lobby. If the kid was asleep, he wouldn't wake up. And if he was up, then Jerry would put him to sleep, fast and final.

The pretty overnight clerk was very helpful; after he told her that his boss had asked him to check on his son after they'd had a bit of a blowout, all told through a rather embarrassed grin, she gave him Billy's room number. She couldn't give him the key, though; sorry about that, sir, but it's policy. He'd told her that was no problem. He wasn't here to pack the kid off to boot camp, just to try and talk to him.

"Thanks for your help, Vicki," he said, giving her a smile as he read her name tag.

"You're very welcome, sir," Vicki said, smiling right back. Jerry took the stairs rather than the elevator, aware that he was already most likely on camera but wanting to avoid as much as possible. If necessary, he would deal with that once this was done. But the plan was to get the kid out of the hotel, and he was pretty sure he knew exactly how to do just that.

He knocked firmly on the door to room 315, but got no answer. Undeterred, he knocked again, but with the same result. "Fuck," he said under his breath. "Can't ever be easy." He could force the door, but that was just an all-around bad idea. At this time of the night, it would sound like a tank rolling through the hallway, and it would most definitely bring down some serious attention on him.

But wait. Just wait a minute and think, he told himself. This is what you do, Jerry. You think your way around a problem. Battering your way through something is the kid's way, not yours, so calm down and think. Of course, as soon as he did that, the logical answer presented himself.

He put what he was pretty sure was a concerned look on his face, and went down to see his new best friend, Vicki.

4.

Twenty nerve-wracking minutes later, he was once again standing in front of the door to room 315, this time with the night manager. Vicki had bought his woeful tale of family arguments, legal troubles, and drug addiction hook, line, and sinker. It had probably helped that he'd been able to inject the absolutely truthful angle of the poor hired schmuck who was hopelessly caught in the middle of this particular mess, namely himself.

"You understand, I can't let you in the room," the manager said as he pulled the key card from his pocket. "I can check on him for you, but unless--"

"No, it's okay," Jerry said, sounding appropriately worried now. "If he's okay, then the rest is between him and his old man. I just need to make sure he didn't OD or something."

The thought of a guest dying of a drug overdose, and on his shift, was just the right motivator for the man; he unlocked the room and stepped inside. "Sir?" he heard the man say. "Hotel management, sir. There's been some concern about—oh my God."

That sounded like very bad shit to Jerry, and he pushed the door open before it could latch. What he saw both simplified matters for him, and at the same time complicated them immensely.

William Marcus Denison was, without question, one dead motherfucker. He lay on the bed, pants around his ankles and shirt torn open. Jerry had to do a double-take to make sure that what he saw on the boy's chest, arms, legs, and throat were, in fact, bite marks. Ragged, torn holes in the flesh, not to put too fine a point on the matter. The manager, who by now had been all but forgotten, started for the room phone, but Jerry stopped him.

"Don't touch anything," he said, catching the man by his arm and dragging him out of the room. He let the room door swing shut and latch, effectively sealing off the room. The presence of the man took away any real decision he could make, and so he did the only thing he could reasonably do at the moment.

He pulled his cell phone from his jacket pocket, and dialed 911. Once the cops were on the way, he had no choice but to wait for them, so he filled the time by making the only call he'd wanted to make less than the one to the police. He called Harlan, and told him everything he could, mindful that the manager was still standing next to him, possibly in shock but still able to hear.

"Harlan?" Jerry said after a long pause. "Are you understanding me?"

"Yes," Harlan said, but he sounded distant, as if he were terribly distracted by something in the room. "Yes, I understand. How did it happen?"

"I have no idea," Jerry said, looking back at the closed door of room 315.

"I'm on my way," he said.

"That may not be the best idea, Harlan," he said, but he'd already disconnected the call. In the distance, he heard sirens approaching.

"I don't—nothing like this has ever happened here," the manager said, looking as if someone had just slapped the man with a very large trout. Jerry remembered the way Billy had resembled nothing so much as a dried up apple doll, bite marks all over his body.

"Buddy," Jerry said, resigning himself to official contact as the first officers got off the elevator. "I'm pretty sure nothing like this has ever happened anywhere."

CHAPTER TEN

1.

Lilith sat in the middle of the living room floor, her legs crossed under her and her palms resting on her knees. She didn't need to send her consciousness out to the world to watch the events happening in the local hotel, because one of the responding police officers was of her line. She'd placed her touch on the man as she walked through town earlier, thinking that it was a stroke of luck to find one of her sons in a position of authority.

It was a stroke of luck, on more than one front. He was on the scene, and saw everything. And Lilith's energy was low; sending herself out into the world like that drained her, leaving her weak and vulnerable. The energy she received from her special children helped quite a bit, but only time would really replenish her. She could see everything through her child's eyes, and what she saw troubled her.

The problem with having her children in positions of authority was that they tended to be smart and conscientious, meaning discrepancies and unusual circumstances caught their attention immediately. And if the body of a strong, healthy young man dried up like so much dead grass, and with multiple bite marks, didn't qualify as unusual, she wasn't sure anything would.

It was a problem, but not an insurmountable one.

There were ways to deal with it, but the real problem was that she was so drained. Virtually anything she did would leave her dangerously exhausted and vulnerable, and given what she'd seen earlier, that was a risky proposition.

It wasn't the first time she'd encountered someone from the third lineage, but it hadn't happened in many lifetimes. They were understandably rare, and very dangerous. Her children were always accessible to her, and even those of the Other mother were sometimes open to her, because of the husband she shared with the Other. That link, tenuous as it was, was often enough to at least allow her to understand those children of the Other. But this one, this man, was like a closed book to her. She could feel his presence, even now, but beyond that he was a mystery to her. The only thing she knew for sure was that he was dangerous.

She had encountered five others in her many lifetimes; all men, and each a fierce warrior, brave and strong. That alone made them dangerous. What was worse, they were immune to her influence. And, in her experience, men who could not be influenced with her love were not likely to succumb to fear, nor could they be bargained with.

But worst of all, she had seen at least one of these men slaughter her special children. As they were immune to her influence, they were also unaffected by her special children's charms. There was something else, something she couldn't recall, although it seemed to be very important that she remember it. She settled down and focused her mind, searching through centuries of memory, but it was no use. It wouldn't come to her, not like this. She was too drained, too tired to recall what she must.

Like it or not, it was time she fed, and fed properly. She loved how selflessly her children fed her, but it wasn't always enough. But it was so horrible, what she had to do to feed. To do that to one of her own; almost unthinkable. But it had to be done; she could not properly love and protect her children if she were weak and helpless herself. And while her children could only properly feed on those of the Other, she could only feed on her own.

She stood up and went to the bedroom, where all her daughters slumbered. No, not one of them; they were too important to what she needed to do. Too valuable to sacrifice. There was Ruth Ann, but that seemed ill advised; the others had come to love her as a sister, albeit one they had yet to fully meet. She would not cause them that much pain, not even to feed.

Resigned, she blew a kiss to her daughters, ensuring they would sleep, and went out into the early dawn light to hunt.

2.

As a mother, she liked to think that all of her children were good, at least at their core. But countless centuries of experience told her that this simply wasn't true. Her children were human, and as such ran the gamut from good to evil, and everything in between. On the rare occasions she did need to feed, she chose to see it as an act of loving correction; regrettable punishment that was her duty as a loving and caring mother.

She thought about Ruth Ann, still sleeping away the last effects of the poison she'd been using for years, and it made her heart ache. What was worse, it was one of her own sons that provided her with the poison she'd been slowly killing her beautiful body, mind, and spirit with for years. She reached out and touched the sleeping Ruth Ann's mind, and found her memories of Garrett Brown.

Garrett dealt in many poisons; the crystal rock Ruth Ann loved so, the various white powders, the pills. He was not particular about how he was paid for his wares, either; he'd happily accept their pride and dignity in exchange for his poison. She saw through Ruth Ann's mind and memories how often she'd utterly debased herself to this man for the privilege of destroying herself with his products.

It was not acceptable, and Garrett needed to be corrected. It was this thought she held onto as she made her way to his trailer. She didn't bother knocking; Garrett was wide awake, thanks to his own habits. She let herself in, and found Garrett sitting on a dilapidated couch, wearing equally worn boxer shorts and a spectacularly disgusting tank top shirt. His bare feet were filthy, thanks mostly to walking on carpet that was probably a few generations away from intelligence of its own.

"Hello, Garrett," she said, looking around the filthy trailer. It was, if anything, far worse than Ruth Ann's had been; at least there had been nothing growing in there. The smell, though; that was truly unique. The air was thick with the acrid stench of the burned crystals and rancid food, combined with some impressively aggressive body odor. It seemed Garrett had little interest in personal hygiene.

"Yeah?" Garrett said, looking up at her with bloodshot eyes. "What's up, baby? You looking for a little something?"

"Yes," Lilith said. "I am. Something very special."

"Yeah?" Garrett said, smiling to expose teeth that were well beyond saving. "Whatcha lookin' for, baby? 'Cause I got it all, you know?"

"Oh, I know you have exactly what I need, Garrett," she said. "And I need it, badly."

"Well, have a seat, and tell Daddy G what you need, sweetness," he said, patting the filthy couch cushion next to him. She thought privately she'd rather swim through hot garbage, but just declined with a smile and a small shake of her head.

"I'm in a bit of a hurry, Garrett," she said.

"Well then, let's get down to it," he said. "I got whatever you want. Ain't free, though. You got cash?"

"I don't use money," she said, still smiling. This didn't seem to faze Garrett at all. He just leaned back on the nasty couch and smiled.

"Well, green ain't the only way to pay for something, sweetness," he said. "Maybe you give me a little something, I give you a little something in return."

"I'm going to give you something," she said, and he grinned. "I'm going to give you some advice, Garrett. The things you make these poor women do, just so they can continue killing themselves, are horrendous and unacceptable."

Garrett rolled his eyes. "I ain't got time for this shit," he said. "You want something, or not? If not, get the fuck out."

Before Garrett knew she was moving, she'd crossed the disgusting carpet and picked him up by the chin. She was angry with him, but she made herself control it. Punishment from anger was a man's way; a mother corrected her children with love. She would be stern, because that was what he needed, but it came from love and not anger.

Garrett made a small, gasping noise as her fangs, long unused, descended. "I want you to know, I wish I didn't have to do this, Garrett," she said. His eyes went wide, and she sank her fangs into his throat. She let his blood flow into her mouth, not missing a drop. It carried his life essence with it, and she felt it infuse through her entire body as she drank.

When she was full, she let what remained of Garrett fall back to the couch. She had a choice to make; leave him as he was, and let him return as one of her dark children, or put him out of his misery.

"I'm sorry, Garrett," she said, standing over him. Unbelievably, his eyes followed her; he was still alive. "But I can't allow you to come back. You're too dangerous to the other children." With real regret, she took his head in both hands and twisted, wincing as the bones of his neck snapped. She twisted harder, and the head came off in her hands.

"I love you, my son," she said, and kissed the

decapitated head on one cheek. With his life force flowing through her, she saw his whole life, a sad story of neglect, abuse, poverty. Of seemingly endless nights with no food, no love, no hope. Nights spent in fear that the door to his bedroom would open in the middle of the night, and Travis would come to him. Travis was his stepfather, and starting at only eight years old, had raped Garrett at least weekly until he left home at thirteen. The pain of his tragedy tore through her to her heart, but it couldn't be helped now.

At least his suffering was over, she told herself as she searched the filthy trailer for what she needed. As it turned out, it was unnecessary; Garrett had a small lab in the back of the trailer, where he made his crystal poison. It was full of flammable chemicals; all she had to do was strike a match and let it fall. But first, there was something else to consider. Poor Curtis was still in the trunk of Jennifer's car. She was sad that she'd actually forgotten poor Curtis, who'd so kindly fed Jennifer when she woke. Full of Garrett's life blood, the trip back to Ruth Ann's trailer took her mere moments, and Curtis himself weighed almost nothing. Satisfied with her night's work, she struck a match and dropped it onto Garrett's disgusting couch.

She walked away from Garrett's trailer as the flames began to grow, and by the time the meth lab exploded, she was gone.

3.

Jim stepped off the elevator on the third floor of the Marriott, and was immediately relieved to see Mark was already here. Granted, the call had come in almost three hours ago, and Mark had been on duty for at least thirty minutes by now, but it was still a relief.

"Mark," he said as he approached. Mark finished his marching orders to the crime scene tech about a piece of evidence, and turned to him.

"Sorry to grab you on the way into the office," he said,

but Jim just shook his head.

"What's the situation?" he said. "Is that ID solid?"

"It's Denison," Mark said, nodding. "Room's in his name, paid for with his card. And you can tell who it is just looking at him. Well, kinda."

"Anything missing?" he asked, wondering if the Universe could have possibly dealt out a little ironic justice.

"Far as I can tell, it's all here," he said as they stepped into the room. Jim ignored the body on the bed for the moment; the crime scene guys were busy with it, and he didn't want to look at him just yet. Mark pointed to a clear evidence bag with a wallet inside. "ID, half a dozen credit cards, about six hundred bucks in cash. Couple of joints in his shirt pocket. If it's a trick roll, it's the worst one in history."

"Couldn't be that easy," Jim said, shaking his head. "Any idea on cause of death?"

"Karma?" Mark said, making a couple of the techs look up at him in confusion. Jim just gave him a slight shake of the head, and Mark buttoned it. "Either of you guys wanna take that one?" he asked the techs. "I'm not smart enough to explain it."

Jim knew damned well that wasn't true, but he let his officer punt to the techs. "You see anything odd, Chief?" one of them said, motioning to the body and the bed it lay on.

"You mean besides the dead guy?" Jim said. "It's very early son, and I didn't sleep much. Best to just spell it out for me."

"Right," the tech said. He touched the skin on Denison's arm, and it sunk in. Rather than rebounding like even dead tissue should at this early stage, it sank in and stayed. "Body's entering rapid deterioration, minus the smell. And he's all but completely drained."

"Drained?" Jim said, sure he wasn't understanding him correctly. The tech nodded.

"Best I can tell, there isn't even enough blood left in his

body to pool in the lower extremities," he said. He double-checked with his partner that everything had been photographed, and then pulled off one of Denison's tennis shoes. The foot, which due to gravity and his position should have shown signs of discoloration and swelling, was as pale as the rest of him. "Nothing on his back or buttocks, either. Chief, do you know how much blood is in the average adult male body?"

Jim just shook his head, trying not to look as annoyed as he was. "Guy his size, he would have right about five and a half liters of blood in him," the tech continued. He shined his pen light on the various small bloodstains on the bedspread. "I've seen more blood from my kid's nosebleeds than what's on this bed. So I guess the sixty-four thousand dollar question is..."

"What happened to the blood?" Jim said, shaking his head. "I actually just said that."

"Chief," the county ME said as he came into the room uninvited. Ray Creek did not, as a rule, feel he needed an invitation to go anywhere. "What kind of dinky dow shit is this? Call notes said something about an exsanguinated body, but no blood pool?"

"Welcome to the Twilight Zone," Mark said, making the techs chuckle. Once again, Jim just gave him a small head shake to cut it out. "Still no word from Curt, Doc?"

"No, and when you find him, he'd better hope for his sake he's been abducted by aliens," Ray said. "Otherwise, I'm gonna kick his ass before I fire him."

"Sure not like him to just bail," Jim said, and Ray nodded, then shrugged as if to show just how hard it was to find good help.

"Okay, you clowns," Ray said, and the techs backed off. "You've slow-danced with the gentleman long enough. Let's get him bagged and back to the office so we can get to know him a little better."

Jim had to stifle a chuckle of his own, even as he looked at Mark and desperately begged him with his eyes not to laugh; it would only encourage the old fart further. Miraculously, Mark kept a straight face the entire time as Ray and the techs bagged the body, and two of the ME's assistants brought in the stretcher.

"Gentleman, the service elevator, please," someone said. "The other guests."

"Oh, shit," Mark and Jim said at the same time. If there was anything on God's green earth guaranteed to earn someone Ray's entire, devoted, and thoroughly unpleasant full attention, it was telling him how to do his job.

"Ain't my concern," Ray said, directing the assistants to the elevator right in front of them. "Closest path to the exit is right through that lobby, and that's where he's going. I ain't about to traipse all over hell and back just for you."

"It's okay," Jim said as he saw a prim, prissy little man he assumed had to be the general manager. "Go on and get him back to the lab, Doc."

"Wasn't asking anyone's permission," Ray said, and stepped onto the elevator just before the door closed.

"Sheriff, this is--"

"Chief," Jim corrected him. "And while Dr. Creek can be a little rough, he's right, sir. The more the body is transported or handled, the more likely key evidence can be disturbed."

"But the guests," the manager said.

"Sir, if you'll come with me, we'll see if we can't keep them from being disturbed any more than necessary," Mark said, and Jim gave him a subtle nod. He'd placate the man while gathering what little witness statements there might be.

"Chief," someone said, and he heard heavy footsteps accompanied by a creaking duty belt and jangling keys as Jake Faulkner, a tall, somewhat heavy-set but capable man who worked the overnight shift, came running up to him. "You need to hear this," he said.

"Go," he said, and he gave him the basics right away, with no preamble or backstory, just the way he liked it.

"Call just came into county dispatch," Faulkner said. "Large explosion and fire. FD's on the scene, say they've got it under control. Report of at least two bodies."

"And this concerns us?" he said, confused. "It's a county scene, right?"

"Sir, it's Garrett Brown's trailer," he said, as if that was all he needed to know. It was, of course; Brown was well known to his department, and probably two dozen others as well.

"Lab explosion?" he said, and Faulkner nodded. "Any ID on either bodies?"

"Just preliminary," he said. "One looks to be Brown, which isn't a surprise since he never leaves the place. The other one, at least according to what was left of an ID card in his pocket, is Curt Standhope."

That woke Jim up; Curtis Standhope was the assistant ME who'd gone missing with Jennifer Bennett's body. "What the hell?" he said, because it was the only thing that fit.

"I got this if you want to roll out there," he said, already knowing exactly what he wanted to do. "Just waiting on the CSU guys to finish now that the body's gone."

"After they finish, go through and document everything," he said. "You have a camera in your unit?"

"Yeah," he said. "And plenty of SD cards."

"We don't issue those," he said, and Faulkner shrugged.

"I buy them by the carton off Amazon," he said. "If it makes you feel better, I'll submit the expense report."

"Might as well," he said. "Budget's already shot to hell, anyway."

Faulkner laughed. "Don't I know it," he said. They both knew he wouldn't submit the expense ticket, just as they both knew that if he did, the city would take forever to reimburse it, if at all. They were too busy with important things, like the small fleet of city cars they gave to various employees, repainting year-old parking lines on the square, and buying even more freaking lights for the annual Christmas parade to deal with piddling trifles like the PD paying for necessary equipment and supplies out of their own meager salaries.

Jim looked at his watch. "You're supposed to be off duty an hour ago," he said, and Faulkner shrugged.

"Kinda feels like an all-hands situation to me," he said. "And I get the feeling you're gonna need Mark most of the day."

"Wrap up here, and go get some rest," he said. "That's an order, just in case I forgot what they sound like."

"Yes, sir," he said, smiling. He knew Faulkner was just cheerfully insubordinate enough to take his time and do the job right, then probably take one or two swings through town before calling it a day. He also knew it would do absolutely no good to argue with him. "Chief, I know we're not supposed to have any sort of personal feelings about this sort of thing," he said. "But if there was anyone in town who had it coming, it was that young man."

"I know," he said. "But we don't get to make that call. We work it just like any other case."

"When half the town is a suspect, where do you even start?" he said, and Jim had to grudgingly agree with him. It certainly didn't help that he'd essentially boiled the entire problem down to one sentence.

Confident the scene was in good hands, he went downstairs to find his lead officer, and try to figure out what in God's name was happening in his town.

CHAPTER ELEVEN

1.

Ray Creek, Chief Medical Examiner for the entire county, was in a spectacularly foul mood, and he was willing to share the wealth. Curt was his right hand man, in more ways than one; the young man had been stepping up more and more lately, performing many of the more routine autopsies. Under supervision, of course, but he still did the grunt work. It occurred to him that he'd come to rely on that more than was probably wise, given the fact that the younger man had apparently absconded with a body.

And not just any body, either. Ray cursed himself under his breath as he got the autopsy theater ready, with the unfortunate soul who'd been picked to assist him doing her best to help and stay out of his way at the same time. Get your shit together, old man, he told himself. It's not the girl's fault.

"Laura, could you do me a favor and grab the digital recorder out of my desk?" he said with what he hoped was a warm smile. There was an audio recording system in the autopsy theater, but it was just a few years shy of ancient, and notoriously unreliable. He tapped the mic that hung overhead in demonstration. "I don't trust the Dinosaur, here."

"Yes, Dr. Creek," she said, scurrying to his office. She

was a good kid, even if the ink on her pathology degree wasn't quite dry just yet. Certainly the brightest of his assistants, and the administrator inside him decided she was the one to tap for the assistant ME position. Always assuming he could keep from showing his ass enough to avoid scaring her off, that was.

Laura brought the recorder to him, holding it out in both hands like a sacrificial offering. "Okay," he said with another smile. "I was hoping you'd get to work with Curt a bit more first, but you're ready to jump in, I think."

"I'll do my best," she said, and he nodded.

"Of course," he said. "It's not your qualifications I wanted Curt to work on. I wanted him to teach you how to ignore me when I'm being a grumpy old bastard." That brought a smile, and she visibly relaxed.

She was good, he thought as he turned to the table. She'd laid the body out on the table, and not done a single thing to it since. He remembered the first time Curt, who had actually worked as a mortician's assistant before finishing his degree, had assisted him. Before he could remind him not to, Curt had actually washed the body.

"Well, at least the drain filters are on," Ray had said, shaking his head. It had worked out okay in the end; the body had been that of a transient homeless man who'd died of exposure. Had it been a criminal case, the entire autopsy findings could have been called into question. Ray had always had a rough tongue, but he'd had better control of it back then. Curt had stood in front of his desk, back ramrod straight, and taken his dressing down like a man. It obviously hadn't been pleasant for him, but he'd never made such a colossal mistake again.

Have to be a little gentler with this one, he reminded himself. Women crying had always made him extremely uncomfortable. "Well, I suppose we should get started," he said. Laura nodded and turned on the Dinosaur for him, the switch to which was absurdly placed on the far wall instead of anywhere remotely helpful, like on the mic itself.

"Body is that of a Caucasian male, tentatively identified as William Denison, twenty-six years old. Body appears to be in a state of advanced decomposition, although a most unusual sort. Skin is dry and brittle, showing multiple small cracks, commonly associated with extreme desiccation. There are multiple—shoot, not multiple. There are seven laceration-style bite marks on the body. One above the femoral artery, midway up on both thighs. One at each wrist, and one at each elbow. The seventh is located on the anterior right side of the throat, and all appear to have damaged blood vessels at each point. It is noteworthy that virtually no blood was found at the scene."

He sighed and stepped away. He looked up at Laura, who was busy taking notes. "Please note that the bite marks do not appear to be human in origin," he said, and pointed at the tear on the inside of his left elbow. "The punctures appear to be of varying depth, more consistent with an animal bite."

"Extended canines?" Laura asked, and he nodded. "But these look like human incisor marks, Doctor."

I'll be goddamned, he thought as he looked closer. In the small portion of tissue that hadn't been torn, he could clearly see what did indeed look like incisor marks. Human incisors. "Make a note of that," he said. "Good catch."

The young woman smiled and continued to write as he went on with the external exam.

2.

She let the children sleep in; they were still growing into their full powers, and children needed rest to grow. She also needed some time to herself, in order to take care of things they could not. Emma was up, tidying the trailer and doing a pretty good job of staying out of her hair.

The kids were in the backyard, laughing and playing in

a way that made Lilith smile despite the distraction. She wouldn't ask them to quiet down for the world; they had always been terrified of disturbing their father, and uninhibited play was a new sensation for them. She'd never let anyone or anything get in the way of that.

But she did need a little isolation, and just the fact that Emma was awake inside the trailer was enough to break her concentration. She wasn't doing it intentionally, and so Lilith couldn't possibly be annoyed or angry at her.

"I have some errands to do," she said to Emma, who had just finished wiping down the spotless kitchen counters.

"Is there anything I can help with, Mother?" Emma said, the hopeful look in her eyes nearly making Lilith weep with love.

"I'm afraid it's the sort of thing only I can do," she said. She cocked her head as she felt someone stirring. "But your sisters are waking, and I have something very important for them to do. All but Jennifer; I'm afraid she can't go on this errand. She'll be more than happy to stay with the children, though. Right, love?"

"Of course, Mother," Jennifer said, standing in the kitchen doorway and stretching. "I'd love to."

By the time she finished explaining their errand to Emma, the others had risen as well, and were all sitting around the small kitchen table, cozily bumping shoulders and jostling each other. They were in high spirits, and why not? They'd just fed well, and avenged their sister in the bargain.

"Mother, I have a question," Kris said, and she looked vaguely uncomfortable, as if she were being impudent. "Will we need to feed like that often?"

"No," she said, smiling. "In fact, it won't be strictly necessary for some years. Decades, even. All of you are technically still alive. All but Jennifer, something that breaks my heart. I wasn't able to stop that, and I can't ever apologize enough."

"It wasn't your doing, Mother," Jennifer said. "You helped us make it right." Lilith went to the girl and put her hands on her cheeks, caressing her beautiful face.

"You will need to feed," she said. "Not often, though. Once every ten or twelve days. Don't worry, though. You won't need much."

"So I won't have to kill anyone else?" she said, and the little glimmer of hope in her voice made Lilith smile.

"That, my sweet, is entirely up to you," she said, leaving it open for whatever interpretation Jennifer wished to apply. She kissed the girl's cheek, and turned to Emma.

"We'll get it done," Emma assured her without being asked.

"I have no doubt," Lilith said. "And when I return, we'll find out exactly what happened to your poor sisters, and why."

With that, she left them to hunt down Jerry Hartman, and went to see what she could learn about this stranger, the man who was a son of neither her nor the Other.

3.

Jerry was beginning to wonder if he wasn't maybe in some moderately deep shit.

He couldn't blame Harlan for his suspicions, not really; he'd stated his opinion about what should be done with Billy on numerous occasions. The fact the man's son was now dead certainly made him look suspicious, particularly since he found the body.

He sat in Harlan's office, waiting somewhat patiently for the man himself to arrive. He himself had gotten out of the police station only forty minutes or so ago, and had come straight here. Harlan was apparently still giving his own statement.

He had a brief moment to wonder if he was currently being wrapped up in a bow and handed over to the cops in a pretty package, but dismissed it. There was no conceivable way Harlan could sell him down the river without ending up in the cell next to him; they were too far intertwined in each other's affairs by now.

That had been a mistake from the beginning, he now understood. He'd operated a series of fairly successful small-time enterprises over the years, and had made decent money in each. But the key word in that particular scenario had always been small-time; not big enough for the big boys in those same rackets to care about him, not flashy enough to attract attention from the cops. He'd had his little piggies in all sorts of pies over the years, everything from drugs to guns to, and this was the funny part because the margins were bigger than dope or iron, contraband cigarettes. He could clearly remember making ridiculous amounts of money on truckload after truckload of Marlboros, Newports, and so many generic brands he couldn't possibly name them all. That had been a sweet gig, but ultimately it drew the worst sort of attention, which was federal.

But that racket had financed his relocation, and help him set up in his first local endeavor, which was basically renting warehouse space to guys with things they didn't want anyone to know about. That, he understood, had been where shit started going sideways, because that was what brought him into Harlan Denison's circle of influence.

He stood up and shook off the second-guessing; it was useless now. He could nit-pick all his mistakes later. Right now, he needed to focus on the current situation. And that current situation could only be perfectly described as a shit show.

Almost from the beginning, Billy Denison had seemed bound and determined to fuck up every single operation he and Harlan were involved in, and it had driven Jerry absolutely batshit. When Jerry found himself sitting on twenty kilos of high-grade coke, little Billy had helped himself to some of it. That had cost Jerry almost sixty grand, which would have been the least of his problems.

For nearly a kilo of uncut coke, the guys who'd paid him to store it would have happily cut off many of his most treasured body parts to get it back.

Harlan had paid for the coke, but that was all. It had still fallen on Jerry to make it right with the Columbians, which had cost him a decent chunk of change and a large portion of his pride. He'd come very close to taking both directly out of Billy's ass, but once again Harlan had intervened.

Looking back, he could remember dozens of times when Billy had been just stupid and reckless enough to nearly fuck everything up. If Jerry had something valuable in the warehouse, something Billy wanted, he could almost count on some or all of it going missing unless he was very careful. Harlan had been pissed when he found out the guys he hired to watch his warehouse had orders to beat the shit out of Billy if they caught him anywhere near the place, but Jerry had stood his ground.

"Sooner or later," Jerry had told Harlan after he'd finished yelling, "that boy of yours is going to fuck something up you can't fix, Harlan. When he does, it won't be either of you on the hook for it, either. It'll be my ass they take it out of, and you're lying to yourself if you think I won't spread it around."

Harlan had let the issue drop, but from that point on, he'd kept a closer eye on Billy. Well, almost, Jerry thought. He'd at least managed to convince the boy to leave the business side of life to him, which had probably suited Billy just fine. He was more into the "getting loaded and doing stupid shit" side of life, and he'd excelled at it.

It occurred to him that there was very little reason for him to be sitting here, waiting for Daddy Denison to come chew his ass. It wasn't like Denison was at all connected; he was a small town big shot, but little more. The only real connections he had were Jerry's, and he wasn't in the habit of sharing his address book. Not that any such book existed, but he liked the analogy. Point being, if Denison needed to call a hitter, he talked to Jerry. If Jerry was gone, he might or might not find some second-rate dipshit, but the odds of said dipshit doing anything beyond taking Harlan's money and laughing on his way to score some rock were so low as to be incalculable.

And it was definitely time for Jerry to get gone. The very idea of ordering more merchandise had been insane, even before the little asshole had gotten himself killed. Now, with not just local but probably state and even federal heat coming down, he'd sooner skin his own dick than be in the same time zone as more of that shit.

He decided to give Harlan another ten minutes. Ten minutes wasn't going to change anything, one way or the other, but it would let the housekeeper tell Harlan he'd waited for an hour. And an hour was a nice, round figure he could get behind. On impulse, he helped himself to one of Harlan's cigars, cutting it with the gold guillotine cutter sitting next to the humidor. It was part of a set, but the lighter that went with it seemed to be missing. That figures, he thought. Guys at his plant busting their asses and destroying their bodies for a couple bucks above minimum wage, and Harlan has a fucking matched gold lighter and cutter set probably worth six or seven grand, easily. Unfazed, he simply lit the cigar with his own lighter. No gold Davidoff lighter, but the black Bic disposable in his pocket produced fire just the same.

After the allotted ten minutes had come and gone with no Harlan, nor any word of him, he got up and walked out of Harlan's office, making sure to let the housekeeper know he was leaving. She seemed worried as she reminded him that Mr. Denison very much wanted to speak to him.

"Don't worry, Sharon," he said, remembering her name at last. "He knows how to find me, and I think I'd be more use out there, figuring out what happened to poor Billy than sitting in the office, don't you?"

"Poor Billy," Sharon repeated, and you didn't have to

be psychic to see exactly how the old woman felt about poor Billy Denison. He decided to take a small chance; after all, it never hurt to make friends where you could.

"Between you and me, no one's gonna miss him, except maybe Harlan," he said, and she looked around nervously to make sure no one was listening in before nodding her head in agreement.

"He used to be a sweet boy," she said. "Mrs. Denison, God rest her soul, hired me the day he came home from the hospital, you know. Something happened to him, Mr. Hartman. Something while he was away, at school. He was always a little wild, but a good kid at heart. I just don't know what happened."

He finally grew into his full potential as an asshole, Jerry thought but did not say.

"You're going to look for whoever did this, aren't you?" she said, eyeing him sharply. "I'm an old woman, but not a fool, Mr. Hartman. I know who my employer is, and what he is. I see a lot more than he ever thinks about. You're not just a foreman out at that plant, young man."

"No, ma'am," he agreed. Again, a small risk, but it seemed sweet old Sharon might be handy to know. "I guess you could say I'm a troubleshooter."

Sharon nodded, and patted his arm. "Then you find the trouble that got to that boy, and you shoot it," she said, and left him alone at the front door. Jerry had a strong suspicion it was so he wouldn't see her crying.

Fuck, he thought. He wanted nothing more than to pack his shit and get gone, never even think about this little shithole town again. But a little-known fact that might surprise a lot of people who really knew him was simply that he had a fairly deep vein of responsibility in him, and more than a little empathy. He'd killed before, of course. It was almost unavoidable in his line of work. But that had been business, never personal. If he'd gotten around to killing Billy like he'd wanted, that would have been business, too.

But it seemed the little jagoff's death was personal to some. To Harlan, who he didn't give two shits about, and to Sharon, who he was more than a little surprised to find he liked, it was very personal, indeed.

"Fuck it all," he said, standing on the front step and scrubbing a hand over his face. "Fine, fine. I'll take care of this, and then I'm gone."

He was almost to his car when something slammed into him from behind. His forehead bounced off the ground, and the world grayed out. He groaned and tried to get to his gun, but a hand gripped him by his short hair and slammed him down onto the ground again, face-first, and he finally passed out.

4.

She knew nothing about this child of neither line, so Lilith did the only thing she could; she walked, and followed the feeling inside her. It was currently screaming at her to turn and run, to flee this place. That told her much about this man, or at least his lineage. There was only one who could inspire such feelings inside her. It was not quite a new feeling, but one so rare it was unfamiliar, and it took her some time to recognize it.

She was afraid. No, she thought. Don't belittle it. I am terrified. There is a Son of Sekhmet here, and my children are in great danger. She herself was also in some danger, of course, but she was a Mother. Her first thought would always be for her children.

She followed the feeling of dread coming from deep inside her to the town square, where she seemed to want to go anywhere but to the police station. That was it, of course. The sons of Sekhmet were fierce warriors and protectors, and such men were often drawn to law enforcement. Evil bastards, she thought, but shook her head.

She knew better, of course; Sekhmet herself was a protector, a Mother. She and her children had come into the world at the same time as Lilith, and had once roamed the land in great numbers. Time and the Other's cheerful fecundity had diluted both her line and Sekhmet's, but neither had been completely eliminated. She suspected neither could be eliminated; after all, even goddesses came from somewhere, and whatever brought them into being must have some sort of plan.

She was temporarily distracted when one of her children, a young woman in a fairly silly hat, offered her something. "Have a cone," the girl said, smiling. "No charge."

"Thank you," Lilith said, smiling. She took a tentative bite, and smiled at its cold sweetness. "This is lovely. What is it?"

"You've never had ice cream?" the girl said, laughing. Lilith laughed with her, because it wasn't mean laughter, only surprised.

"I've been away for a long time," she said. "They didn't have ice cream where I was."

"Well, welcome back to civilization," the girl said as a group of children, shepherded by two tired-looking women, approached. "Have a good day."

"And you, as well," Lilith said, smiling as she enjoyed her ice cream. What a wonderful treat, she thought. She reached out to her children around her, feeling for memories related to ice cream. She found thousands, all of them happy and excited. A few were decidedly naughty, but that only made her smile more. Well, weren't her children human? And sex was a wonderful part of the human existence. Let them enjoy it how they would, so long as they hurt no one.

Although, she had to admit that while some of the things she saw seemed rather interesting, it also seemed like a waste of delicious ice cream.

She finished the ice cream cone, dropped the wrapper in a nearby trash can, and went back to trying to discover who the son of Sekhmet was. She watched a strong young man go inside, but she could feel her mark on him already. A tired-looking woman not in uniform went in the front door, but she was a child of the Other mother. Curious, she reached out to the young man with her mark, feeling his mind. Ironically, his name was Mark.

She saw through Mark's eyes as he waved to an old woman at the front desk, to the tired-looking officer now dressed in street clothes, and then she saw a man. A large man, strong and tall. There was a look of hard steel in his eyes, and she couldn't help but feel the same slight tremor of lust that went through the young man, and herself by default. Young Mark was a lover of men, and he apparently had good taste.

She and Sekhmet were vastly different, but she could not deny that the old bitch made good-looking children. Surely Sekhmet had daughters, as well, but she'd never met one. Only her sons, and she'd learned early on to avoid them whenever she could. She ignored the man and focused on Mark's mind until she had what she needed.

The son of Sekhmet was none other than Big Jim Harlow, Chief of Police and former soldier. That fit with everything else she knew about Sekhmet's sons. She knew without meeting him or touching his mind, something she wished desperately she could do, that he would not hesitate to kill if pushed. Had almost definitely killed already, in fact.

She pulled away from Mark and walked away at a sedate, calm pace that belied the terror in her heart. Her daughters were still young, still learning about their new lives and their abilities. Jennifer was stronger than the others, but she was no match for this Jim Harlow. The sons of Sekhmet were very good at finding and killing her special children.

She was just thinking it was time to put some obstacles in his way when a thought came to her from across the ether. It was Kris; she was with the others, and she was excited.

We have him, Mother. We found him.

Lilith smiled as she felt all of her children; Melanie was full of rage as she began to understand what Hartman had done. Teresa was soul-shakingly sad. Melissa wanted to kill him right there, but she would wait. Only Amber was a blank to her, which was the only really troubling part.

"Thank you, my sweets. Please, take him to the trailer, and make sure he cannot leave." She felt them do as she asked, and reached out to Amber directly.

"What troubles you, baby girl?" she asked. People passed her on the street, but none seemed to notice her. Men swerved at the last minute to avoid walking into her without knowing why, and not thinking about it later.

I saw something when I hit him, Amber said. *Another man.*

"We'll learn all he knows when I talk to him, love," Lilith said. "For now, make sure he cannot escape, and be careful. He's a killer."

Yes, Mother.

She was turning to walk back to the trailer when a voice she hadn't heard in thousands of years spoke up behind her.

"Leaving so soon, Lilith?" the woman said. She stopped, frozen in her tracks, then turned around to face her with a smile.

"Hello, Eve," she said with genuine warmth. "It's been too long."

CHAPTER TWELVE

1.

"Doctor?" he heard Laura call from the autopsy theater. "I think you'd better get in here." It was a confused, worried sound, and he wondered what in God's name he'd have to hold her hand through now. He'd left her to take blood and tissue samples for testing before beginning the internal examination. He also needed a break; his hip was screaming eighteen shades of blue murder at him for all the extra work he'd asked it to do today.

Reluctantly, he put on his best patient smile, reminding himself to talk to her like he would his granddaughter. "Yes?" he said, limping his way back to the theater. "Is there a proble—what the fuck?" he almost shouted, completely forgetting his reminder to himself and all thoughts of his granddaughter.

"I—I don't know what happened," Laura stammered. "I was trying to get blood samples, and--"

She gestured at the table in confusion and disgust. Where the body should have been, where it fucking well had been when he stepped away, was nothing but an oblong pile of dust roughly shaped like a young man's body.

He took a deep breath, counted to ten, and then back to one before speaking again. What he wanted to do was to shout at the top of his lungs that the goddamn joke was over, and if that body wasn't back on the table in the next sixty seconds, a lot of people were going to be walking around with their nuts shoved up their asses.

What he said instead was, "Laura? Are you telling me that this is what's left of the body?"

"I don't know what happened," she said again, and this time she was near tears. "I started to do the cardiac draw, and—"

"And poof?" he said, raising one eyebrow. Oh, it was a hell of a joke, alright, and he suspected one Curtis Standhope was behind it. Well, that would be easy enough to prove, he thought. The audio recording equipment might be next door to shit, but the video gear was almost brand-new. He limped his way over to the computer, outside the sterile zone, and sat down with a sigh.

"Someone's gonna wish they'd gone into telemarketing," he said to no one in particular, and pulled up the most recent video footage. It was digital, and although black and white, extremely high resolution. He watched himself do the external exam, saw Laura taking notes. The detail was amazing; he could see the back of his neck well enough to know it was time for another haircut, and Laura's name on the ID card pinned to her coat was clearly visible. She had scrubbed in since then, because she wore the blue tunic and sterile gear.

He watched the body the entire time as she stepped out of view, then came back a moment later in the proper gear. He watched the body closely as she selected the proper needle and syringe and slid it home into the chest. Even as the needle moved, the reaction began.

Ray watched in a mixture of disbelief, horror, and fascination as the body disintegrated right before his eyes on the monitor. Laura stood frozen over what remained of the remains, looking as if she wasn't quite sure what she'd just seen.

"Fuck," Ray said, perhaps a little too loudly, but under

the circumstances, he figured it was allowed. To her credit, Laura didn't even flinch when he swept the mug of pens off the desk in a fit of anger. It shattered on the floor, sending dozens of gimme pens from various vendors and the city itself scattering over the spotless floor.

2.

"You know what I don't get?" Mark said as he sat in the chair across from Jim's desk. He had his yo-yo out and was lazily making it sleep. It dropped down, spun merrily for what seemed like an impossible amount of time, and then came straight back up the string at a twitch of Mark's finger. The yo-yo thing had annoyed the shit out of him at first, but it quickly became apparent that it was just what Mark did when he was thinking. It was also a hell of an icebreaker with kids. "Garrett Brown blowing himself to hell, sure. Meth cooks tend to be meth users, and careful isn't a word you can usually use with them. I suppose I can even buy someone burning him out. Maybe get rid of the competition, or he just pissed off the wrong person at the right time."

"He pretty much pissed people off all the time," Jim said, and Mark nodded.

"And like I said, meth heads aren't known for being models of control," Mark said. Jim wanted to tell him to put the fucking yo-yo away and get to the point, but he knew it was a lost cause. Mark had a first-rate mind, and a way of thinking around corners. The trick, Jim knew, was to let him get there on his own. "I'm honestly a little surprised the place didn't burn more than it did. Basically the lab blew itself out when all that shit exploded. Barely anything in the rest of the shithole touched."

"Including both bodies?" he said, and Mark nodded.

"Barely singed," Mark said. "At least, according to the FD. Waiting for Doc to get a look at them to be sure, but I guess he's got his hands full." They both sat quietly for a moment as they realized exactly why Ray was so shorthanded, and then Mark went on. "And nothing in there is remotely out of place for what you'd expect to find in a meth trailer. Lots of trash, lots of glass. You know what doesn't fit? What has no business in Garrett Brown's fuckhole trailer?"

"Curtis Standhope's body," Jim said, and Mark nodded. The yoyo snapped down, walked along the floor, and jumped back to him.

"Get that man a cigar, and a blowtorch to light it with," Mark said. "Curt's body. Now, I've known Curt since we were kids. Guy rarely even drank, and even then he stuck to beer. Never knew him to even smoke a little reefer. So how does a guy like him end up in a meth trailer out in the boonies? Answer? Whoever took Jennifer Bennett's body brought him out there. But that's not even the best part," Mark added, grinning. "You wanna hear the best part?"

"I'm quivering in anticipation," Jim said.

"Take a wild guess what first responders said they saw on Curt's neck?" Mark said. "Here's a hint. He and Billy Denison finally have something in common. Well, beside the fact they both wanted the Bennett girl something bad."

"Bite marks?" Jim said, wishing he'd actually made it to the scene. But the fire was out by the time Mark got there, and he had it under control. Like it or not, he had his own fish to fry. Above and beyond all the day-to-day bullshit he had to deal with as part of the chief's chair, he wanted to follow up on Faulkner's report from the Denison scene.

"You win again," Mark said. "Now, I'm not a bite mark expert, but from what I saw, it looked one hell of a lot like the one on the Denison asshole's neck. Again, have to have Doc do the full workup and a comparison to be sure, but I'd bet tender parts of my anatomy those two bites are the same."

"The fuck?" Jim said in frustration, and Mark smiled.

"Oh, come on," he said. "Tell me you don't see it."

"Fine, I don't see it," he said. "What am I not seeing?"

"Dead guys with bite marks, drained of blood," Mark said, pocketing his yo-yo and ticking the items off on his fingers. "Bodies that disappear from the morgue. Jeez, man, didn't you ever watch a movie as a kid? Read a book, maybe?"

Jim looked at him for a moment, and shook his head. "If you even say the word 'vampire,' you'll be washing cars until you retire," he said, and Mark laughed.

"I do that anyway," he said. "Come on, man. How could you not think it?"

"Because this isn't a movie," he said. "Or a book. We're stuck in reality, where shit doesn't make much sense most of the time. Maybe Daddy Denison made the body go away, hoping to make the case go away."

"How the hell could he do that?" Mark said. "Just walk in and snatch the body?"

Both of them looked at each other for a moment, and the realization hit them both at the same time. "We are very stupid men," Jim said, and Mark stood up.

"I'll call my buddy at County," he said. "See if he'll get us the security tapes from the morgue."

"Ask nicely," Jim said. "Technically, Brown's trailer is about ten feet past the city limits. Their sandbox."

"I'll smile and say 'pretty please,'" Mark said, and Jim laughed. He had his own suspicions about who Mark's "buddy" at the sheriff's department was, and how close they really were, but it was none of his business.

There was one question Mark hadn't gotten to, and it was driving him crazy trying to figure it out. Where the hell was Jennifer Bennett's body? His thought was interrupted when a man walked into the station, this time without any of the usual bravado that accompanied him. This morning, Harlan Denison did not look like the local mogul and probable crime figure he'd been earlier; he looked like a broken man.

Feeling like he'd just been given his very own boulder to roll uphill, he grabbed a legal pad out of his desk, picked up the file on Bill Denison, and went to interview the man who was most likely just a grieving father, but possibly a suspect as well.

3.

There was no longer any doubt. Jerry knew damned well he was in moderate to severely deep shit. The fact he'd been knocked out, hog-tied, and apparently tossed into a trunk was highly indicative of the level of said deep shit, which he guessed to be at least chin-high.

But he had a few things going for him. One, whoever had tied him up apparently didn't know jack from shit about it; the bindings on his wrists had a lot of give. He had been slowly exploring the knots as best he could with his fingertips, and he was pretty sure he could slip them. But of course, that was a small comfort when stacked against the rest of his current predicament. Even with his hands free, he was still locked in the trunk of a moving car, and his head still felt like it was full of scrambled eggs.

This, naturally, begged the question; who the hell had buffaloed him? He was having a bit of a hard time focusing, but he still couldn't think of anyone who would have both a reason to take him out and the ability to get it done so quickly and professionally. He thought briefly of Harlan, but dismissed it. The closest thing he had to hired muscle was either his son's idiot friends, who were currently occupied with rotting away in a gravel pit, or some of the less than outstanding citizens at the plant. The only problem with that idea was that none of the morons from Surima were even remotely good enough to get the drop on him like that.

And that, good friends and dear neighbors, was at the heart of the problem. Whoever had taken him down had done it fast and hard, giving him no time at all to react. He hadn't seen who it was; all he knew was that they were small, fast, and God-awfully strong.

He worked over these questions in his mind as he

worked at the ropes binding his wrists. The ropes gave way fairly easily; the nagging questions did not. With no real way to address those, he decided to focus on the more immediate concerns.

Judging by the cramped quarters he found himself in, the car was both compact and fairly old. He felt for the release lever most newer trunks had inside for just such an occasion, but found none. He was trying to get to his front pocket for the small, single AA cell flashlight he kept there when he discovered another point in his favor. Whoever had tied him up had apparently not only been ignorant of restraint, but overall not even remotely qualified to be kidnapping anyone. They hadn't bothered to remove either the gun or the knife in his waistband, or the snappy little MicroTech switchblade in his pocket.

The game had just changed. Rather than try to pop the trunk lid, he scooted back as far into the trunk as he could, his gun ready. When that lid popped open, someone was going to die.

4.

Thank God, Emma thought as she parked in front of Ruth Ann's place. I'm home. Finally, home.

The girls had all beaten her back, and probably by a fair bit; they were all sitting outside, watching as the kids played. Jennifer looked up, and immediately called them over.

"Okay, kiddos," she said. "Just about time for you to start that homework."

"Aww, do we have to?" Carrie said.

"Yeah, come on, Auntie J," Aiden said. "Can't we watch a movie first?"

"No arguments," Jennifer said sternly, but she smiled. "Go on, get started." Both of them ran inside to the trailer, and Emma nodded.

"Thanks," she said, and Jennifer hugged her. "Auntie J," she added, and Jennifer smiled.

"Their idea, not mine," she said.

"Oh, we're all Auntie something-or-other now," Melanie said as they hugged. She exchanged hugs all around, a little surprised at how relieved she was to see them all again. It had only been a few hours, but she'd been worried about them all as they took off from the hotel.

"We were getting worried," Teresa said.

"Yeah," Kris said, giving her a light and playful slap on the butt as they hugged. "You had us scared, Sis. What gives?"

"I had to be careful," Emma said. "I couldn't risk coming straight here, in case someone was watching. And of course, I couldn't risk getting pulled over with a guy tied up in the trunk."

"I guess we should get him out of there," Melanie said. "Wouldn't want him to suffocate or anything."

"Speak for yourself," Melissa said, and they laughed. It was a nervous laugh, because they all knew better. Mother wanted him in the trailer when she came back, and that was exactly where he was going. They went to the trunk and listened. Their senses were much better than Emma's, but she didn't hear anything.

"I think he's still out," Kim said.

"You didn't kill him, did you?" Emma asked Amber, who shook her head.

"No," she said. "I can hear his heartbeat. He's gonna have one hell of a headache when he does wake up, though."

Emma nodded and flipped through her keys until she found the right one, and inserted it into the trunk lock. "Do you think Mother would mind if one of us takes the kids out for a bit?" she said. "I don't want them anywhere near this guy."

"Of course she wouldn't," Teresa said. "She'd want them safe. I could take them for ice cream, maybe a movie."

"Sure," Jennifer said, smiling. "You get to be the fun auntie, and I'm the hard-ass." Teresa stuck her tongue out at Jennifer, who gave her a playful swat on the butt for it. Emma was laughing as she twisted the key in the lock, and then all hell broke loose.

5.

"You're looking well," Lilith said as they found a bench and sat together. "This form suits you."

"I always wanted to be a blonde," she said, touching her golden hair. "You've been busy this time around, Lilith."

"I've stuck to our agreement," she said carefully. Eve nodded, and patted her hand.

"I know," she said. "And I feel like I should apologize for my children. They haven't been kind to yours."

"We love them the best we can, and hope they do right," Lilith said. "It's not your fault. Tell me, how is our husband?"

Eve laughed. "Living it up, as usual," she said. "Last I heard, he's somewhere in South America. Senoritas and margaritas." They both laughed at that. "You know, I think sometimes the only reason he was faithful as long as he was, is simply that there was no other choice." The laughter left her voice.

"I suppose you're here about Jerry Hartman," she said, and Eve sighed.

"He's important to his father's plans," she said.

"Did he send you here to intervene on his behalf?" she asked, one eyebrow raised. "I've never known you to do anyone's errands for them."

"I wish it were that simple," she said. "He's destined to do something very important. Well, not him specifically, but the child he'll father one day. Actually, he's slated to do that in about eight months from now."

"He slaughtered thirteen of my daughters," Lilith said. "Just shot them, then dumped them in a pit to rot. If I

163

hadn't found them, they'd still be there."

"And I am sorry for your pain, Lilith," Eve said. "I'd take it back if I could. Could you not--"

"The damage was too severe," Lilith said, wiping a stray tear. "They could not come back, not even with my blood."

"They'll be with our Father," she said. "You could go see them. How long has it been since you've been home?"

Lilith laughed. "I'm pretty sure that's not allowed, Eve," she said. "The old man doesn't forget that fast."

"He misses you," Eve said. "And so does our husband."

"I already have him," Lilith said. "My special children have him now, and they're waiting for me."

"Then all you have to do is let him go," she said. "Hurt him, if you must. He should be punished. But Lilith, you can't kill him. He's too important."

"Not to me," Lilith said. "And if Adam, or our Father, wants him so badly, they can come and take him from me themselves." She stood up.

"I don't care about what Adam wants," Eve said. "And Father will do whatever he wants to do, without bothering to ask anyone. As usual. I'm not here for them, Lilith. I'm asking you, please. Don't kill him. Not yet, anyway."

"He has to be punished," Lilith said.

"And he will be," Eve said. "I give you my word. He'll suffer for what he's done. Lilith, if you could just see what I have, what our husband has planned for him, you--"

"I don't care about Adam's plans," Lilith snapped. "Or our Father's plans, for that matter. The last time I allowed myself to follow his plans, I was shunned and ejected from the Garden. As were you, if I recall."

"That was my mistake," Eve said, and Lilith laughed.

"Right," she said. "Free will. Never mind that he all but shoved that damned fruit down your throat, or that you ended up taking all the blame for it, because God forbid his precious first son should ever take responsibility for his own actions."

Eve sighed. "This is not why I came to you, Lilith."

"No?" Lilith said. "Isn't it? Aren't you tired of being led by the nose? Of both of them constantly manipulating you? Sending you to do their dirty work? Leaving you to watch over their children while they do whatever they please? Let them take care of themselves for a change, Eve. Come with me. We both know our children can do so much better than they are. Let's show them the way, together. Clearly their father's influence isn't working."

Eve gave a bitter chuckle. "I came to ask you to come with me," she said. "Come home, Lilith. Make amends with Father. With us together, he'll listen to what we have to say."

"And then dismiss it, and do whatever he damned well wants, just like always," Lilith said, shaking her head. "A mother's place is with her children. You used to know that."

She saw the hurt on Eve's face, and made an effort to control herself. "I don't wish to hurt you, Eve," she said. "I'm sorry. But how long have we watched, and waited, just hoping their way works? I can't do it anymore, Eve. I'm sorry."

Eve rose and hugged her. "Please," she said. "At least be careful, Lilith. You know there is another here. One not of our lines."

"A son of Sekhmet," she said, and Eve gasped. "I've seen him."

"Then you should come with me," Eve said, sounding frightened. "Lilith, we're not immortal. If he learns what you are, he could kill you."

Lilith nodded. "I know," she said. "But I can't leave my children alone to deal with him. And besides, I may not be immortal, but I'm not helpless, either."

"No," Eve said, smiling as she touched Lilith's hair. "You never were. I always admired that about you, Lilith.

You've always been so strong. I think that's what scared him, you know. He could feel your strength, and it made him feel weak."

"Men are so fragile," she said, and they both laughed. Eve hugged her. "I wish you'd come with me. You should see my daughters, Eve. They're so beautiful."

"I'm sure they are," Eve said. "Protect them."

"What will you tell him?" she said, and Eve smiled.

"Nothing he hasn't been expecting," she said. "I think he asked me to come because he knew we could at least talk without trying to kill each other."

Eve slipped her arms around Lilith's waist, and she let herself be drawn closer. "You know, there are other reasons to come home," she said. "It's been so long since we were close, Lilith. I miss you."

"I miss you, too," she said. When Eve kissed her, she didn't resist. After the kiss was over, Lilith touched her cheek. "But my place is here. I won't tell you where yours is."

"You might be the only one," Eve said, and Lilith smiled.

"That's always been your problem," Lilith said. "You've spent forever letting them tell you your place, you've never stopped to consider the truth."

"And what's that?" Eve asked, her soft, voluptuous body pressed close to Lilith. The contact was definitely tantalizing, as it was meant to be, but she was stronger than that.

"The only one you should be listening to is yourself, Eve," she said, and gave her another light kiss. "When you do that, I hope you'll find your way back to this world again. Your children would do better with your influence."

"I'll think about it," Eve said, and Lilith smiled again. "Will you at least consider what I ask?"

"I'm sorry," Lilith said. "But what I said stands. If our husband wants him so badly, he can come and try to take him."

"Take care of yourself," Eve said as Lilith backed away.

"I always do," she said. She touched a finger under Eve's chin. "You really do look good as a blonde."

She turned and walked away, and by the time she couldn't resist looking back any longer, Eve was gone.

CHAPTER THIRTEEN

1.

Jerry didn't fidget or shift his position once he was set up. The gun, a Glock 19, was ready in front of him. He had sixteen rounds in the gun, and a spare magazine, but he figured if he ran out of rounds before he was able to get gone, he was probably dead anyway. He heard a key sliding into the lock of the trunk lid, and made himself take slow, steady breaths. He wanted to open up as soon as the lid cracked open, but he made himself wait.

The lid opened partially, and then stopped as he heard several women laughing at something. He could only see two of them, but he was sure he heard more voices than that. Gotta be smart, he told himself. Get ready, and take advantage. If they're laughing like that, they aren't taking this seriously.

He saw two more bodies step in close to the others, and he nodded. That's good, he thought. Cluster up nice, girls. Daddy's got a big surprise for you.

The lid opened, and Jerry started shooting. He did it methodically, moving from left to right. The first two bullets hit the girl on the far left in the stomach, and the rest rose steadily. The next shot landed in a cute little blonde's chest. One hit a set of massive titties, and the last two caught a shorter brunette in the face.

His ears ringing from the gunshots in the enclosed

trunk, he didn't hear the screaming as the confusion set in, but he didn't need to hear it to know it was happening, and take advantage of it.

Limping slightly from a cramp in his left leg, he jumped out of the trunk and took off running, firing behind him blindly to keep their heads down as he bolted. The gun clicked empty, and he kept running. There was a road up ahead, and he saw where he was almost immediately. The plant was less than two miles away. A pleasant half-hour stroll on any other day, an impossible distance while he was being chased. He needed wheels.

He turned toward town instead, which was only about a half mile or so away. He managed to reload the Glock on the run, but didn't put it away until he saw the city limits sign.

In all the confusion, he couldn't believe no one had chased after him. There was no way he'd gotten all of them.

Fucking amateurs, he thought as he tucked the gun back into his holster, straightened himself up, and calmly started walking back to his apartment.

2.

Emma saw it happen in slow motion, and even when the bullets caught her in the stomach, she still couldn't believe it was happening. She just stood there, vaguely aware she was starting to bleed, as Kris fell down. Teresa was knocked backward, but it wasn't until she saw the back of Amber's head explode that she started screaming.

She was vaguely aware that Hartman was currently hauling ass at an impressive pace away from them, and started to go after him. She made it two paces before she fell down.

"Holy shit," Kris said, sitting up and pulling her shirt up. Emma watched as the bullets that had smashed into her, now deformed, fell out into her lap as the wounds closed themselves. Teresa sat up shortly afterward, her own wounds healing. Emma let out a sigh of relief, and then someone was kneeling behind her, catching her as she grew dizzy.

"Emma," Melanie said, cradling her head. "Oh God. Emma, come on. Stay with us, sis. Stay here."

"What the fuck?" Teresa said, and then she saw Emma. There were two holes in her stomach, just above the navel.

"Move," Melissa said, ripping her own shirt off and kneeling down in front of her. She folded the shirt into a pad and pressed it against the wounds. "Mel, feel her back. Look for exit wounds."

"What?" Melanie said, crying. Undeterred, Melissa simply slapped her across the cheek. It worked; Melanie's eyes flashed bright for a moment, but she stopped crying and started paying attention.

"Hey, no fighting," Emma said, but her voice sounded distant, even to herself.

"Melanie," Melissa said, her voice softer. "I need you to feel her back for exit wounds. Can you do that?"

Melanie moved her hand, and shook her head. "I don't feel anything," she said.

"Don't," Emma said, but it was hard to focus. "Don't let the kids see this."

Before anyone could say anything else, Emma fell back into Melanie's arms, and was still.

"No," Melissa said, feeling for a pulse at her wrist. Behind her, Kris and Teresa were crying softly. Jennifer paced back and forth, arms folded around her slight waist.

Melissa heard someone sobbing, and it wasn't until someone screamed that she realized it was her. "No," she said, still crying. "No, come on. No, God damn it. Mother!" she screamed as Emma died in Melanie's arms.

It wasn't until Lilith arrived, eyes blazing and looking absolutely terrifying some two minutes later, that anyone noticed that Amber hadn't gotten up yet.

3.

Melissa's scream tore through Lilith, making her cry out as she fell to her knees. She saw it all through Melissa's eyes then; Kris and Teresa healing from gunshots, and her poor Emma, dying in Melanie's arms. Completely unaware that anyone might be seeing her, Lilith rose and flew into the air, rushing to her children. As she flew, she felt for each of them. Poor Emma, of course, was gone. Teresa and Kris would survive their injuries. Melanie and Melissa were uninjured, but she couldn't feel Amber.

"No," she sobbed as she landed, aware on some level that at least part of her real form was visible from the look on their faces. Two small faces appeared at the door, and Lilith looked up, the last traces of her real form disappearing.

"Mother?" Kris said as she and Teresa held onto each other. "Mother, what do we do?"

"Help her," Melissa said, looking up at Lilith with tears in her eyes. "Please, Mother. Bring her back to us."

She looked at each of them in turn, and knelt down next to her poor Emma. "Teresa, will you take Aiden and Carrie inside, please?" she said, struggling to keep her voice calm. "They shouldn't witness this."

"Of course, Mother," Teresa said, and immediately went to the children. She could hear her reassuring them that Mother would help her, that it was all okay because Mother was here now. She hoped she wasn't lying to them.

It was a bad idea, at least from a strategic point of view. With a son of Sekhmet here, she needed all her strength. But she wasn't a general, wasn't a strategist. She was a mother, and her child needed her.

"Jennifer, I'll need your help," she said. The small girl immediately came to her. "Melanie, trade places with her." Both did as she asked without question. She looked up at Jennifer.

"This will be unpleasant," she said. "You'll need all your strength to hold her once it starts. Can you do it?"

"We'll help," Melanie said, and Lilith nodded. The four of them held poor Emma as Lilith held up one hand. The nail of her index finger grew long and thick, tapering to a wickedly sharp point. Before anyone could ask questions, she slashed her own wrist deeply, then held it to poor Emma's lips. She nodded to Jennifer, who held Emma's head back so the blood could drain down her throat.

"It won't take long, one way or another," Lilith said. "She's only been dead a few minutes. Be ready, my children. She will fight when she comes to." If she comes to, she thought but did not say.

But after five minutes of no reaction, she knew the truth. She touched Emma's forehead, felt none of the beautiful soul that had resided in her, and wept as she closed the poor thing's eyes. She could hear her other children sobbing as she stood up.

They all came to her, and she stood there with them, mourning their losses.

"Mother?" Jennifer said, confused and hurt. "Is she?"

"She's gone," Lilith said, tears streaming down her face. "Amber, too. All gone. Taken from us. Was it the Hartman man?"

"He surprised us," Kris said. "I'm so sorry, Mother. It's my fault."

Lilith shook her head. "No, my lovely," she said. "The fault is mine. I should have dealt with him myself. I knew he was dangerous, and I sent you after him. That mistake has cost us dearly, but it will be rectified soon."

"What do we do?" Jennifer asked, her voice small and weak. It hurt Lilith to hear that in her, and she let the hurt fuel her anger.

"We take care of them," she said, bending down to pick up Emma's body. Melanie lifted poor Amber and placed her gently in Jennifer's arms, and they all followed her out back. Inside, she could hear the children sobbing, asking for their mommy, and the pain in Lilith's heart seemed to grow until it would explode.

"We'll need shovels," she said absently. One of them, she was never sure who, left and returned a moment later with two shovels from somewhere. She took one, and Jennifer the other.

Once it was done, she stood at the grave with the others surrounding her. Their pain and grief were powerful emotions. It wasn't a true feeding, but it would give her the boost she needed for what came next.

"What do we do now, Mother?" Teresa asked, her face streaked with tears.

Lilith looked up at them, and knew her eyes were glowing from the looks on their faces. Far from frightened this time, she saw them responding. Behind them, Aiden and Carrie stood hand in hand. They were not crying anymore; they looked angry.

"It's no longer safe for us here," Lilith said. "Especially for the children."

"I know a place," Melissa said, wiping her cheeks. "My family has a little farm, not far from here. No one lives there, though. It was my grandpa's."

"Go there," Lilith said. "Kris, Teresa, Melissa, Melanie. Take the children, and Ruth Ann. Keep them safe, no matter what happens. Will you do that for me?"

"Yes, Mother," Teresa said. Lilith kissed the girl's cheek, and then turned to the children. She knelt down in front of them.

"Is our Mommy coming back soon?" Carrie asked. Lilith stroked her hair.

"I'm sorry," she said. "But you're not alone, my sweet. You'll never be alone. We are all family, my beautiful little one, and no one will ever hurt you."

"I want to come with you," Aiden said, his face hard and angry. "That man hurt Mommy. He hurt my aunties."

"Yes, he did," Lilith said, putting her hands on the boy's shoulder. "And he'll be punished for it, I promise."

"I want to help," he said, and it broke Lilith's heart to

see the hate inside him. "I'm gonna take him up, good."

"But you will help," Lilith said. "I have a very special job for you, young man. Are you up to it?"

"Yes," he said, his small and perfect face hard and serious.

"I need you to take good care of your sister for me," she said. "She's going to need her brother with her. Can you do that?"

Aiden nodded, and put one arm around his big sister's shoulders. Lilith knew this would usually result in squabbling and cries of "he's touching me, make him stop." Now, Carrie hugged him fiercely, burying her small face in his chest as she cried.

Lilith kissed them both on the forehead, and rose. She nodded to Kris, who led the others back into the trailer.

"We're hunting him, aren't we?" Jennifer said, and Lilith nodded.

"We are," she said. "But first, there are things I must tell you. Things you need to know."

She hugged the girl tightly, caressing her hair and just loving the feel of her. "There is a man in town," she said. "If we're not careful, if we draw his attention, he could kill us all."

"Who is he?" she said. "If he could kill you, or my sisters, we should kill him first."

"No," Lilith said firmly. "We will stay clear of him, for now. I just want you to be aware, there is a greater risk than Jerry Hartman waiting for us in town." She held Jennifer at arm's length, struck by the girl's strength and beauty.

"His name is Jim Harlow, and he is a son of Sekhmet," Lilith said. "He is a direct descendant of the goddess of war, and he could destroy us all."

4.

Jim Harlow, blissfully unaware of his divine genealogy, was feeling more frustrated and tailspun than anything.

Harlan Denison had been sitting in front of him for the last forty minutes, and so far he'd spun a tale that would make Agatha Christie say it was more than a little far-fetched.

"He's had his hooks in me for years," Denison said.

"That would be Jerry Hartman?" Jim asked. It wasn't the first time he'd asked, or the twenty-first, but Harlan didn't even seem to notice. He just nodded.

"That greasy bastard rents a warehouse from me a few years ago, and before I know it, I'm caught up in God only knows what," he said. "Before I can even blink, he's practically taken over half my factory, he's running drugs and guns and probably whores out of half my property. And what could I do? He made it all look like it was done in my name, you know? All the property's in my name, all the money comes out of and goes into my accounts. Hell, for all I know, that really does make me an accessory. I don't know and don't care. He's gone too far this time, Chief. I think he killed my boy. You understand that, Chief Harlow? The son of a bitch killed my only son. I don't care what you do to me, but he's gotta pay."

Jim double-checked that the recorder was working for what felt like the hundred and first time, and wondered exactly how much of this spectacular line of bullshit he was supposed to buy. "Mr. Denison, are you telling me that your employee, Jerry Hartman, has been engaged in multiple criminal enterprises, with your cooperation?"

"My coerced cooperation," Harlan said, and Jim could almost see the twinkle of inspiration in his eyes. He knew it was bullshit, Denison knew it was bullshit, but there was nothing else he could do. Denison's story covered every base he could think of, and made him look exactly like what he was portraying himself to be; an unwilling accomplice, cooperating under threat of violence.

Oh, go ahead and say it, Jim thought. Let's get this bullshit over with. "I think," Harlan said, and here he choked back a sob Jim wasn't entirely convinced was false.

"I think that's why he killed Billy. Because I told him enough was enough. I was done with all of it. The guns, the dope, the whores, all of it."

"And what signaled this sudden stroke of virtue?" Jim asked, unable to keep the sarcasm out of his voice.

"I know what you think of me, Harlow," Denison said, leaving off his title. "And to an extent, you're right. I let Billy run wild. I covered for him, paid his fines and got him out of all sorts of trouble. I wish to God I hadn't, but I did what I thought his Mama, God rest her soul, would have wanted. I see now that was a mistake. She was always the disciplinarian, you know. Maybe if I'd taken a firmer hand with the boy," he said, letting the thought trail off. "But when I found out what that bastard had done yesterday, I was done. There has to be a line, and I drew it."

Here we go, Jim thought. Here comes the big, fat lie that will make it impossible not to follow up on this. "And what, exactly, did Mr. Hartman do that you found so offensive?" he said. Denison looked at him a little sideways, probably because Jim couldn't be bothered to hide how much he hated the man.

"I found out there were women being held at Surima," he said. "Held against their will. Girls, really. From South America, somewhere. He was whoring them out, I guess."

"You're talking about human trafficking," Jim said, unable to hide his surprise. It wasn't that either Denison or Hartman was capable of something so horrible that surprised him; it was that they'd been able to do it right under his nose, apparently, and him none the wiser. Well, he thought, as big fat stinkers go, that's gonna be hard to top. It worked, though; that was the bitch of it. He couldn't ignore even the remote possibility of sex slaves being held in his jurisdiction. The only question was, did he call the Feds, or check it out himself?

But that wasn't a question he needed to ask; there was no way he was calling in the FBI based on nothing but

Harlan Denison's admittedly imaginative attempt to cover his own wide ass. "So, there are young women being held against their will and used for sex at Surima?" he said.

Denison shook his head, and this time Jim didn't think he was faking the sick, washed-out look on his face. Harlan Denison had a streak of bullshit a mile wide and two deep, but no one was that good. "He killed them," Denison said. "Soon as I dropped the bomb on him. Killed them all, and dumped them in the gravel pit just behind the plant. That's just a guess, but I know he's talked about it before."

Fuck me, Jim thought. He's got me. I have no choice but to check it out. "I know you can't do much just on my word," Harlan said. "So I brought you evidence." He reached into his jacket and pulled out a sheaf of papers, folded neatly into thirds.

"And what's this?" Jim said. "Blueprints for his death ray?"

"Shipping manifests, invoices, ledger sheets," Denison said. "Records of money transfers. Follow the money, Chief. The company names are fake, but that shouldn't be much of a challenge for you, smart as you are."

That last dig was all Jim could take. He reached out and turned the recorder off. "Why don't we cut the shit, Harlan?" he said.

"I don't know what you mean, Chief," Denison said.

"Cameras are off, audio's off," he said. "There's no one in observation. See?" He stood up and stepped out of the interview room, then reached into the open observation room and turned on the lights. The one-way glass lit up, and he knew Denison could see inside as he came back.

"It's just us talking," Jim said. "Off the record. How much of this is bullshit, and how much of it is you trying to get out from under this Hartman guy?"

"Oh, I want out," Harlan said. "And I really do think he killed Billy. Either he did it himself, or he set it up.

And he's really doing all the things I told you, Jim. Check it out. The warehouse out by the highway, the back room at Surima. Couple of other places; they're in the paperwork. I'm serving up every single operation he's got that even remotely touches my name, because that's all I know about for sure. Now, why don't you go do your job, and arrest the son of a bitch?"

"I will," Jim said, standing up. "But just so we understand each other. When I can prove you were involved in any of this—not if, but when—I'm coming for you, Harlan. I want you to know that. When the cuffs hit your wrists, I'll be the one closing them. You can count on that."

"Go find Hartman," Denison said. "The rest will shake out how it shakes out."

Jim nodded, and started for the door. "And Harlow?" Denison said, stopping him. "I don't imagine he's gonna come in quietly. Watch yourself."

"I'm touched you care," Jim said, resisting the urge to roll his eyes.

"Oh, I don't," Denison said. "But everyone knows you're the toughest son of a bitch around. If he takes you, who's left to stop him?"

5.

Since no one specifically told him to stick around, Harlan decided it was time to get the hell outta Dodge. He kept expecting someone to stop him as he walked out of the police station, and he actually jumped once when he heard someone call out "Hey!" His heart eventually crawled back down out of his throat as he saw the young man waving to someone as they pulled over, but by the time he made it to the car, he was sweating.

He didn't dare go home; if there weren't cops there waiting, there would be soon enough. What was worse, Jerry could be there. Probably would be, and by now he no doubt at least suspected that Harlan had sold him out.

At any rate, it was clear that his time here was over. He felt bad about not going back to the house; there were things there he desperately wanted to take. Pictures, mostly; of his wife, and of Billy. Mementos of his old life, in other words, which he grudgingly supposed he shouldn't take with him into the new one. There was some cash there, naturally, but nothing he'd ultimately miss. Most of his funds were tucked safely away in Switzerland, where he could access them at any time. He knew a guy in Kansas City who could get him new papers, and from there he could catch a flight to just about anywhere.

Once he was out of town, he pulled his cell out of his pocket and tossed it out the window into a ditch. So long, folks, he thought. Been fun while it lasted, but shit's just getting too thick around here for me.

CHAPTER FOURTEEN

1.

Jerry almost made it to his apartment. He was close; it was just up the street, at the top of a steep hill. The whole complex was a barely acceptable shithole, but he'd stayed in worse. It was a place to sleep and eat, that was all.

He was halfway up the hill when he saw her. She was standing at the top of the hill, dressed in nothing but a white shift dress. He didn't know her, but at the same time there was no question she was there for him; the woman walked toward him, hips swaying slowly as the slight breeze blew her dress around. He was telling himself to run, to get the fuck outta Dodge and not look back, but he couldn't move. He was too busy watching the way her nipples poked through the thin cotton of her dress and enjoying the glimpse of some truly world-class legs as she walked toward him. By the time she reached Jerry, he was just staring, unable to do much of anything.

Later, he would marvel at the irony of what happened next; what should have been the last cog in a trap that ended his existence saved his life instead. A hand grabbed him from behind, and it woke him up.

He didn't have time to register that the hand was small, or that it seemed unbelievably strong. He didn't think at all, just reacted out of instinct. As soon as the hand landed on his left shoulder, he grabbed it with his right hand and drove an elbow straight back. On a man of average size, that shot would have landed squarely at the base of the breastbone, driving all the wind out of him. But the person who grabbed him was neither average sized nor a man, and his elbow strike crushed in most of Jennifer's face with a sickening crunch.

His body and mind now both screaming that he was in danger, Jerry did what he did best; he attacked. He slammed his right palm into the woman's upper chest, letting the momentum carry his hand up. The inside edge of his hand hit her in the throat, driving her back. It drove her back, her hands moving up to her throat, and he pressed the advantage.

He drove a hard side kick into her midsection, collapsing the woman onto the ground. Strong, petite hands grabbed him by the shoulder, and he let her turn him around. He used the movement to hide his next move, and when the hard straight punch landed in her chest, she was caught completely by surprise. It was a textbook punch, ending with a snap two inches or so behind the target, and she folded onto the ground.

Jerry ran. His apartment was close, and there were weapons there. At any rate, there was nowhere else to go; he couldn't remember where he'd left his truck, even if he could shake these two long enough to get to it. And he wasn't going to shake them, he knew that. Already they were both getting to their feet, and would no doubt be coming right after him. His apartment was on the ground floor, at the end of the building, and he'd never been so thankful to be paranoid in his life. He'd paid extra to get that particular apartment because it was the one closest to the street, and easiest to escape from.

Slow down, he told himself as he felt in his pocket for the key. Do not rush, do not fumble those fucking keys, or you are as good as dead. He made himself grip the keys tightly, and actually steadied his right hand with his left as he inserted the key into the lock.

Once inside, knowing it was probably pointless but unable to do much of anything else, he locked the door, threw the deadbolt, and hung the security chain. If nothing else, it'd buy him a few precious extra seconds.

And when you kept a loaded gun in every room of the house, a few seconds was all you needed. The closest gun was the Mossberg 12 gauge in the hallway closet, and he grabbed it. He kept it loaded but the chamber empty.

He racked the slide, took up a position, and waited for the door to be battered down.

When, after five minutes that felt like days, he heard tires crunching on the gravel and saw flashing red and blue jackpot lights through the window, he thought he'd never imagined being so happy to see the cops pull up outside his door.

Because those weren't just a couple of random chicks, he knew that much. There was something about the barefoot woman in the dress that scared him, and scared him badly. He was self-aware enough to admit that. She might be a foot shorter than him, and couldn't weigh more than a buck twenty, but she fucking terrified him just the same. But strange as that was, the truly weird part of the encounter had been the girl who'd snuck up behind him. It was beyond strange; in fact, it was pretty goddamned peculiar, because he knew who she was. He recognized her, mostly because he'd been keeping an eye on Billy Denison long enough to know the little shit had a thing for her. Completely one-sided, of course; she had good taste and too much good sense to want anything to do with Billy.

He wasn't particularly imaginative, but neither was he a fool; he believed what he saw with his own eyes, and there was no doubt in his mind that a dead girl had almost killed him just now.

So when none other than Jim Harlow banged loudly on his door and called for him by name, Jerry did the only thing he could. He put the shotgun away and opened the door, keeping his hands out and visible.

"Boy, am I glad to see you," he said as Harlow turned him around and cuffed him. Hands removed his gun and knife from his belt.

"That's a new one," the other cop, Gillette he thought, said. "Usually, they pretend they have no idea what we want."

"Not even an offended 'What's this all about?' for us?" Harlow said, and the other one laughed.

"Honestly?" Jerry said as he scanned the street for any sign of either woman. "As long as you promise to put me in a safe, sturdy cell, we can all get along fabulously. You would not believe what I just saw."

"Probably not," Harlow said as they led him to the car. He read Jerry's Miranda rights from a card, and Jerry agreed he understood them perfectly well. He was aware that his left shoulder was aching something terrible, and a flash of inspiration hit him.

"Do me a favor?" he said as they sat him in the back of Harlow's car. "Pull my shirt down, over my left shoulder. Is there a bruise there?"

Gillette looked at his boss, who just shrugged. When he pulled Jerry's shirt aside, he could see what looked like the beginning of a deep bruise, shaped like a hand. A very small hand, he saw. "Well, that can't be good," he said.

"What's that?" Harlow said. "You gonna claim we did that?"

"No," Jerry said, shaking his head. "They don't usually let guys with baby hands be cops. No one would believe it, anyway. No, it's bad news, because it means I wasn't hallucinating any of it." His own bruised knuckles said the same thing, but he was at least glad to have more corroboration.

"Let me guess," Harlow said. "Denison strong-armed you into running his illegal activities. You're just an innocent pawn, right?"

"Nah," Jerry said. "Harlan Denison couldn't scare me

into locking my windows at night. No, we've got bigger problems than that, Chief."

"Oh, do tell," Gillette said, rolling his eyes.

"Well, for starters, there's a tiny dead chick running around town, and she's strong as a fucking sumo wrestler. How's that one strike you, Sunny Jim?"

"Watch your feet," Harlow said, and Jerry tucked himself into the backseat of his cruiser as Harlow shut the door on him. It was better than nothing, but unless a childhood full of horror movies, books, and comics had seriously let him down, it wasn't going to be nearly enough. He'd meant what he said about the sturdy cell.

When a ghost, or a vampire, or whatever the fuck those two chicks were was after you, the more reinforced concrete and iron bars between them and you, the better.

2.

"Mother, is that him?" Jennifer asked as they watched Hartman being driven away. "The one you spoke of?"

"That's him," Lilith said.

"Can we get to Hartman through him?" she asked, and Lilith shook her head.

"No," she said. "I won't put you at risk, Jennifer. Go back to the others and keep them safe."

"But, Mother, I--"

"Do as I say," Lilith said, her eyes lighting up as she growled. Jennifer lowered her head and whimpered, but she nodded.

"Yes, Mother," she said. "I'm sorry."

"No," Lilith said, lifting the girl's pretty face with one finger under her chin. "I'm sorry. I shouldn't have snapped. But I won't let my children take my risks for me. I'll get Hartman, don't worry. Now, please. Go and make sure your sisters are safely settled in."

"Yes, Mother," Jennifer said. "Please, be careful. If Jim Harlow is as dangerous to us as you say, please be careful. I don't want to lose you."

"My child," she said, hugging her. "I will always be with you, no matter what. I love you, Jennifer."

"I love you, Mother," Jennifer said. She watched as the girl ran, faster than most anyone could see. Once she was well gone, she turned her attention back to the matter at hand.

She walked toward the center of town as Harlow took Jerry Hartman away. She didn't need to rush; she knew where they were going.

"Get comfortable, Jerry," she said, smiling. "I'm coming for you."

3.

"So, I guess this is where we talk about why I'm here," Jerry said as Harlow sat down across the table from him. The room was decorated in what Jerry always thought of as "cop chic;" heavy wooden table bolted to the floor, two cheap metal and plastic chairs, and a big-ass mirror on the wall that fooled no one who'd watched TV since the sixties or so.

"By all means," Harlow said, leaving the file in front of him unopened. "Anything in particular you want to talk about?"

"Usually this is the part where I say I want a lawyer," Jerry said, "but something tells me I'd just get stuck with a wet-assed public defender."

"Denison dropped a whole bag of dimes on you," Harlow said.

"Well, color me surprised," Jerry said. "I bet it was a thrilling tale of coercion and blackmail, with Harlan as the unfortunate victim. That about the size of it?"

"Close enough for government work," Harlow said. "You got a different story to tell?"

"Would it matter?" Jerry asked, and Harlow smiled.

"Let's just say I'm not inclined to take Harlan Denison's word for much of anything," he said. "Did you kill Bill Denison?"

185

"No," Jerry said simply. "I was going to, don't get me wrong. But someone beat me to it. Several someones, I'd say, judging by all the bite marks. But you've got a bigger problem than Billy boy, Chief."

"I'm listening," Harlow said.

"I doubt that very much," Jerry said. Harlow sighed and sat back in the chair.

"You actually have anything to tell me, Hartman, or you just stalling while we wait for the buddy movie to begin?"

"You won't want to believe it," Hartman said. "Hell, I just saw it happen with my own freakin' eyes, and I don't want to believe it. But it's real, and it's happening, so we're gonna have to deal with it."

"We?" Harlow said, smiling. Jerry waved his hand in the air as best the handcuffs holding him to the table would allow.

"Pick apart my semantics later, Chief," he said. "We, you, me, the friggin' National Guard. Doesn't matter. What does matter is that there's something out there, something not natural, and odds are it's coming here for me."

"Right," Harlow said, and Jerry saw the humor sparkling in his eyes. "This is the part where you tell me the only chance we have of living through the night is for me to let you walk out of here, probably with a fast car and a bag of cash."

"Shit, no," Jerry said, shaking his head. "I hit that fucking thing hard enough to kill a man, and she never even blinked. I'm safer in here."

"She?" Harlow said, grinning. "Should we put out a BOLO for Xena, Warrior Princess? Or maybe Buffy the Vampire Slayer?"

"You ever killed anyone, Chief?" Jerry asked. Harlow's grin never faltered.

"None of your business," he said. "We're talking about you, Jerry. How about it? You ever killed anyone?"

"Twenty-six," he said without hesitating. "Sixteen women and ten men." The look in Harlow's eyes was unmistakable; he was torn between calling bullshit, and thinking he'd just made the arrest of the decade. "I'm only telling you all of this because I need you to take me seriously, Chief, and I know you won't do that if you think I'm spinning lies to cover my ass."

"Don't suppose you'd care to give me a list of names, where to find the bodies?"

"Sixteen of those bodies are in the gravel pit behind Surima," he said. "I never bothered to learn names, most of the time. It was never personal enough to learn their names, you understand. It was business, and they were a liability. The rest are well outside your jurisdiction."

"Write it all out anyway," Harlow said, and Jerry shook his head.

"Later," he said. "Right now, I need you to hear what I'm saying. There is some sort of supernatural entity in your town, and it's coming here. You need to lock this place down, and get ready to fight."

Harlow just shook his head. "I knew you were jerking my chain," he said. "Tell you what, I'll lock you back in your cell, and then we'll go check the gravel pit for those bodies."

"Yeah, do that," Jerry said with a touch of enthusiasm. "The cell has to be more secure than this room."

"You'd never make it past the door," Harlow said, his eyes and his voice going cold. "I promise you that much."

"You're still not listening," Jerry said, trying to be patient. "I'm not worried about getting out. I'm worried about something getting in."

"Bullshit," Harlow said simply. "You're just setting up your psych defense."

He was about to walk out, and Jerry knew he only had one card left to play. No point in being delicate about it, he supposed, and went for it. "Tell me, Chief. You ever find Jennifer Bennett's body? You haven't, have you?"

Harlow stopped in his tracks. "You telling me you had something to do with that?"

"No," Jerry said. "But you haven't found the body, because she's up and walking around."

Harlow turned and planted ham-sized fists on the table in front of him, and Jerry understood that if it came down to a fight between them, he'd probably be nothing but a pink mist in no time flat. That was fine; he wasn't insecure about such things. It was actually comforting, because it meant that he might actually have a chance at surviving the shitstorm that was no doubt coming for him. And they were coming for him, there was no question in his mind about that. He'd seen it in the beautiful woman's eyes. She intended to murder him.

"You listen to me closely, Hartman," Harlow said. "A lot of people in this town loved that girl. You start talking shit about her, and maybe something bad happens to you, understand?"

"I'm not talking shit," Jerry said. "I'm telling you straight. I saw that girl up and walking around not an hour ago, Chief. This little souvenir is from her," he added, gesturing to his shoulder and the deepening bruise there. "And I hit her. I hit her hard. Smashed an elbow into her face, probably shattered most of it. Punched her in the chest hard enough to cave it in. She barely noticed. That sound remotely human to you?"

"Sounds like a lot of horse shit," Harlow said, and Jerry nodded.

"I know," he said. "But that's exactly what happened. Now, you want to hear what the other one looked like, or just chuck me back in my nice, safe cell while you chase your tail?"

Harlow sighed, sat back down, and folded his cement-slab arms across his chest. "Assume I give a shit," he said. "Who or what do you think is coming here?"

"I have no fucking clue," Jerry said. "But she's about five-four, maybe one-fifteen. Killer figure. I mean, absolutely perfect. Great legs, too. Long dark hair. I'm telling you, she looked like she should be on a magazine cover somewhere instead of walking around barefoot in this shithole."

"Barefoot?" Harlow said, and Jerry nodded. Of course, he thought.

"You really are a good cop," Jerry said. "You homed in on the weird part right away. She'll be hard to miss. You don't see knockouts like that often."

"So we're looking for a beautiful woman and a dead girl," Harlow said, nodding. "Got it."

"There's something else," Jerry said. "Don't look at her for too long."

"What?" Harlow said, laughing.

"I'm serious," Jerry said. "I knew the minute I saw her blocking my way, she was there to kill me. I just knew it. But she almost got me anyway, because I couldn't stop staring."

"You just knew she was going to kill you," Harlow said. "You psychic or something?"

"You spend a little time in my life, you learn pretty quick to recognize that look," he said, and Harlow just shrugged. "She was there to kill me, no doubt in my mind. She's probably on her way here to do it now."

"Well, then I guess we should get you back to the cells, where you'll be safe," Harlow said, all but rolling his eyes.

"I think that'd be a very good idea," Jerry said. "Might not hurt to put up a crucifix, maybe spray the place with some Holy water if you've got it."

"I'll get right on that," Harlow said, unlocking his cuffs. He briefly considered making a run for it, but decided not to bother. One, he believed Harlow completely when he'd said he'd never make it to the door. And two, that meant he'd be outside when whatever the fuck that was showed up.

Instead, he let the big man lead him back to what was probably the safest place he could be at the moment.

4.

Lilith stood outside the police station in the afternoon sunshine, oblivious to the other people around her. A young girl, no more than twelve, almost ran into her, but swerved away at the last minute without actually seeing her. A man, his mind currently working over the thorny problem of how to tell his wife he'd slept with the babysitter, walked past her without looking up, although he felt a distinct chill as he passed.

She reached out with her mind and her senses. She could feel Hartman inside, foolishly sure he was safe behind bars. There were two or three others, but none of them mattered. The only other person beside Hartman himself that mattered to her was in his office, preparing to head out. The son of Sekhmet had just called a local man to bring out some dogs that were apparently trained to detect corpses, and she'd felt a slight chill when she knew he'd sent them to the gravel pit. She had little hope they wouldn't find the bodies of her daughters, but that couldn't be helped. Perhaps they could trace them back to their families.

That wasn't her concern at the moment; what concerned Lilith was that possibly the only man for thousands of miles who could actually hurt her was about to leave, and Hartman would still be inside. She smiled and found a bench to sit and wait. She sighed as she felt something familiar in the back of her mind, a presence she knew.

"You might as well come out," she said to the air. "Both of you."

She saw Eve first; that blonde hair was hard to miss. She liked the slinky little dress she wore this time. It showed off just enough to make you want to see more. Behind Eve was the one face she hadn't thought she'd ever see again, at least outside of home.

"Hello, Sister," Sekhmet said as Lilith rose to greet

190

them. "It's been far too long."

"Yes," Lilith said, and after a moment, the three of them embraced. She stood back and looked at her long-lost sister, admiring her fierce beauty and strength as she always had. She hadn't bothered to alter her looks, unlike Eve. Then again, her appearance had never been Sekhmet's defining aspect, either. Her hair was still black as coal, her complexion still golden brown.

"You're not wearing your armor," Lilith said, looking at her simple, modern outfit. Tight jeans, a black strap t-shirt that showed off her ample bosom and finely muscled arms.

"I wasn't expecting a battle, Sister," Sekhmet said. Behind them, a group of young mothers with small children felt the immediate and strong urge to leave, packing up complaining children and hustling away. "Was I mistaken?"

"I hope not," Lilith said. "But there is something I must do, and I cannot allow anyone to stop me."

"The Hartman man," Sekhmet said, nodding.

"A child of mine," Eve reminded them, and Lilith nodded.

"Yes, I know," she said. "And he must die, Sister. I am sorry for that, but he must be punished."

"Then let the laws of man punish him," Eve said. "Please, Sister. Our Husband--"

"Your husband," Lilith corrected her. "He threw me over for you. Remember?"

"How could I forget?" Eve said bitterly. "If you aren't reminding me, he is."

"I don't care one way or the other about the Hartman man," Sekhmet said. "And I care even less about Adam's plans and schemes. I care about my sisters."

"Then help her to see reason," Eve said. "Because one of your sons is here."

"I know," she said. "And he's a fine warrior. Very strong, very powerful. And compassionate, as well. Makes a mother proud."

"My daughters were strong," Lilith said. "And beautiful. Then Jerry Hartman slaughtered them."

"And how many have you slaughtered in return?" Sekhmet said. "Both of you, for that matter? How many of each other's children have you both taken over the years? And for what? To set right a wrong neither of you are responsible for?"

Lilith fumed, then sighed, and finally smiled. "I've forgotten how well you do that, Sister," she said. "You were always good at pointing out our foolishness."

"You've both been making fools of yourselves over that man for millennia," Sekhmet said. "Personally, I never saw the appeal. Don't you think it's time to end this?"

"What do you suggest?" Eve said.

"Honestly, I think you should both go kill Adam together, then we'll celebrate," Sekhmet said. Lilith knew by the look on Eve's face it wasn't a welcome suggestion for her. About Adam, she herself was more ambivalent. Still, she had to admit she found the idea of killing Adam distasteful.

"But, as neither of you will ever do that," Sekhmet continued, "perhaps there's another way to settle this. One where neither of my beloved sisters dies. Because you will die here, Lilith. If you continue on this quest, my son will become involved. And he will kill you."

"As needs be, they will be," Lilith said. "I won't let this man go unpunished."

"Please, Lilith," Eve said. "Let's at least hear her out."

"My proposal is simple," she said. "Walk away, the both of you. Eve, you'll see to it Hartman faces man's justice. Lilith, you'll take your creatures with you, and leave this town."

"My daughters," Lilith corrected her, and Sekhmet nodded.

"Your daughters," she said. "My apologies."

"Accepted," Lilith said. "But I'm not leaving while Hartman lives."

"Sekhmet, could you influence your son to leave it be?" Eve said. "Simply look the other way?"

"I could," she said, "but I will not. Unlike you two, I don't meddle with my children's destinies for my own petty reasons."

That one stung, but Lilith held her tongue. "Perhaps you're right, Sister," Lilith said. "Perhaps we have become too intimately involved with our children's lives."

"I don't criticize," Sekhmet said. "I know it's done out of love." All three of them nodded at this. Across the street, an old man carrying a plastic shopping bag stood up straight and tall for the first time in years and walked down the street with his head held up high. Eve saw this and smiled.

"There are benefits to us being here," she said, and Sekhmet nodded.

"And drawbacks," she said. "Tell me, Lilith. Your special children. Do their families know what's happened to them? Or do their feelings not matter to you?"

"I made them strong," Lilith said. "I made them beautiful."

"They were already both, long before you meddled in their lives," Sekhmet said. "What you mean to say is, you made them more like you."

"How dare you?" Lilith said, her voice hard as she seethed. "I gave them a new life, new power. Who are you to question me?"

"I question anyone I see acting foolish," Sekhmet said coolly, her eyes never leaving Lilith's. "And I dare simply because you don't frighten me, Lilith. Don't forget who you speak to, or I'll be forced to remind you."

"Enough," Eve said as the two of them stared at each other. "Both of you."

Sekhmet bowed slightly, and Lilith nodded her agreement. "Forgive me," Sekhmet said.

"No reason," Lilith said. "I think perhaps you're right. I should step back, let my children do as they will. Although, they know what this man did to their sisters, and they're howling for his blood. I only kept them back because--"

"Because of my son," Sekhmet said, nodding. "And yes, it was a wise move. He poses a threat to them, but they also pose one to him. If nothing else, they have the numbers to simply overwhelm him."

"You'd let her children just take him?" Eve said, looking at Sekhmet.

"I let Lilith do nothing," Sekhmet said. "And I have no dominion over her children, no more than I do over you or yours."

Eve was crying. "Will he at least be allowed to fight back?" she said. "Or will they just murder him in his cell?"

"Of course," Lilith said. "They don't want to execute him. They want to hunt him." This made Eve shiver, but she nodded.

"When will it happen?" she said. Sekhmet looked at Lilith, who smiled just enough to show the sharp point of fangs.

"My children have always loved the dark," she said.

"Sunset, then," Sekhmet said.

"But he has to know the stakes," Eve said, surprising them both. "He has to be told what he's facing, and how to survive. Otherwise, it really is nothing but an execution."

"Agreed," Sekhmet said. Lilith felt a chill of alarm, but suppressed it. Like it or not, Eve's suggestion was a fair one.

"I'll tell him," Eve said, but Sekhmet shook her head.

"I think you've both interfered enough with this world," she said. "I will go to him, and to Lilith's daughters."

"And what are we to do?" Lilith said. "While you send our children after each other?"

"What you should have been doing this whole time," Sekhmet said, and now there was no denying the anger in her voice or on her face. "You'll sit back, and watch."

With no real choice, Lilith took Eve's hand and watched as Sekhmet disappeared from their view.

"I suppose we should talk," Lilith said.

"There's nothing to talk about," Eve said, pulling her hand away and turning to sit down on a bench and wait.

CHAPTER FIFTEEN

1.

Jerry sat in his cell and contemplated his future. It could pretty much be summed up in one word, and that word was bleak. He'd just voluntarily confessed to over two dozen murders. The fact that he had actually committed them was almost irrelevant at this point; what mattered was that Harlow and Gillette were likely just hours away from finding at least sixteen of those bodies. But, strange as it was, that wasn't even his biggest concern at the moment.

What worried Jerry was what was no doubt either already outside waiting for him, or on its way now. That the beautiful woman he'd seen was an it and not a she was a given for him; he'd known beautiful women all over the world, but none had been able to—well, to hypnotize him like that. That was what it boiled down to; she'd hypnotized him, and the dead chick had nearly gotten him. What that might entail was something he couldn't stop wondering about, no matter how he tried.

And what the fuck was the Bennett girl now, anyway? He knew she was dead; there had been no question of that. Even in backwoods podunks like this, doctors didn't make colossal mistakes like that. She was dead, and now she wasn't. Or was she? His mind raced, considering all the weirdest possibilities. Was she a vampire? A zombie?

Maybe some kind of vengeful spirit?

"Break it down," he told himself. This was something he did when he was stuck dealing with a large and complex problem. He broke it down into the simplest possible terms, and dealt with each one. He knew she had died, and now she was walking around. He knew she was physically real; he had a bruise on his shoulder to prove it, and he'd felt solid contact when he drove his elbow into her face. He'd even heard the crunch as her nose shattered.

So not a ghost, then. A vampire? It was mid-morning when they attacked, so unless the wide world of myth, legends, and Hammer films was grossly mistaken, probably not a vampire. A zombie? That was a little trickier; she was clearly newly back from the dead, but zombies did not, as a rule, have perky tits.

"Doesn't matter," he said with a sigh, and leaned his head back against the wall. Except that he had a feeling it might matter a great deal. The legends about monsters were almost as varied as the civilizations they came from, but all had at least one thing in common. When the monster showed up, you had to know what it was to know how to kill it.

He was wishing he had a notebook and a pen so he could at least write some of this shit out when the door to the holding area opened. Something about that itself was different, but it wasn't until he saw his visitor was alone that he understood what. He hadn't heard anyone actually unlocking the door; no jangling keys, no beeps or thumps from magnetic locks. The door just, well, glided open and let his visitor inside.

Jesus, he thought. Hammer got something right, anyway. It seemed that all the monsters were beautiful women. She was tall, nearly six foot, with long dark hair and golden bronze skin. Ample, firm breasts encased in a black tank top preceded her approach, and held his full attention. That in itself was odd; he was a leg man, through and through.

"Jerry Hartman," the woman said, and her voice was liquid silk. It flowed and purred in his ears, promising all manner of sinful delights and excruciating tortures in equal measure.

"Have we met?" he said, feeling like an idiot. "You obviously know my name, but I'm afraid I'm at a loss for yours." Not that I'd forget meeting a woman like you, he thought, and she actually smiled as if he'd said it out loud.

"I'm afraid I've never had the pleasure," she said. "But I understand you met one of my sisters earlier today."

"Right," he said. He stood up and walked to the bars of the cell. "So, did she send you to kill me?"

"No," she said with a smile. "Believe me, Mr. Hartman. If I were here to kill you, you'd already be dead."

"I do," he said, and he did. He had no illusions about his situation, and he knew damned well that if this woman, or whatever she was, wanted to kill him, the bars between them would not even slow her down. "So, what happens now?"

She reached out and touched the lock, and the cell door popped open. "You have until sundown, Mr. Hartman," she said. "You could use that time to run, although in all honesty it wouldn't do much good. Also, it would be very disappointing."

"And what happens at sundown?" Jerry said, taking a tentative step out of the cell. He half expected Harlow to come barreling down the hallway and tackle him at any moment, although he knew Harlow was probably out at Surima now, collecting enough evidence to get him the needle.

"My sister's children will come for you," she said.

"And I'm supposed to roll over like a good little boy, let them do whatever they want, right?" he said, and she shook her head.

"Of course not," she said. "You may fight back

however you will, with whatever weapons you have. There will be no restrictions on you, or on them."

"Like a duel?" he said, and she chuckled. The throaty, rich sound made something deep inside him stir, and he was suddenly desperately horny.

"In a way," she said. "The stakes are simple. If you survive the night, you're free to go on with your life for as long as you can. You'll still be a wanted man, of course, but I imagine that's hardly a new idea for a man like you."

"And if I don't?" he said. "Do I become one of whatever the fuck they are?"

"No," she said. "You'll simply die, like any mortal. The long answer is complicated, involving bloodlines and genetics, and is actually fairly boring."

"Maybe to you," he said, and she laughed again.

"You're an intelligent man, Mr. Hartman," she said. "I like that. And you're brave. You would have made an excellent warrior, I imagine. But you're not asking the right questions."

"What are they?" he said, almost breathless.

"They're children of Lilith," she said, as if that explained everything.

"Oh, right," he said. "Lilith. Heard about her big fair every year. Sounds like fun." The woman smiled.

"They're strong," she said. "Even the smallest and weakest of them is stronger than ten men. You've experienced that for yourself."

He rubbed the bruise on his shoulder, and nodded. "They can take a hit, too," he added, not without respect.

"Yes," she said. "But they aren't invincible, and they aren't immortal. Everything can die, Mr. Hartman. Even goddesses."

"Is that what you are?" he said. "Your sister?"

"As close as you'll be able to understand in the time you have left," she said. "But as neither I nor my sisters will interfere, that is of no concern to you."

"I've heard that one before," he said, and she laughed.

"I'm sure you have," she said. "But it's the truth. I'll see to it."

Jerry nodded. "What's your name?" he said. "I mean, chances are I'm already dead. Might as well know who all the players are."

"Sekhmet," she said, and he nodded.

"I recognize it," he said. "An Egyptian goddess."

"The legends get some things right," she said. "Or at least, close enough. Your time is limited, Mr. Hartman. I'd suggest you use it wisely."

"Right," he said. "Any idea how I'm supposed to get out of here without being shot?"

Sekhmet laughed again, and even as terrified as he was, Jerry wanted to put her against the wall and do her right there, in the holding area. He thought trying that might be unwise at best, and suicidal at worst, but it was still tempting. "You're a very resourceful man, Mr. Hartman. I imagine you'll think of something."

"Not even a hint, huh?"

She laughed again. She was going to have to stop doing that. "What fun would that be?" she said, and disappeared before his eyes. She didn't leave; didn't walk out or duck into a secret passage. There was no puff of smoke or big flash distraction; one minute she was there, the next she was gone.

"Well, shit," he said, shaking his head. Hoping he wasn't about to get shot to death, he made his way out the open door from the holding cells to the jailhouse offices. Un-fucking-believable, he thought. She made it sound like it would be so hard.

The entire office was empty. He grabbed a random jacket and ballcap off the coat hooks by the door, slipped them on to cover himself as best he could, and simply walked out. They'd taken his watch and cell, of course, but the clock over the door said it was nearly two-thirty. By his estimate, he had maybe four hours. Four hours, at most, and then a group of monsters was coming after him.

But not immortal monsters, he thought. They can die.

Keeping this thought in the forefront of his mind like a talisman, he started the slow and painful process of making his way out of town. He had several emergency stashes nearby, where he had weapons, papers in various names, and cash hidden away. The trick, he knew, was going to be getting to one without getting caught.

But he'd been in tight spots before, and he still had his one comforting thought. They can die. They can die, and they're going to die tonight.

Every last one of them.

2.

"Wondered where these assholes had gotten off to," Jim said as they stood at the edge of a gravel pit behind the Surima plant. Grady, Taylor, and Hollister were lying at the bottom, covered in gravel dust and dirt with bullet holes in their foreheads.

"Okay, can I just say it?" Mark said. Jim nodded, thinking he knew pretty much exactly what Mark was going to say. "The body of a homicide victim disappears before an autopsy can be done. Three of the four suspects in that homicide are now lying dead in front of us. Doesn't take a genius to figure out Daddy cleaned up behind Junior again."

"And then killed Junior, just to be sure?" Jim asked, and Mark shrugged. "No, I'm betting this was Hartman. Hell, he admitted it. He killed these three, and a lot more according to him."

"I don't think there are any more bodies down here," one of the techs said, "but the ground's pretty disturbed. We did find some bits of cloth, though. My guess? There were a lot more bodies here, but they've been moved."

"Bob," Jim said, and Bob Anderson came forward, drinking a can of Dr. Pepper and looking bored. "The boys up for a bit of a walk?"

"Sure," Bob said, looking back at his truck. His three

bloodhounds, Amos, Andy, and Duke were sitting quietly in their cages. Amos was happily gnawing away at a rawhide, while Andy and Duke were lying still, nearly asleep. Jim nodded to the tech, who brought him one of the scraps of cloth they'd found.

Bob got the dogs out, short-leashed them, and showed them each the scrap of cloth before telling them to seek. The dogs sniffed around the perimeter of the gravel pit, and then nearly dragged poor Bob behind them as they took off toward the small green belt behind the pit.

"Easy, now," Bob said as they continued to pull him. Jim and Mark followed closely behind until they came to a large patch of ground that had been recently disturbed.

"Oh, Lord," Bob said quietly, pulling the dogs back. He'd been doing search and recovery for the county for more than fifteen years, and he knew what a hole that size had to mean.

"Better get the techs over here," Jim said, and Mark nodded. He looked pale.

"Jim, you think this is--"

"I think the cadaver dogs hit on this area," he said. "And we need to investigate. That's all I'm thinking right now." That's all he could stand to think at the moment, but he didn't tell Mark that. "Go on, go fetch the techs. And call the staties; we're gonna need a lot more men down here."

"On it," Mark said. "How long until the press gets wind of it, you think?"

"I don't know," Jim said. "When they do show up, keep them back. Your favorite words are now 'no comment,' understand?"

"Got it," he said. Jim put his sunglasses back on and started for the car. "Uh, you're leaving me with this?"

"You can handle it," Jim said. "Just go slow, make sure they take pictures of everything. By the book. Got it?"

"Yeah, but where are you going?" he asked.

"I'll swing by and check on Hartman," he said. "And I

want another word with Harlan. If he thinks I'm buying what he's selling, he's fucking insane."

"I'll keep you updated," Mark said, and Jim nodded.

"Just don't use the radio," he said. "That's one mess we don't need."

Mark gave him a tired salute and went back to the green belt where the few crime scene techs present were beginning the slow and painstaking process of excavation.

Jim got behind the wheel of his cruiser and started the engine. He sat there for a moment, and muttered to himself "What the fuck is going on here?"

He knew of at least two people who had answers, and he was done asking politely for them. To hell with Hartman, he thought as he put the cruiser in drive. He's locked up. Time to go see Daddy Denison. He did call the station, where Brenda said he was tucked in just like a little baby, fast asleep.

"Please tell me you didn't go back there all alone," Jim said, trying to sound firm but mostly just sounding scared to death.

"The day I can't handle one idjit in a cell is the day I retire, Jim Harlow," Brenda said, and her always polite but utterly practical voice said he would be wasting his time pushing it any further.

Satisfied Hartman was under wraps for the time being, he headed out to Harlan Denison's house.

3.

Sekhmet, unseen in the corner, watched as Hartman dressed in stranger's clothing and walked out of the police station. The woman who'd been here when she walked in was currently sitting in a broom closet, unable to speak, move, or even blink. Seeing her true form was hard on most humans, but she had to give the woman credit; most didn't even survive it. She heard a phone ringing, and picked it up.

"Why, yes, Chief," Sekhmet said in the woman's voice.

"I just checked on him. Brought him his lunch. Fast asleep."

She listened with a mixture of pride and humor as her son chided her for going back into the cells alone, touched at his concern for her. She assured him that she was fine, and she knew how to be careful. She thanked him for his concern, and put the phone down once he'd ended the conversation.

She smiled as she went to the closet. "Brenda," she said, remembering the woman's name. She said it softly, gently, but she still flinched at the sound of her voice. "Shh, little one. You'll be fine. You're strong. I need your help, Brenda. Will you help me?"

Brenda whimpered and pulled away at her touch, but she didn't take it personally. She was obviously in no condition to play any great part in Sekhmet's plan, but that wasn't a great concern. There were plenty of ways for her to help, after all.

"I know," she said as Brenda flinched again. "You poor thing. You're terrified, aren't you? There's no need, you know. It won't hurt, not a bit."

Brenda looked up at her then, and Sekhmet helped her to her feet. "I want you to know, I take no pleasure in this part," she said, touching the woman's cheek. "But my son isn't invested in the game yet, and I need him to be. Finding you will do that nicely, I think."

Brenda still didn't comprehend, and when Sekhmet drove the improvised dagger, made of a sharpened piece of Jerry's bed frame, into her chest, she looked genuinely surprised. She knew about forensics, about fingerprints and DNA, because her children knew. When they tested the chunk of bedframe, it would have both Jerry Hartman's fingerprints and DNA all over it. Of her, of course, there would be no trace.

She left Brenda lying on the floor in front of her desk, where she'd be seen as soon as Jim Harlow walked into the station. The homemade knife, the open cell door; it would all tell him exactly what she wanted him to see. There was only one small detail left to tend to, and she went about it now.

She dropped the lighter she'd taken from Harlan Denison's home near the open holding cell door, where it would be found with a thorough investigation. Not too obvious, though, or it would be suspicious. Her children were brave, strong, and prone to action, but they were not fools.

Satisfied that two of the players in the game were on their way to the playing field, she went to make sure the rest were properly motivated. She'd been waiting so long for this to play out, and now that it was here, she could hardly remember ever being so excited. She was so excited, in fact, that it nearly overrode the distaste she felt at what had to come next.

4.

"I'm sorry, Chief," Harlan's housekeeper said. "He's not here."

"I see," Jim said. He thought briefly about just pushing his way inside, but decided against it. He had no warrant, and wasn't likely to get one based on what he had so far. If pressed, Harlan could easily lay all the bodies they'd found so far at Hartman's feet, which wasn't a surprise since he was convinced Hartman had actually done the killing. That he'd done so on Harlan's orders was a different matter, one he couldn't prove just yet. "Any idea when he's expected back?"

"Honestly, Chief Harlow, I thought he'd be back by now," she said, looking genuinely worried. "Mr. Hartman was by earlier for him, but left when he didn't show. That's unusual, because he always sees Mr. Hartman."

"Yeah," Jim said. "Thick as thieves, aren't they?"

"I know what Mr. Hartman is," she said. "I'm not a fool, Chief. And I know you think he killed Billy, but I don't."

"Ma'am," he said. "I think Bill is just the tip of this iceberg," he said, knowing it was a mistake the moment it came out. He cut her off before she could ask by handing her his business card. "I want to talk to Harlan, today. I need to make it very clear, Ma'am. I'm not asking. He can come in on his own, or I can come and find him. Make sure he understands that."

"I will," she said, taking the card. He knew damned well she had no real influence over Harlan, but he'd made his point. Well, almost.

"Ma'am," he said. "If you know where he is, the smart thing to do would be to tell me. I don't want to see good people go down with him. And he is going down, make no mistake about that."

"I wish I did know," she said. "Even though I know it'll mean my job when you catch up to him, I want to know where he is. I'm worried."

"Yes, ma'am," he said. "If you talk to him, convince him his best bet is to come in voluntarily. He can bring his lawyer, if he wants."

Satisfied he'd done what he could, at least until he could get a warrant for the house, he started walking back to the car. He was barely behind the wheel when the radio squawked.

"Unit One," the voice said. It was high, and shaken, and he didn't like the sound of it at all. He liked it even less when he recognized it as Jake Faulkner. The hell was he doing on the radio? He wasn't even on shift until eleven.

"Unit one, go ahead," Jim said into the radio. "That you, Jake?"

"Yes, sir, it's me," Jake said, and the radio went silent for a moment. "Chief, I got a hell of a mess here. Okay to call you direct?"

Fuck me, Jim thought. Jake was a decent officer, smart and tough. If he was shaken up this badly, and he didn't want to use the radio, then it had to be very bad shit, indeed. "Go ahead," he said. A moment later, his cell rang.

"Chief Harlow," he answered, purely out of habit.

"Chief, it's me," Jake said, and over the phone it was much easier to hear the distress in his voice. "You'd better get back to the house, pronto."

"What's up?" he said, keying the ignition and starting to back up into a three-point turn. "Thought you weren't on until eleven, anyway?"

"Yeah," Jake said, blowing out a shaky breath. "Came in early to catch up on reports. I found—Jesus fucking Christ, just get here, Jim. It's bad."

Jim didn't bother asking for more clarification; he simply ended the call, turned on the jackpots and the siren, and hauled ass back to town.

5.

"I'm here, Sister," Lilith said as she stood outside the cabin. Sekhmet stepped out of the trees, and began walking toward her.

"Thank you for coming," Sekhmet said. "Is Eve here?"

"I'm afraid she needed a little time away," Lilith said. "I don't think I give her enough credit sometimes. She's already mourning her son."

"She pretends not to care, because she cares too deeply," Sekhmet said. "I sometimes wish I had her capacity for emotion."

"It's as much a curse as a blessing," Lilith said. She knew that all too well; how much pain had she experienced on behalf of her children? Sometimes she went through it so they did not have to, but often it was merely empathetic pain.

"I know you feel their pain, as she does," Sekhmet said. "That's why I asked to speak to you. To warn you. You need to prepare yourself, Sister. Your daughters may well kill him tonight, but not all of them will survive the battle."

"I know," Lilith said. "That's why I wanted to do it myself. To protect them."

"But you can't protect them," Sekhmet said. "Sometimes in battle, the soldiers you kill are your own."

"Always the warrior," Lilith said, and gave Sekhmet a smile. "Has he been prepared?"

"He knows what he needs to know," Sekhmet said. It wasn't quite an answer, but she knew from long experience it was all she would likely get from her. "And he's preparing, even now."

"As we should be," Lilith said. She sighed and corrected herself. "As my daughters should be."

"For what it's worth, I don't have much sympathy for the man," Sekhmet said. "He could have been a fine warrior, but instead he's little more than a murderer. But he's motivated, and he's prepared. I don't think your daughters are, though. Am I wrong?"

"I don't know," she said, looking back at the cabin. She could feel them in there; still mourning the loss of Emma and Amber and loving each other and the children. But she couldn't feel the spark of hate she knew they'd need. They were outraged, yes. But there was no hate, and that worried her. "They still grieve."

"Grief can be a motivator," Sekhmet said. "But revenge is better. Colder."

She heard something in Sekhmet's voice, but she'd let her guard down. She'd been too connected to her children, too involved in her own grief and anger to think clearly. She turned to her, but it was too late; the arrow in Sekhmet's hand pierced her body with ease, sliding through bone and muscle like wet tissue paper until it found her heart.

"I'm sorry," Sekhmet said as she caught Lilith before she could fall to the ground. "But I've worked for so long to bring this to fruition, and I need all my players properly motivated."

"Why?" Lilith said, gasping as she felt her life, her true

life and not this shell, fading away. Sekhmet's arrows killed anything they pierced, human or otherwise.

"Because it's what I do," Sekhmet said, smoothing her hair. "And don't fret; your death will serve a purpose. By the time they enter the battle, they'll be wild as harpies. It will be glorious."

With the last of her strength, Lilith reached up to Sekhmet's face. She didn't strike; didn't tear flesh with her nails or gouge with her strong fingers. She caressed her cheek instead. "I forgive you, Sister," she said, and the last thing she saw was a single tear rolling down Sekhmet's face before everything stopped.

Crying, she removed the arrow and made it disappear, then waved a hand over the wound. It changed shape from an incision to a round hole, with burned edges. Another, larger hole appeared in her back, under Sekhmet's hand.

She didn't have to manufacture tears as she carried Lilith's body up to the cabin. When the first of them saw her carrying her sister's body, they all came running outside.

She listened to their wretched sobbing, their pathetic whines and cries of "mother" until she couldn't stand it anymore. "Get up," she said to the smallest of them, the girl who Lilith had brought back from beyond death. "You are daughters of Lilith, and it's time you behaved like it."

They all looked up at her harsh words, with tears streaming from their eyes. One of them started to speak, and Sekhmet slapped her across the face. It was a hard blow, one that would have killed anyone but one of Lilith's special children. As it was, it knocked the redheaded girl to the ground, but she was up again in an instant, eyes flashing and fangs bared.

"There," she said. "That's better. Now, you can stand there sniveling, or you can rise up and take your revenge. Which one will it be?"

"Who killed her?" the redheaded one said, her eyes blazing with hate.

"See for yourself," Sekhmet said, dipping her finger into Lilith's blood. An entirely unnecessary gesture that meant nothing, but to them it would seem like more of Lilith's magic. She daubed the blood onto the girl's forehead, at the same time showing her exactly the scene she'd crafted. When the girl saw Jerry Hartman shooting her in the heart, she howled with rage.

The link between them carried the images to the others, and soon they were wild with hate and grief.

Wild as harpies, she thought, and smiled.

"Where is he?" the smallest one said. "I'll tear his heart out."

"Soon," Sekhmet said. "For now, see to your mother, and I'll find him."

"He's ours," the redheaded one snarled. "Our kill."

"Of course," Sekhmet said, smiling. "When the time comes, you'll have him, and the man aiding him."

"Denison," the small one snarled, and Sekhmet shook her head.

"He's of no consequence," she said. "Hartman has another partner."

"Who?" she asked.

"His name is Harlow," she said, hoping her smile didn't reach her face.

"The cop? Isn't he yours?" the small one asked. "Mother warned me about him."

"If she'd only listened to her own warning, none of this would have happened," Sekhmet said. "I don't interfere in my children's lives. His fate is his own to make."

"Not anymore," one of them said from the back. She had beautiful chocolate skin, and long hair in intricate braids that must have taken her servants hours to do. Her eyes were burning intensely, and Sekhmet could feel the waves of rage boiling off her. The others didn't know it, nor did she, but she was the strongest of them all, her rage and power the most pure.

"Tend to your Mother," Sekhmet said. "I will find this man Hartman for you. When I return, we'll hunt."

She left them to bury Lilith's body, and to make the rest of her arrangements.

CHAPTER SIXTEEN

1.

"Tell me again," Jim said as he watched the ME's assistants taking Brenda's body out of the station. Jake sat on one of the small benches near the door, his hands clasped in between his knees to keep them from shaking.

"I came in early, thought I'd catch up on some paperwork," Jake said. "I even--" He stopped, then ran a hand over his face. "I even stopped and grabbed a dozen glazed from the grocery store. Her favorites."

Jim nodded; Brenda's love-hate affair with glazed donuts was legendary. "I came in, and saw her on the floor. Checked her for a pulse, although I think I knew it was pointless. What the hell was that in her chest, anyway?"

A fuckup that never should have happened, Jim thought. He'd known the beds in their three holding cells had needed replacing for months, but the city just didn't have the money to do it, or at least they didn't according to their illustrious mayor. "Piece of bedframe," he said instead, and Jake just nodded.

"I saw the door to the holding cells open," Jake said. "So I drew my weapon and checked it out. Number two was open."

"Hartman," Jim said, nodding. Jake looked up.

"Jerry Hartman?" he asked, and Jim nodded. Jake

212

didn't need to ask any further; he was a good officer, and he'd had the same bad gut feeling about the man Jim himself had. "What'd you collar him for?"

"Suspicion of homicide, trafficking, a few others," Jim said. "You need me to call Shelly or anything?" he asked, but Jake just shook his head.

"She's, uh, at her mother's for a few days," he said, scrubbing his cheeks again. Jim noticed he hadn't shaved, which wasn't like Jake at all. "She and the girls."

Jim nodded. Brenda's taste for donuts wasn't the only inside joke at the station, although it was the only one he'd ever seen concrete proof of so far. Still, there were others, and he'd stalled asking about them long enough. "Jake," he said, sitting down next to him. "I hate to, but you know I have to ask."

Jake nodded. "Home life sucks," Jake said, and shrugged. "Pretty sure Shelly's not coming back. Probably has a whole mess of good reasons for it, too. I'm no saint."

"Was there anything between you two?" he asked carefully, keeping his voice low. He'd rather do this in his office, but that would automatically fire up the rumor mill a hundred times worse than it already was. Jake shook his head.

"No," he said. "Not like you're thinking, anyway. Never got that far."

"But that's where it was headed, wasn't it?" Jim said, and Jake sighed.

"Maybe," he said. "Hell, probably. But I didn't do this, Jim. Hartman did."

"Probably," he said. "But there are some questions that need answered, Jake."

"Like how'd he get out of the damned cells in the first place," Jake said with a tired sigh. "I know. You check the camera feeds?"

"On the fritz again," Jim said, which wasn't a surprise. The CCTV system was as old and broken-down as everything else around the place. And Jake would have known that, he thought. It wasn't a welcome idea, but it wouldn't go away. "Brenda's keys are still locked in her desk," he said, and Jake nodded. "And mine are still on my belt."

"Just say it, Jim," Jake said. "I'm tired, and I think maybe I need to make a phone call. To a lawyer," he added.

"Might be best," Jim admitted. He motioned for Jake to follow him into his office. "Close the door."

Jake did, looking beaten down. "I suppose I could point out that I don't have any blood on me," Jake said. "Or that the GPS on my phone will show where I've been pretty much every minute of the last twenty-four hours or so. Or any one of a hundred things that we all know to check."

"But because you'd know we can check, you'd know a way around it," Jim said, finishing the thought for him. Jake just nodded. "It's just a formality, while we wait for the forensics."

"Yeah," Jake said, nodding. "That's where it always starts." He removed the badge from his uniform shirt and put it on Jim's desk, then took the wallet carrier with his second badge and ID out of his pocket and placed it next to the badge. "Gun's mine. I bought it. Go ahead and say the rest of it, Jim. Let's just get it done."

"You're suspended with pay, pending the outcome of the investigation," Jim said, feeling like an utter horse's ass. "You know the drill."

"Yeah," he said. "You've got my ten-card on file. You want a cheek swab before the techs bug out?"

"Sure, Jake," Jim said, and that cinched it for him. Jake didn't do this. He hadn't really thought he had anyway, but now he was sure. Of course, Jake was a cop, too. He knew better than most that not every crime had DNA evidence, but the odds were that this one would. Breaking a chunk of steel off a bed frame, even a really dilapidated one like the ancient cots in the holding cells, was bound to leave a man with cuts on his hands.

He followed Jake out into the main office, where a tech took his cheek swab and placed it in an evidence bag. Jim signed for it, and let the man get on with his work. "Listen," Jim said. "If you think of anything, anything at all, that you think I need to know, don't keep it a secret, okay?"

"I think," Jake said, taking a deep breath, "I think I'll run anything through my lawyer first, Chief Harlow. My apologies, but I think that's the safest course of action."

"Of course," Jim said, more than a little disappointed but not entirely surprised. He'd all but just accused the man of murder. And not just any man, but one of his own officers. One smart enough to know that talking to the cops without a lawyer was virtually never in your best interest.

"Chief Harlow," one of the evidence techs said from the door to the holding cells. "Found something."

Jim and Jake both turned at the same time, but after a second or so Jake stepped back. Mark came in as Jim was examining what the crime scene tech had found; a gold lighter. "Jesus wept," he said. "Is it real?"

"Afraid so," Jake said. "Hi, I'm the main suspect. Nice to meet you."

"Can that shit," Jim said. "We both know better. Just go home until I can sort this shit out." Jake nodded.

"Looks like a pretty expensive lighter," Jake said, pointing at it.

"Davidoff," Mark said. "Nice. You into high end lighters, Jake?"

"How high end?" Jim asked, letting the tech put the lighter into an evidence bag. That got Mark's attention, fast.

"That's probably about an eight hundred dollar lighter," Mark said, holding out his hand. "May I?" The tech handed it to him, still in the bag, and he took a closer look. "Scratch that. This baby's a couple grand, easy."

"So, who do we know that's got that kind of money to throw around on something so stupid as a lighter?" Jim said.

"Probably the same guy who's hired man just skedaddled," Mark said, nodding. "But how'd he get the door open, let alone the cell?"

"I don't know," Jim said. "But you can bet your ass I'm gonna ask them both about it when I catch up with them."

2.

Jerry watched from the treeline opposite where the cops and the CSI-types were having their little field day. He'd almost bailed when he saw the party going on, but stopped. His best emergency cache was here, about two hundred yards from the main factory in a storage shed. He'd already retrieved it, and probably should have made tracks by now, but he was curious. Jim Harlow had torn out some time ago, and he didn't need three guesses as to why. He should have understood as soon as he saw the empty police station, but at the time he'd been a little punch-drunk from meeting a goddess. The police station was never empty; even if it was only the cute little receptionist, there was always someone there. Overnight, one of the officers was on desk duty to catch calls. And a goddess wouldn't think twice about killing one little receptionist, would she? Especially if she was in the way.

But in the way of what? He could almost feel it; something at the edge of everything. Something moving him around, like a chessman on a board. Probably moving others, too. It was all just a little too convenient; everything from Billy shitting the bed by killing the girl at the worst possible time to his incredibly timed rescue by Harlow. From his admittedly stupid decision to bury those bodies so close to Surima, effectively taking a giant shit right next to the dining room table, to his extremely convenient escape, it all stank to high heaven. All of it seemed to be designed to move him into a position that wasn't his choice, which of course made it the wrong position.

And now, he had less than two hours before sundown, when apparently a whole gaggle of monsters would be after his ass. That seemed almost too crazy to be real, but he believed it implicitly. The only question was, why? Why were they after him? And more importantly, why was he going to be around when they showed up?

The most obvious reason was that he'd killed someone he shouldn't have. That had become almost a reflex action by now, something he was at least self-aware enough to recognize as a problem. But who? Surely it couldn't have been those three assholes Harlan had sent him to help clean up the Surima operation; he couldn't imagine anyone giving two squirts of runny shit about any of them. Ditto the girls; they were no one special to anyone here. Hell, he doubted anyone outside of the few locals who paid for the privilege of screwing them even knew they were here. And it was a sure damned bet that none of those morons wondered who they were, or where they came from. Still, that seemed like the most likely motive; it was by far the worst thing he'd ever done. He was more than a little surprised to find it actually bothered him. After all, he'd had no choice; it wasn't as if he could just give them bus tickets and send them on their way. But it did bother him, and not just because those dead bodies represented a significant lost investment, or even a cozy spot on death row for him.

For the first time in a long time, he felt like he'd done something wrong.

No matter, he decided. What's done is done, and can't be undone. All he could do now was survive, and to do that he needed a plan. The only problem was, he had no idea what he was planning for. If he hopped in a vehicle, he could be over a hundred miles gone by the time dark fell.

But he had a feeling that wouldn't be far enough; hell, he wasn't sure the other side of the world would be far enough away. And since running wasn't really much of an option, that left fighting. But again, the question was what was he fighting?

He decided it was time he found out.

Gathering his gear, he made his way back out through the woods, avoiding the highway. Even if the goddess hadn't killed anyone at the station, he was a fugitive now, and he had a feeling cops weren't the only ones looking for him. If he was headed for some stupid, High Noon-type showdown, then he might as well do it in style. He was outnumbered, hunted by cops and God only knew what, and his resources were beyond limited. But he had at least one advantage, and he intended to use it.

He could pick the battlefield. And he had just the place in mind. All he had to do was get there in time. And to do that, he needed wheels. He briefly considered stealing the cruiser parked behind the plant, but quickly decided against it. It would be ballsy as all hell, and it had a certain flair he liked, but it also most likely had a GPS unit that could be tracked. Same with the crime scene vans.

But the second shift at the plant had just started, and the parking lot was full of old trucks and cars, most of them barely held together with duct tape and hope, that wouldn't be missed for several hours.

Unaware he was grinning, he began making his way carefully down to the parking lot.

3.

Sekhmet watched as her son organized his men, sending them out to hunt for Jerry Hartley and Harlan Denison. It made her proud to see him this way; strong and decisive. His men, and the women as well, all respected him. They'd do as he asked, not just because he was their commander, but because it was him.

Oh, her children made such fine warriors. But, it seemed his training was overriding his instincts, and she couldn't have that. Instead of hunting these men himself, he was using his own men to find them and bring them in, probably to submit to man's justice.

She slid in behind him unseen, and gently laid a hand on his large shoulder. "This is not what you should be doing, James," she said. Although he was completely unaware she was there, she felt his body stiffen under her hand, and she knew he felt her influence. It was the same influence that had sent her sons charging recklessly into battle for centuries, often overcoming seemingly insurmountable odds.

"This fight isn't for your men. It's for you, my son. The Denison man is of no concern. Hartman is your quarry. And there are others, as well. Others only you can defeat. You must go, my son. Go, and fight."

She reached up and touched his forehead, and gave him all the knowledge he would need. He knew now what Lilith's daughters were, where they were, and how to defeat them. But of course, it couldn't just be that simple, or he wouldn't trust it. Her children were not fools.

Instead, she masked it with an urge to check out something for himself. It was where the Hartman man was going, and of course where he went, Lilith's daughters would follow.

It was going to be a glorious battle.

4.

"Mr. Hartman?" Sharon said as she opened the door. Jerry pushed his way in, closing and locking the door behind himself. "You—you shouldn't be here, Mr. Hartman. The police were here not long ago, and I think they'll be back."

"Probably," he said, looking out the front window. "We can always hope, but somehow I don't think they're gonna be much help."

"Sir?" she said, but he ignored her and started through the house, locking windows. "Sir, I--"

"Ma'am," he said as he hustled through the kitchen to lock the back door. "I'm sure you've got a million questions. I do, too. But right now, we need to lock this place down. Now, you can either help, or you can stay out of the way. Honestly, now might be a good time for you to go on home."

"What is going on here?" she said, near tears. "Where is Mr. Denison?"

"I have no idea, and frankly I don't give a shit," he said. He grabbed her by her bony shoulders and looked her in the eye. "Sharon, is it?" he said, and she nodded. "Okay, Sharon. Here's the deal. Right now, there is a whole pack of pissed off I-don't-know-whats coming here. They're coming for me, but if you're here, I doubt they're gonna stop to ask for your life story first. Sun won't be down for a good thirty minutes or more, so you've got time. Now, I like you, so I'd rather you get in your car and haul ass out of here. But I don't have time to fight with you about it."

She looked at him for a moment. No, she wasn't just looking. She was studying him, scrutinizing him like she would a naughty child caught in a fib. "Do you think Mr. Denison is alive?"

"I honestly don't know," he said. "But the fact he's still not here doesn't look good." He honestly didn't give two shits if Harlan was alive or dead. Honestly, things would go much simpler for him if Harlan was dead, although that was given the huge assumption he was alive himself come morning.

Sharon took a deep breath, and nodded. "My shift was over forty-five minutes ago," she said. "And Mr. Denison hates paying overtime." She went to the pantry and fetched a massive old-lady purse and a windbreaker. "I left his dinner in the fridge. Tell him all he needs to do is warm it up in the oven. Thirty minutes at three-fifty should do it."

"I'll let him know," Jerry said, and watched as the old girl left.

He shook his head and unshouldered his pack, laying out what weapons he had. "What next?" he muttered. "A goddamn quilting bee in the backyard?"

The three pistols and the knife were a good start, but he needed more firepower. Thankfully, Harlan was a big fan of the Second Amendment. He tucked one pistol into his waistband, and went to Harlan's office. More specifically, he went to the large gun safe in the closet.

"Jackpot," he said as he looked at Harlan's prodigious collection of illegal weapons. He ignored the fancy Heckler and Koch rifles, the finicky M4 carbines, and the anachronistic but nifty little Thompson sub-machine gun, and grabbed a rifle he recognized as a solid workhorse.

He was just inserting one of the loaded magazines into the AK-47 when he heard tires crunching on gravel. He had a brief moment of panic, but locked it down. Did monsters and goddesses drive? He didn't know, but it seemed unlikely.

He went to the front door and looked out the small window, thinking it would either be Harlan finally coming home, or maybe a cop. It was a cruiser, but the jackpot lights were off. He pulled the AK's charging handle, chambering a round. He briefly considered just opening up, but changed his mind when he saw the unmistakably massive form of the only cop in town that legitimately scared him.

Rather than being frightened, he was actually glad to see Big Jim Harlow. If anyone could help fight whatever the hell was coming, it would be him. Always assuming the big bastard didn't just shoot him on sight, that was.

Reluctantly, he safetied the AK and set it down, and stepped out onto the porch with his hands up as Harlow approached.

"Get on the fucking ground," Harlow said, stalking toward him with his hands clenched. "I won't tell you again."

"Chief, we need to talk," Jerry said. He started to explain what was coming, but those words were as far as he got before Harlow blasted him with a hard right to the mouth. He didn't fall so much as just collapse bonelessly to the porch, almost unconscious.

"Jesus," Jerry said, groaning as he tried to sit up. He managed to scoot back to the door, and leaned against it. "Hmm," he said, holding up a finger as he reached into his mouth and pulled out what was rattling inside. It turned out to be three teeth. He dropped them onto the porch and spat to clear the blood from his mouth. "Feel better?" he asked.

"You're under arrest, Hartman," Harlow said. "Get up so I can beat the shit out of you properly first."

"Lovely thought," Jerry said, spitting again. Christ, that hurts, he thought. Damn near took my head off. "But right now, we've got bigger problems."

"Why'd you kill her?" he shouted. "She wouldn't have tried to stop you. Couldn't have even if she wanted to. She was no threat to you."

"The receptionist?" Jerry asked glumly.

"Her name was Brenda, asshole," Harlow said. "And you're gonna pay for what you did to her." Harlow started for him, and Jerry held up his hands.

"Hold on," he said quickly, or as quickly as he could with all the little cartoon birdies flying around his head. Christ, he'd never had his bell rung that hard in his life. "Just, hold on a damned minute. Something's off here, Chief, and I think you're smart enough to see it, if you can calm the fuck down and look at it."

He had a brief moment to think he might actually be getting through to him, and then he saw a group of women walking across the lawn toward them.

5.

"If you can calm the fuck down and look at it."

That was what Hartman had just said, and despite his full intention of thoroughly beating sixteen shades of hell out of the man, it made him stop. My God, he thought as he finally understood what had been happening. It had never been this bad before. He'd gotten caught up in the whirlwind again, and this time he hadn't even known it.

He was still contemplating this when Hartman pointed behind him, his face pale. He saw Hartman's finger trembling, and it made him look behind him.

Five women were walking toward the house. No, he realized as he got a better look at them. Five teenage girls. No again; four teenage girls and someone who shouldn't, couldn't be walking around.

"Jesus fucking Christ," he said, his hand dropping to the Glock on his belt out of habit.

"Inside," Hartman said, getting slowly to his feet. He started to argue, but stopped when he got a closer look at the girls. More specifically, at their eyes.

All of their eyes were glowing bright orange. One of them, a cute little blonde he recognized from around town but whose name he couldn't recall, hissed at him. Actually hissed at him, revealing sharply pointed canines that actually extended as he watched. Fuck me, he thought, and followed Hartman into Denison's house.

Hartman locked the door, first at the knob and then with the three deadbolts. "What the fuck?" he said, wondering if he'd actually seen what he knew he had. "What the actual fuck?" Hartman leaned against the door as they started to batter on it. He watched as it jumped in the frame.

"A little help here?" he said, and Jim's paralysis broke. Something pinged in the back of his mind.

"Salt," he said. "We need salt."

"The fuck?" Hartman said. "You're gonna season the bitches to death?"

He ignored Hartman and ran through the house to the kitchen. He dug through the kitchen cabinets, found nothing he needed, and growled in frustration until he tried the pantry door. He grabbed the large bag of pickling salt from the lower shelf and ran back to the front room, where Hartman was doing his best to try and hold the door and reach an AK propped nearby at the same time.

Jim set the bag down, pulling his pocketknife and flicking the blade open. He sliced off the top, reached in and grabbed two large handfuls, and looked up at Hartman. "Stand back," he said.

"Are you fucking crazy?" Hartman said as the women, for lack of a better term, continued to bang on the door. "Do you have even a single fucking clue what you're doing?"

"I have no idea," Jim said, but that wasn't true. He had no idea where it came from, but the knowledge was there in his mind. Salt and silver would burn them. They were tough, but not invincible. Damage the heart and the brain enough, and they would die. "Do it anyway."

Hartman shrugged, stepped away from the door, and grabbed the rifle. The door lasted another five seconds before the frame shattered and it was flung inward. Jennifer Bennett stepped inside, eyes glowing and sharp canines exposed. She looked from Hartman to him, and Jim swore he heard her growling.

"So it's true," she said, her voice rough. "You're working together."

"What?" Hartman said, shocked into inaction by the sight of her. Jim ignored it all and threw a handful of salt at her, expecting it to do nothing more than patter against her like sleet on a windowpane.

Some of it did bounce off her shirt, but everywhere the salt struck skin, it stuck. He watched with a mixture of horror and elation as it began to actually melt into her flesh, accompanied by a sound that made him think of bacon frying in a cast-iron skillet.

Jennifer screamed as steam began to hiss off her exposed skin, and she ran back out the door. Hartman, who was apparently shocked but not completely out of it, raised the AK and let out a short, controlled burst. Half a dozen slugs caught her in the middle of her back, knocking her completely off the porch.

Jim stepped outside, drawing his Glock. He tossed his other handful of salt at the girls, who jumped back to avoid the worst of it. Some of it struck them, however, and they shrieked as they brushed it off.

Hartman opened up then, spraying them with bullets in one long, rattling burst until the rifle clicked empty. He watched as one of them fell down, missing most of her head. The cute little blonde, he saw. She wasn't cute anymore. None of them were; they looked like fucking nightmares.

He was about to take aim at another one when something stirred at his feet. He looked down to see Jennifer Bennett's hand creeping toward his boot as she stared up at him with hate in her eyes. He lowered the Glock and fired twice, obliterating the top of her head. Out in the yard, the girls screamed curses at him as Hartman reloaded the AK and raised it.

"Inside," Jim said, firing at them. It wasn't quite blind fire, but it was hardly controlled. Still, he managed to hit two of them in the upper body, knocking them back but not down. He turned to yell at Hartman, but the man was already inside, holding the door open for him. He backed through it, firing the Glock dry as he did. Hartman shut the door as Jim dropped the Glock on a nearby sofa and pushed it up against the broken door. It wouldn't hold them out for long, if at all, but it was better than nothing.

"So," Hartman said, breathing hard. "You ready for that talk now, Chief?"

6.

When Ruth Ann woke, she was alone.

No, that wasn't quite right. Her new sisters were gone, but she could feel someone with her. Mother was dead, she felt that immediately. But that didn't mean she was completely gone.

"I'll always be with you, my sweet," she heard someone whisper in her ear, and she smiled. She stood up and stretched, aware that all of her old aches and pains were gone. She ran a hand through her hair, and it felt wrong. Curious, she found her way into the bathroom and took a good look in the mirror. What she saw made her smile.

Her hair was no longer the chemical wasteland of fried roots and split ends that it had been; now it was the lustrous, thick golden honey color she remembered from high school. Her face hadn't been in much better condition, but now the sores and the ghosts of old scars were gone. Her nose, which had been broken and never set right at some point she no longer remembered, was straight, and her eyes were clear and bright. And when she smiled, her teeth were whole and perfect, and almost brilliantly white.

"Thank you, Mother," she said, crying tears of joy as she saw herself. "You made me so beautiful."

"You were always beautiful," Mother whispered in her ear. "I have something special for you to do, my child."

"My sisters," she said. "Should I go to them? Help them?"

"No," Mother said, and she felt an invisible hand wipe away her tears. "Their path is set, and cannot be changed. But there is another task, one only you can do now. Will you help me, Ruth Ann?"

"Anything for you, Mother," she said, standing up straight. "How can I help?" She listened as Mother told her what she needed to do and smiled.

"Can you do it, my child?" Mother asked, and she smiled.

"I can," Ruth Ann said. "And it would be a pleasure."

CHAPTER SEVENTEEN

1.

Melanie watched it happen, as if in slow motion. Jennifer backing away, her skin hissing. The Hartman man firing his damned rifle. The Chief of Police, Jim Harlow, executing Jennifer, like a sick dog that had to be put down. And Kris. Kris's beautiful face disappearing in a mist of blood.

She heard screaming; a high, wailing shriek of pain, grief, and horror. It wasn't until she felt hands shaking her arm and someone asking what they were supposed to do that she realized she was the one screaming. She turned and saw Teresa gripping her left arm, crying and shouting something she didn't understand. The left side of Teresa's face was still smoking from whatever they'd thrown at them.

"Mel," Teresa said, crying. "What do we do?"

"Kill them both," she snarled at her friend. Not just her friend anymore; her sister.

"But they--"

"They can't watch every door and window," Melissa said, and Melanie nodded.

"Circle around back," Melanie said, her eyes glowing. "Find me a way into that house."

She watched as Melissa took off to the right, and Teresa the left. She stood there, motionless, staring at

Jennifer's body on the front porch. She watched in horror as Jennifer began to, well, melt. Her body first softened, then liquified, and finally just drifted away as so much mist on the night breeze. She choked back a tear as she turned and saw the same thing happen to Kris. Soon there was nothing left of either of her beautiful sisters.

And very soon, there would be even less left of the men in that house.

2.

She watched. It was what Eve did best.

She watched as Hartman and Harlow fought off Lilith's daughters, surprised that they knew to use salt.

How would they know that? Neither of them struck her as particularly superstitious. Certainly not Harlow, who seemed to be stubbornly, peculiarly practical. The way he'd executed Jennifer showed her that much. And that was exactly what it had been, an execution. Both men could have easily escaped back into the house at that point, but that hadn't been enough for him. He wanted to make sure.

Sekhmet's children were almost always ruthlessly practical. Killing her had been the best option, and he'd taken it without a moment's hesitation. But the burning question that remained was, how did he know what to do?

She felt out with her senses, not at all surprised to find she wasn't alone. "Get out here," she said, angry and frustrated.

"I thought you'd left, Sister," Sekhmet said.

"You were supposed to," Eve said, her voice hard as she stared at her. "I never trusted you, Sekhmet."

"Probably the wise course of action," Sekhmet said. "Where is Lilith?"

"Don't," Eve said, staring her down. "Don't you dare lie to me now, Sekhmet. I saw it all."

"And what, exactly, is it you think you saw, Sister?" Sekhmet said.

"You killed Lilith," she spat, her eyes burning red as her hair blew around her face. "You stabbed her with one of your arrows, then you told her daughters Hartman was responsible."

"Did I?" she said, smiling. "Or did I do as Lilith asked me to do? Come now, Eve. You should know better than this. Do you really think Lilith is so easily beaten?"

"You're lying. She trusted you," Eve said. "How could you do that?"

"You don't understand the whole situation," Sekhmet said. "You're angry, and you're not thinking clearly."

"I understand enough," Eve said, producing the item she'd left to retrieve.

"Where did you get that?" Sekhmet said as she held up the khopesh. It was heavy, made of solid gold. "You can't have that."

"Why not?" Eve said. "You killed Lilith. Why shouldn't I kill you?"

"Because she's right," another voice said from behind her. She turned, already knowing who it was. There was no mistaking that voice, or his presence. "You don't know the whole situation, Eve." Adam strolled toward them, hands clasped behind his back in that extremely annoying pose he loved so much.

She held the khopesh out in front of her, turning to face both of them as much as possible. "One of you had better start explaining," she said. "Why did you kill Lilith?"

"I'm afraid it was necessary," Adam said. He pointed to where Melanie stood staring at the front door of the house. "They were too busy reveling in themselves and each other to do what they were supposed to do."

"And what was that? Kill Hartman? Harlow?"

"Yes," Sekhmet said. "Or at least, die trying."

"Why?" Eve said. "Why do all this?"

"Because it's entertaining," Adam said, smiling. Sekhmet slipped an arm around his waist, and the two kissed briefly. "We may or may not have a small wager on who wins."

Eve growled and swung the khopesh at them. It whickered past the tip of Adam's nose as he drew his head back. But Eve wasn't a warrior. She overbalanced and almost fell down. Sekhmet delivered a sharp kick to the back of her knee, sending her to the ground as Adam stepped on the sickle-shaped blade of the khopesh.

"Settle down," he said, sounding bored. He bent down and picked up the sword as Eve stared up at them both.

"I'm going to stop you," she said, her eyes burning furiously.

"No," Sekhmet said simply, "you won't. You might try; I'll give you that. But in the end, you'll do what you've always done, Sister. You'll submit. You may as well do that now, and save yourself a lot of pain. I don't want to hurt you, Sister. But you won't interfere in my game."

"A game," Even said, standing up. "You killed Lilith for a game. You unbelievable bitch."

That made Sekhmet laugh. It was a hearty laugh, full of promised sex and potential violence. "Priceless," she said. "Tell me, Eve. Where was all this concern for Lilith when Father drove her from the Garden? Or were you too busy planning your new life with Adam?"

"You did seem very eager to take her place," Adam said, smiling. She started toward him, intending to smack the smug expression right off his face, but stopped short when he pointed the kopesh at her. "Easy, wife."

"Never call me that again," Eve said, and he laughed. She took three steps back as Sekhmet and Adam laughed. She saw one hand, the one not pointing the sword at her, land lightly on Sekhmet's breast, and she responded by lightly brushing his crotch.

"Oh, it wasn't all bad, was it?" Sekhmet said, grinning. "I know you and Lilith had a very special arrangement. Nothing says we can't have the same, Eve. Come with us."

She looked at them both, and shook her head. "I wonder what our Father would say about your games," she said, and Adam laughed.

"He hasn't taken any interest in anything we do for a very long time, Eve," he said. "For all we know, he's dead."

"You'd better hope so," Eve said. "Because if he's not, then I'm the least of your problems." She faded out of sight and ran toward the house. It wasn't foolproof; Sekhmet could feel her energy every bit as well as Eve could sense hers. But Adam, being typically male even for one of their kind, was utterly clueless to most feminine energy.

Then again, when it came to women, Adam was pretty much clueless about almost everything.

3.

"Seriously?" Hartman asked him for what had to be the tenth time. "Salt? Fucking salt?"

"Guess so," Jim said, sprinkling it across the doorway in the kitchen. "Worked, didn't it?"

"But how?" he asked. "And how did you even know?"

"I don't know," he said, hoping Hartman understood he was answering both questions at once. "Maybe I saw it on TV or something. Maybe I read it in a book."

"Or maybe," a voice said from the dining room, "someone gave you just the right answers, at just the right time."

Both men had their guns up and pointed in an instant, and Jim understood that when it came time to take Hartman down, it was likely to be a bloody affair. They both stood ready as a woman walked into the kitchen. Not just a woman, but one hell of a woman, he realized. Long legs, perfect breasts, and the sort of face he expected to see on a magazine, not in Harlan Denison's kitchen. Her light blonde hair hung down to her waist, swept back in a sensible ponytail that seemed somehow sexier than it

231

should. She wore jeans and a black t-shirt under a worn and well-broken leather jacket, but to Jim she would have seemed more at home in some sort of designer cocktail dress.

"Close your mouths, boys," she said, rolling her eyes. "You'll catch flies."

"Sorry," Hartman said, and was there a look of recognition in his eyes. "She sent you, didn't she? The goddess who almost killed me earlier."

"In a manner of speaking," the woman said.

"The what?" Jim asked.

"Goddess," Hartman said. Jim laughed.

"It's not really the right word," the woman said. "But I guess it'll do for now. And Lilith didn't send me, not exactly. It doesn't matter right now. What matters is keeping the both of you alive."

"And you're here to do that," Jim said, not bothering to hide his sarcasm. "You're gonna take on those—those things outside?"

"If I have to," she said. "Personally, I think we'd be smarter to just get the hell out of here."

"No good," Hartman said. "They'll just find us again."

"Probably," she said. "They're very good trackers, and they have your scent. Both of you."

"What do you mean, someone gave me just the right answers?" Jim asked. "I haven't talked to anyone about any of this. Hell, I didn't know anything about any of this until just now."

"You didn't talk to her," she said, shaking her head. "She talked to you. You probably didn't even know she was there. Sekhmet always does her best work behind the scenes."

"Sekhmet? Lilith?" Hartman said. "An Egyptian goddess and Adam's first wife?" She turned to Hartman with a look that could only be real appreciation.

"A well-read man," she said, nodding. "I like that. Too bad about the rest of your personality, though."

That made Jim chuckle. "Yes, and no," the woman continued. "The legends at least come withing spitting distance of the truth sometimes. It's a lot more complicated than that, though. Family always is, isn't it?"

"I wouldn't know," Hartman said.

"I know all about your parents, Mr. Hartman," the woman said.

"Doesn't make them family," he said.

"Fascinating as all this is," Jim said as something hit the door again. "Think maybe we could feel our feelings later?"

"Check the back," the woman said, and Hartman nodded. He looked out the window over the sink.

"One out back," he said. "Nope, make that two."

"Leaving one up front," Jim said, checking the chamber of his sidearm. "I say we go right through her."

"You could," the woman said. "Or we could actually be smart about it instead."

Hartman laughed as Jim turned red. "Aww, did she hurt your feelings, big guy?" Hartman said.

"Eat me," Jim said. "Raw."

"Boys," she said, sounding irritated. "Perhaps you could settle your own affairs later, after we survive?"

Jim nodded, feeling oddly like he'd just been called into the principal's office. "How do we do that?" he asked.

"First, by understanding what it is you're up against," the woman said. "And who's behind it all."

"You know, I'm just dying to know all this," Hartman said. "But is now really the time for the big exposition scene?"

"You salted all the doors and windows, right?" she said, looking at Jim. He nodded.

"Everything on the ground floor, anyway," he said. "I mean, it's not like they can fly, right?"

Right on cue, he heard glass breaking upstairs. "Well, shit," he said, pulling his gun as they turned to the sound of running footsteps on the stairs.

"Don't bother," the woman said, and actually moved them both behind her. He thought this was odd, even with the whole goddess schtick; after all, she was five foot three and probably barely cracked a buck-twenty. Then again, the girl who came down the stairs wasn't exactly Hulk Hogan, either.

She was average height, and pretty in that way unique to natural redheads; bright eyes, freckled cheeks, and a smile that would ordinarily be cute as hell, if he couldn't see the tips of sharp fangs poking out from under her upper lip.

"Auntie," the girl said as the stranger stepped in front of her. "You shouldn't be here."

"Neither should you, Melanie," she said. "There are things happening here you don't understand."

"Makes two of us," Hartman said, his rifle trained on the redhead.

"He killed Mother," Melanie said, pointing to Hartman.

"No," the woman said. "He didn't. He's not capable of killing her, and I think you know that."

"He's killed dozens," Melanie said. "Our sisters. He's evil."

"That's as may be," the woman said. "But he didn't kill Lilith, Melanie. He couldn't. He's not strong enough, not by half."

"He killed Jennifer, and Kris," she spat. "If he could kill them, he could kill her."

"Uh," Jim said, holding up one hand. "Sorry, don't mean to interrupt. But if we're being honest, that was me. And they were trying to kill us at the time."

She turned her bright eyes on him. No, he saw. Not just bright; glowing. Glowing red. "Jesus," he said. "What the fuck are you?"

"Doesn't matter," Melanie said. "None of you will be alive long enough to worry about it." She started toward them, and the strange woman blocked her way.

"No," she said. "That's not happening."

"Get out of my way, Eve," Melanie said. "I won't ask you twice."

The woman, whose name was apparently Eve if Jim was actually managing to follow this crazy goddamn soap opera, just sighed and shook her head. "This has gone far enough," she said. "It's over, Melanie. You're being manipulated. All of you," she added, looking back at Jim and Hartman.

"Manipulated by who?" Hartman, who no one could accuse of being slow on the uptake, asked before Jim could put it together.

"That's a long story," Eve said. "Think you can all keep from killing each other long enough for me to tell it?"

"I'm just curious enough to listen," Hartman said. Jim just nodded.

"Melanie?" Eve said. "Can you and your sisters calm your bloodlust and listen? Are you truly daughters of Lilith, or are you just monsters?"

"We'll listen," she said, still staring a hole in Hartman. "For now."

"Fair enough," Eve said, and Melanie pointed at Hartman.

"He still has a lot to answer for," she said. Hartman just shrugged.

"Well, can't argue that," Hartman said. "Still, if someone's jerking us off, I'd at least like to know who. Otherwise, I just feel dirty."

Melanie and Eve both rolled their eyes, and Jim shook his head.

"You really are an asshole, you know that?" Jim said, and Hartman grinned.

"Yeah," he said. "But I'm good at it."

4.

"Well then," Hartman said as they all sat around Harlan's massive dining room table. "Isn't this just the little domestic scene from Hell?" Jim looked around the table at everyone gathered there, and as much as he might want to belt Hartman in the mouth, he had a point. He sat next to Hartman on one side of the table, and the three women—no, the three girls from outside sat across from them. The woman calling herself Eve sat at the head of the table, and Jim decided he didn't envy her a bit. She was the one stuck moderating this little meeting of the minds.

"Will you still be joking when I rip your throat out?" the one named Melanie asked, and Hartman just shrugged.

"You know, I'd give it fifty-fifty odds," he said. "I'm sort of an incurable smartass."

"Enough," Jim said. "Hartman, do something good for once, and shut up."

He just smiled at the girls across from them, and leaned back in his chair, hands folded across his stomach. Jim resisted the urge to knock him backwards, and turned to Eve. "You said you have information for us. For all of us," he added, looking at the girls. "Things we don't know."

Eve nodded. "First, it's important to know that none of you are here by accident, or by your own devices," she said, which struck Jim as a damned strange opening line. "You were manipulated, all of you. You," she said to Hartman, who at least had the good sense to shut up and listen.

"You were influenced to your actions," she said. "Regrettably, it wasn't difficult. It pains me to say it, because you're of my line, but you're an evil man, Mr. Hartman. It wasn't entirely your idea to kill those young women."

"Our sisters," Melanie said, and Eve held up her hand.

"Please, allow me to finish," Eve said, and Melanie nodded. The other two each took her hand, and she quieted down. She turned her attention back to Hartman, who squirmed a little under her gaze.

"It wasn't entirely your idea, but you needed very little

persuasion," she said. "Would you say that's a fair statement?"

He nodded slowly. "I did what I did," he said. "No point in denying it."

"And," Eve continued, looking at the girls. "His actions were not random. They were intentionally designed to provoke a specific response, in Lilith. It worked, unfortunately."

"Wait," Jim said. "I'm sorry, I'm getting lost already. Who is Lilith? For that matter, who are you? And you're making it sound an awful lot like someone's been playing with us."

"That's accurate," Eve said, nodding. "Tell me, Chief Harlow. Are you familiar with the Bible?"

"Passing fair," Jim said. "Wasn't much of a thing in my family."

"Uh," Hartman said, actually raising his hand. "Believe it or not, but I think I can fill this part in for him."

"By all means," Eve said, gesturing to him. "I'll correct you where you go wrong, if that's okay."

"Please," Hartman said, and she nodded again. "You're Eve, as you said. I take it that means there's an Adam somewhere in the picture?"

"Adam and Eve?" Jim said, shaking his head. "As in the Garden of Eden, the first man and woman, the forbidden fruit, all of it?"

"Well, that's the tourist version, anyway," Hartman said, looking at Eve. She nodded slowly, and he continued. "You see, you dig a little deeper, and you find all the bits that were redacted. This lovely lady is actually Adam's second wife. His first?"

"Lilith?" Jim asked, and Eve nodded.

"My sister," she said. "Well, that's probably just the closest word you'd understand for it."

Hartman nodded. "But you see, Adam wasn't what you'd call a secure sort of guy. Lilith was entirely too independent for his tastes. Had a mind of her own, thought she should be able to do as she pleased."

"Mother was strong and independent," the black girl said. Melissa, Jim thought. Melissa Campbell. Her dad works for the city. Jesus wept.

"Bingo," Hartman said. "So Adam tells God he isn't digging this chick. God says, fine, whatever. Takes a rib from him as payment, and creates a more submissive woman for him."

"So Adam thought," Eve said with a smile that made the girls chuckle.

"Flash forward a few billion years, and here we are, the descendants of Adam and Eve," Hartman said. "At least, that's the popular version. Except, there's always more to the story, right?" He turned to Eve, who nodded.

"Lilith was poorly treated," she said. "By Adam, by our Father. By me." She took a deep breath, and lifted her head up. "I admit, I was jealous of her. Her strength, her beauty. Her independence."

"Siblings fight," Jim said. "It happens."

Hartman looked over at the girls, who were still staring a hole in him. "Care to chime in, fill in some gaps?" he said, and Jim had the distinct impression of a man gleefully poking a bear.

"As Mr. Hartman said," Eve said before they could get started, "the real story is more complicated. Lilith and I were not the only daughters our Father created, and Adam not his only son. Sadly, most did not survive."

"Uh, but you're basically gods, right?" Jim said. "Who kills a god?"

"Other gods," Eve said. "As you said, siblings fight."

"So, a few family squabbles, and most of the line is wiped out?" Hartman said. "Wow. Makes me glad to be an only child."

"I survived because I refused to take sides," Eve said. "Lilith never cared for our family squabbles, as you called them. She was devoted to her children."

"Wait," Jim said. "Her children?"

"There are only four of us remaining," Eve said. "But only two of my siblings are involved now. Adam, of course, and Sekhmet."

"The chick who cut me loose," Hartman said. All of the women looked at him then.

"Probably not the smartest move, referring to a goddess as a chick," Jim said.

"Fine, point taken," Hartman said. "So, the lady who let me go is Sekhmet. You said Adam. Wait, you married your brother?"

"Focus," Jim said.

"My sisters and I are each the progenitors of our own lines," she said. "Through Father's influence and sheer luck, my children are the most numerous. But Lilith's children still exist, though in far lesser numbers. Even fewer are Sekhmet's children. For some reason, I've never known Sekhmet to have daughters. Only sons. Men like you," she said to Jim.

"Men like me," Jim said. "What does that even mean?"

"I think she means bad asses," Hartman said.

"Warriors," Eve said. "Men of power and conviction. Lilith favored daughters, but she had as many sons. It was often Lilith's children at the front of conquering armies, but many of those armies were led by your brothers, Mr. Harlow."

"And we're what, the spear carriers?" Hartman said. "Wow, seems like a ripoff."

"Not the time," Harlow said.

"Sekhmet has always been a powerful warrior, and a better general," Eve said. "She is not to be underestimated."

"Yeah, I got that feeling," Hartman said.

"She has apparently been working behind the scenes of this little play for some time now," Eve said. "Influencing all the players, but most especially you, Mr. Harlow."

"Maybe you could dumb this down a little for us," Jim said. "Because honestly, I'm getting lost in the backstory."

"Very well," Eve said, looking uncomfortable. "To put it simply, Adam and Sekhmet have engineered the conflict between all of you, purely for their own amusement."

"I have one question," Teresa asked. She looked at Hartman. "Did you kill Mother?"

"Who, Lilith?" Hartman said. "Look, we can all agree I'm a bastard. And I'm good at what I do, but you gotta be kidding me. I couldn't get that done if I tried. Hell, I gave her my best shot, and I didn't even mess up her hair."

"It's true," Eve said. "Mr. Hartman was not capable of causing Lilith's death. That was Sekhmet."

"Why?" Melanie asked. "Why would she kill Mother? Her own sister?"

"To get you to do exactly what you came here to do," Jim said. "Kill us. Well, him, specifically."

"Thanks," Hartman said.

"And she maneuvered you here, Mr. Harlow, because you're the only one with the ability to kill them," Eve said, pointing to the girls. "Tell me, what is the surest way to kill one of them?"

"Fire," Jim said with no hesitation. "Salt and silver slow them down, and anything dies with enough brain trauma. But fire's the best way. It causes more damage than they can regenerate." Jim looked up, confused. "How in God's name do I know that?"

"I thought all this started because I killed Lilith's children," Hartman said. "Now you're saying he's the only one who can do it?"

"We use the word children interchangeably," Eve said. "Because to us, you are our children. But the women you murdered were of Lilith's line, but not her direct progeny. These three women, they are literally of Lilith's blood."

"Vampires?" Jim said. "I mean, that's where this is going, right? They're vampires."

"No," Eve said, holding up a hand before the girls could object. "Young Jennifer was probably the closest of them all to what you know as a vampire, and only because she died before Lilith could save her. Those Lilith's children drain can become vampires, but that is rare."

"Six of one, half dozen of the others," Hartman said. "Bottom line, whatever they are, Big Jim here's the only one with a shot at killing them."

"The point being, someone's been yanking all our chains," Jim said, and he was surprised to see the girls all nodding. "They wanted you to come after him, and they wanted me to kill you. Honestly, sounds like they're taking bets on who wins."

"So, what do we do now?" Melanie asked. "Just walk away? Manipulated or not, he killed our sisters. He has to be punished for that."

"He will be," Jim said. "Assuming he doesn't get the death penalty, he'll rot in prison for the rest of his life." He looked at Hartman, and grinned. "And I seriously doubt a pretty boy like him is going to have an easy stretch."

"I can hold my own," Hartman said.

"That's not enough," Melissa said. "Not for what he did."

"Probably not," Jim agreed. "But it's what the system allows."

"We could still kill him," Teresa said. "I doubt even you could stop all of us."

Jim sighed. "I can't believe I'm saying this, especially over him, but if you try, I guess we'll have to find out."

"Enough," Eve said, standing up. "This is what they want, don't you see that? Melanie, Melissa, Teresa? You are daughters of Lilith, born of her blood. You are strong, and beautiful. You are no one's playthings, chess pieces to be moved on a board at someone else's whim."

She turned her attention to Hartman. "And you are my son. You have what might be my Father's ultimate gift. Free will. So far, you've used it to do terrible things. But you can also do great things, Jerry. You know, my husband has big plans for you, my son. You're to father an important leader in this world's future. But that can't happen if you continue to blindly destroy those around you."

"Wow," Hartman said. "Never thought I'd be a disappointment to two moms."

"But right now, all four of you are acting like spoiled children who don't get to break someone else's toys," she said, and Hartman actually shut up. "Ladies, you want to kill Mr. Hartman so badly, you're ignoring what's right in front of you. And you, Mr. Hartman, are so determined to make us all believe you're not scared, you're putting yourself at risk in the name of bad jokes and bravado."

"Fair enough," Hartman said.

"And you, Mr. Harlow. Men of your lineage have led conquering armies, destroyed monsters that preyed upon the weak. The sons of Sekhmet have been warriors and protectors since time began. It was Sekhmet herself who banished the darkness in a horrific battle when Father blithely decreed that there should be light. It was a son of Sekhmet who defeated the giant Goliath, and who led the fight against Hitler. And now, you're willing to kill these women, who are not even aware of why they exist or what they were fooled into doing, over a man like him?" She pointed to Hartman.

"Well, when you put it that way," Jim said. "Like I said, someone's been yanking our chains. I think maybe they still are. I don't know about you girls, but I don't like the feeling."

"Neither do we," Melanie admitted. "I guess the question is, what do we do about it?"

"You tell me, Mr. Harlow," Eve said, looking at him. "What should you do?"

"That's not the question," Jim said. "The real question is, why? What do they have to gain from us fighting? It can't be just amusement, not for all this."

"It's TV as a babysitter," Hartman said.

"What?" Jim said.

"That makes no sense," Melanie said. "Did someone hit you on the head?"

"Think about it," Hartman said. "Hear me out. You're stuck with a bunch of rowdy kids, and you wanna get a little private time. What do you do? You plonk 'em down in front of the tube with some cartoons, and slip away while they're busy."

"I hate to say it," Eve said, "but he might be correct."

"So, all of this," Melanie said, waving a frustrated hand in the air. "All of this was so that Adam and Sekhmet could hook up?"

"I doubt it's that simple," Eve said. "My husband has never been one to go to any length to hide his infidelity. But I agree, they wanted you distracted. Perhaps me, as well. But mostly, I think they wanted to see what you could do. All of you, not just Mr. Harlow."

Jim took a deep breath. "Then," he said. "Maybe we should show them."

"Come again?" Hartman said.

Eve sat down and smiled. "Pay attention, children," she said. "I think Mr. Harlow has the beginnings of an idea worthy of his lineage."

CHAPTER EIGHTEEN

1.

"Jesus," Mark said, looking down at the newly excavated mass grave. Thirteen bodies in all, each laid out neatly next to the other. No, he thought. Not just neatly; reverently. They were laid out with great care, even love. All of their hands were folded on their breasts, and the hair had been brushed away from their faces.

"Goddamned mess, is what it is," Ray said next to him. "Christ, I've never seen anything close to this." Mark grunted and knelt down at the edge of the hole.

"Take a look, Doc," he said, pointing to the closest one. "She can't be more than fifteen."

"Probably isn't," Ray agreed. "You know what this is, young man, same as I do. Hell, you see the same bulletins I do."

"Human trafficking, here?" Mark said. "I mean, I know Harlan said his guy was involved in it, but I figured he was just shading things to cover his ass."

"Looks like he was telling the truth," Ray said as he climbed down into the hole. He pulled on a pair of gloves and turned back to his assistant. "You shoot it all?"

"Got it," the kid said, and Ray nodded. He opened the closest girl's mouth. "Not much in the way of dental care," he said.

"Plenty of folks right here without dental insurance,"

Mark said.

"Yeah," Ray said. "But it adds up. Bet you ten bucks you won't find a single missing persons report on any of these girls."

"No bet," Mark said. He tried to raise Big Jim on the radio again, but there was no response. "Fuck," he said.

"I think that pretty well sums it up," Ray said.

2.

"You know, I'm curious about something," Hartman said as they stood in Harlan's living room.

"I'd imagine you have a great many questions," Eve said.

"You said there are four of you left," he said. "There's you, and Adam, and Sekhmet. Who's the fourth?"

"He is of no consequence to our immediate situation," she said. "And believe me, you don't want to meet him."

"I don't know," Hartman said. "Sounds like a bucket list item to me. I mean, Sekhmet creates badasses. You create the common folk, and Lilith apparently created vampires. What's his deal?"

"Annihilation," she said. "You're familiar with the book of Revelations?"

"Yeah," Hartman said.

"Then you know of the Four Horsemen," she said, and he nodded. "My brother wears many faces."

Hartman looked surprised as Jim turned to them. "Wait, you're telling me your brother is one of the Four Horsemen?"

"No such luck, Big Jim," Hartman said. "I think what she's saying is that he is the Four Horsemen. All of them, all at once."

"Those are just masks he wears," Eve said. "Father created him for a very specific purpose. Be grateful his fate isn't intertwined in this, and leave it at that."

"Works for me," Jim said. "So, are we ready?"

"Ready as we'll ever be," Melanie said. She reached out

and took Melissa's hand, who took Teresa's. "Will this work?"

"It doesn't matter," Jim said, double-checking his sidearm.

"Gonna have to disagree with you, Big Jim," Hartman said. "I think it matters a lot."

"I mean, either way, we're doing things our way this time," he said. "We're not dancing to anyone else's tune, not anymore."

"He's right," Melanie said. "If they want a fight, I say we give it to them."

"It won't be that easy," Eve said. "Sekhmet is dangerous, and she's had all of time to perfect her skills. Adam may not be the warrior she is, but he's not helpless, either."

"But they can be killed, right?" Hartman said, and Eve nodded.

"With the tools I've given you, you can kill them," she said, and Hartman nodded. "And you three, you are strong enough. Lilith's blood is in your veins."

"And I suppose I'm just here for moral support," Jim said.

"You're our most powerful weapon, Mr. Harlow," she said. "Of all of us, you have the best chance of succeeding. But you cannot hesitate. No mercy, Mr. Harlow. I don't know if you're capable of that, or not."

"Guess we'll find out," Jim said, and walked to the front door. He stepped out into the night air, with Hartman and the girls behind him. Eve came forward and stepped out onto the lawn.

"I know you're here," she said to the empty night. "No more games. Come out and face me."

Jim watched with a mixture of awe and horror as the air shimmered, and two people appeared in front of her. One was a man, of average height and build with dark hair and a full beard. The other was a woman who seemed to fairly radiate strength, beauty, and horror in equal amounts.

"That's her," Hartman whispered. "She's the one who sprung me. Pretty sure she killed your receptionist, by the way."

"Hello again, sister," the dark woman said.

"It's over, Sekhmet," Eve said. "They're onto your game now."

"Someone's been telling tales out of school," the man said, smiling. "Whatever happened to the obedient wife I knew?"

"If you thought that, then you never really knew me at all," Eve said.

"So, this is Adam," Hartman said. "You know, I guess I thought you'd be taller."

"Hello, son," Adam said. "I'm happy to see you've survived this long. I have big plans for you, you know."

"Yeah, so I hear," Hartman said. "But you see, the thing is, I'm not a big fan of people jerking me around." He raised the pistol and fired before anyone understood what he was doing.

To Jim, time seemed to slow to a crawl; he could swear he actually saw the bullet moving through the air. But he supposed it wasn't just any bullet, was it?

The nine millimeter slug caught Adam in the forehead, leaving a small hole just between his eyes. He looked surprised, putting a hand to his forehead before he fell to the ground.

"What?" Sekhmet said, sounding horrified. "What did you do? How? You can't do that. It's not possible. Adam, stand up. Adam?"

She turned to Eve. "You did this," she said. Eve smiled and held up her hand, showing Sekhmet the small wound in her palm.

"Blood of my blood, flesh of my flesh," Eve said. "You remember that? One of Father's favorite lines."

"You killed Mother," Melanie said. "You used this man to kill our sisters. Admit it."

"I did," Sekhmet said. "And now, I'm asking you. Pleading with you, actually. Stand down. Don't make me kill you, too."

Jim heard all three girls growl as they charged at her. He watched, almost frozen in place, as Sekhmet produced an arrow from nowhere and promptly stabbed Melissa in the heart. She fell to dust before their eyes as Sekhmet turned to the others.

Melanie and Teresa attacked, but it was every bit as futile. It didn't take long; Sekhmet killed them both just as easily as she had Melissa.

Hartman shot at her, but she seemed to move fast enough to avoid each of his bullets. The gun ran dry, and before he could reload, she was on him. Sekhmet held him up by the throat with ease. "I'm growing tired of you, young man," she said, raising her arrow.

Jim fired twice, each bullet catching her in the back. Sekhmet dropped Hartman and turned to him, her face contorted with pain and fury.

"How dare you?" she said. "You attack me?"

Jim just shrugged. "Guess I'm just ornery," he said.

"I am your mother," she said.

"I had a mother," Jim said, thinking of Carolyn and cinnamon rolls as he raised the gun again. "And you ain't her." He shot twice more, both slugs catching her in the chest to what was apparently no effect at all. He saw Eve moving toward Adam's body, and had just enough time to be confused before the terror kicked in.

"Stop that," she said, stalking over to him and snatching the gun from his hand. "It's annoying."

"You should hear my knock-knock jokes," Jim said. Hartman had apparently managed to get his gun reloaded, because he shot her once in the head. Sekhmet turned to him with a surprised look on her face.

"Ow," she said. "Do you have any idea how much that stings?"

"I do what I can," Hartman said. He was backing up

when Sekhmet waved her hand, and an arrow appeared in Hartman's chest. He fell to his knees, dropping his gun as his hands went to the shaft of the arrow.

"Ain't this a bitch?" he said, and fell backward. She turned back to Jim just as he drew back his fist and punched her in the face. Unlike the bullets dipped in Eve's blood, which had so far been about as effective as spitballs, this rocked her back. She stumbled but didn't fall, and when she looked back up at him, there was blood trickling from one corner of her mouth.

"There," she said, smiling as she stood up. "That's better." He put his hands up, hoping that at least it didn't drag out too long.

He hit her twice more, and each time she staggered backward, but didn't fall. He swung a third time, and she slapped it aside, catching him a hard shot to the side. He felt three ribs snap cleanly with the blow, and when she backhanded him across the face a moment later, it was all he could do to stay conscious. He dropped to his knees, his head ringing. He saw her approaching him, and something else that made him smile.

"I'm happy to see you've finally found your true nature, my son," she said, hauling him to his feet. "But did you honestly think you could win this?"

"Nah," he said, spitting blood on the ground to clear his mouth. "I was just stalling."

"Stalling for what?" she said, smiling. "You can't be expecting a rescue."

"He was stalling so I could get this," Eve said from behind her. She turned just as Eve brought the strangely shaped sword down, cleaving her from the shoulder to the navel.

Sekhmet stepped back, stumbling over Hartman's corpse and falling to the ground. "You," Sekhmet said to Eve as she helped Jim to his feet. "I never thought it would be you."

Eve knelt down beside her, resting Sekhmet's head on

her lap as she took her hand. "I did not want this, sister," she said, crying openly. "But you left me no choice."

"No tears," Sekhmet said, brushing her cheek. "I fell in battle to superior opponents. That is all I've ever wanted."

Jim knelt down beside them both. "Are you really, well, a goddess?" he asked.

She smiled, blood foaming on her lips. "As good a word as any, I suppose," she said.

"Then I'm sorry things worked out this way," he said, and she nodded.

"They happened as they were meant to happen, I think," Sekhmet said. She turned and touched Eve's cheek. "I think perhaps Father has been annoyed with us for some time."

"It's not like Him to wait," Eve said, crying, and Sekhmet laughed.

"Which is probably why He did it," she said, still laughing. She coughed again, and blood began splattering the ground under her from her wound. "Take care of them," she said. "They'll all need a Mother."

Eve nodded, still crying. "I will," she said. Jim watched in horrified wonder as Sekhmet's body began to disintegrate, floating away on a mild breeze out of the west. When she was gone, Eve stood up, wiping her face and pulling her shoulders back. She looked at the fallout; Hartman's body lying in the grass, the piles of ash that had been the girls, and sighed.

Adam's corpse was already gone, replaced by a small patch of wildflowers. Somehow, that was the most fascinating part of it all to Jim; where there had been neatly manicured lawn before, now there was a patch of wildflowers that appeared to have been growing for years.

"So much lost," she said, tears still trailing down her cheeks. Something occurred to Jim, something he didn't entirely want to believe but couldn't ignore.

"I gotta wonder," he said. "You knew it was going to

shake out like this, didn't you?"

Eve looked at him, but there was no anger on her face. "I suspected," she said. "Out of all of them, you were the only one who had any real chance of keeping her occupied."

"Then why were they here?" he said. "If you knew they were going to die, why not just send them away? I mean, Hartman I get, almost. He sure as shit had it coming. But what did those girls ever do to anyone?"

"They were Lilith's children," she said. "It was only a matter of time before their baser natures took control of them. You remember what I said about those Lilith's children drained?"

"They become vampires," he said.

"It was only a matter of time before they released a plague of the undead on your world," she said. "They wouldn't do it intentionally, but it would have happened. I saved them from that guilt."

"By setting them up to get slaughtered," he said. "Lady, you are cold-blooded."

She smiled. "I suppose that is one interpretation," she said. She turned and started to walk away.

"I don't suppose you have any suggestions for how I explain this?" she said.

"Explain what?" she said, smiling. "Your scientists will find Mr. Hartman died of a gunshot wound, from your gun. He has a gun in his hand that's been fired. I imagine you can work with that, Mr. Harlow. As for the rest, what will anyone find? Flowers?"

She stopped and bent down long enough to pick up the strange sword, then disappeared.

"So, that happened," he said, groaning as he got to his feet.

3.

Overall, it wasn't a hard story to tell. It certainly didn't hurt that the house itself looked like a war zone, or that he himself had been beaten pretty much to hell and back. Certainly Hartman's body looked like it had been put through the wringer. It was a simple story; he'd come out to question Denison and found Hartman. He'd attempted to arrest him, and he'd resisted. At some point, Jim had managed to get to his gun; the rest was, as they say, history.

He was currently sitting in his office, trying to catch up on the absolutely frightening amount of paperwork that this whole mess had generated, when Mark knocked on his open door. "You busy, boss?" he said.

"Nothing I can't happily ignore," he said, putting the half-completed forms aside. "What's up?"

"Forensics are back on those girls in the mass grave," he said, handing Jim a report. "We found a .22 in the gravel pit along with those other three bodies. No big shocker, it matched to all of them. Not much in the way of prints on the gun, but the mag was covered in Hartman's prints."

He looked at the photo of the gun. "This thing holds ten rounds," he said. "He had to reload to finish."

"Best guess?" Mark said. "He does the girls, probably on Denison's order. Then the Three Stooges come out to help with the cleanup."

"That solid?" Jim asked, and Mark nodded.

"Got a couple of guys who say they saw them there that afternoon," he said.

"So, after he gets them to do the dirty work, he caps them?" Jim said, and Mark nodded.

"Vegas money says yeah," he said with a shrug.

"Any sign of Harlan?" he asked, and Mark shook his head.

"Nothing so far," he said. "Nothing on his bank account or credit cards, and his cell phone's dark. We got BOLOs out, but he's in the wind. Odds are by now, he's somewhere with a lot of sunny beaches and no extradition treaty."

"He'll turn up sooner or later," Jim said. "Anything else pressing right now?"

"Just those missing persons reports," he said. Jim felt his heart drop into his stomach, but nodded.

"The girls from the high school," he said, and Mark nodded. "None of them have showed up yet?"

"Not a one," he said. "Which tells me they all ran off together."

"You get into their home lives?" he asked, and Mark nodded.

"Starting to," he said. "Pretty even mix of happy homes and fucking nightmare factories. I got one father, a Sam Harrison, I can't even locate. Not at home, hasn't showed up at work. Same with one of our best customers, Brad Norcroft. Him, I don't have a problem believing he just split. Looks like his wife grabbed the kids and bailed."

"And the other one?" he asked. "The Harrison guy?"

"Him, I don't know," he said. "Might be he's with the girls. I gotta say, if half the rumors I've heard about him lately are true, then that'd be my guess. He's got them holed up somewhere."

"We check his house?" he said, and Mark nodded.

"Checked his house, and all the usual out of the way spots, anywhere someone could be staying off the grid. We got nothing. If he's got the girls, he's on the run with them."

"Which means he should be spotted any minute now," Jim said, and Mark nodded.

"FBI wants it," he said.

"Fine with me," Jim said. "They have the resources to run it down. Anything else?"

Mark looked at him for a moment, and Jim braced himself. "You feeling okay, Jim?" he said.

"Yeah, I guess," he said. "Little sore, maybe."

"That's not what I meant," Mark said, and Jim nodded.

"I'm okay, I think," Jim said. "I mean, everything isn't all roses and tea kettles, but I'm good. Not my first shoot, you know."

"Yeah, I do," Mark said. "Doesn't make it any easier."

"No, it doesn't," Jim agreed. "But I'm good, really. He made the choice."

Mark nodded and stood up. "Hell of a few days," he said, and Jim nodded.

"That it has been," he said.

"You think it's over?" he said. "Things gonna go back to normal now?"

"God willing," Jim said. "Be nice to get back to boring, wouldn't it?"

"Hell, yes," he said. "Well, I'm gonna take a spin around town. Holler if you need anything."

"I will," Jim said. He watched as Mark stopped to say hi to the new receptionist on his way out. Her name was Amanda, and from Jim could tell, she was going to work out okay.

Sighing, he went back to work on his reports, wondering if it was ever going to be really over now that he knew what was out there.

4.

"Thank you, darlin," Harlan said as the bartender brought him his third Brahma. "*Obrigado*," he added, remembering where he was. Those Portuguese lessons were paying off, he thought. She smiled as she left him at the end of the bar. Everyone wanted to be in Rio for Carnivale, but to Harlan, that simply sounded like a nightmare of too many bodies and too much noise. He preferred the quiet, not that there was much of it in a city this size. Still, it was easy to get lost here, and that's exactly what he'd wanted.

Brazil was a good idea, he decided as he saw the latest group of beauties come into the bar. He noticed her right away, mostly because she was clearly Anglo and not local. Something about her made her stand out beyond that, though; she seemed more vital, somehow. More alive.

And, crazy as it sounded, she was headed right for him. He sat up a little straighter as she sat down next to him and signaled the bartender. "Evening," he said, and she smiled as she turned to him. He half expected her to brush him off, so when she swiveled on her stool to face him, he was caught more than a little off guard.

"Wow," she said. "A face from home. You are American, right?" she said, sounding nervous.

"Guilty as charged," he said, and she sighed with relief.

"Thank God," she said. The bartender came over, and she ordered a rum and Coke, which Harlan signaled for her to put on his tab.

"Thanks," she said. "So, you on vacation?"

"Something like that," he said. "Needed a change of scenery. You?"

"Just traveling," she said. "Nowhere special in mind. So, are the wife and kiddies on this trip with you?" she said casually, and he smiled.

"No, it's just me," he said. "My wife, she passed on several years ago."

"Oh, God," she said. "I'm such an idiot. I'm sorry."

"No, no," he said. "It's fine. I, uh, imagine you run into a lot of guys who forget they're married when you show up." That made her laugh, and he knew he was in.

"Wow," she said. "You're good, I'll give you that."

He almost fucked up and gave her his real name before he remembered the one he was traveling under. "I'm Jack," he said. "Jack Harlan." She shook his hand, and the touch lasted long enough to promise him a truly incredible night.

"Ruth Ann," she said, her voice full of promise. "And I think I've been looking for you for a long time."

"Is that right?" he said, and she gave him that killer smile.

"Yeah," she said. "You might say my mama told me to look for a man just like you."

THE END

ABOUT THE AUTHOR

Some say he was born from unauthorized genetic testing. Others say he was found alone in the wilderness as a baby and adopted by a Special Forces team as their mascot. Still others say he was born smoking a pipe, although how he managed to keep it lit is still a topic of great debate.

Whatever his origins, Michael Chambers now lives in and works in Seymour, MO. When he's not writing or plotting world domination in a complicated scheme involving demonic mind control and sentient toasters, he enjoys shooting, martial arts, and flying RC helicopters.

Facebook.com/mchael.chambers.author

Twitter.com/Writer_MikeC

ALSO BY MICHAEL CHAMBERS

The Jennifer Blake Series

Blood Eagle	Sins of the Fathers
Faceless	Malevolent
Legacies	Haunted
Lost City	The Darkness Within
Nemesis	Battleground

The Blood Lines Series

Blood Feud
Blood War
Blood Vengeance
Blood Ties
Blood Borne

Stand Alone Novels

Smiling Jack	Possession
Sisters	The Beast Within
Bad Girls	Any Given Weekend
Zombies, Inc	The Farm
Hunted	The Rage
Inner Demons	The Church
Buried Sins	Til Death Do Us Part
Linda	

Novellas & Short Story Collections

Asylum	Chance Encounters
Joey	The Basement & Other Stories
ARES	The Things We Leave Behind
The Clown	